Rm

NO MARKS FOR TRYING

Whilst discussing holiday plans, Diana Holt's husband, Lewis, had suggested they go to Bahia Dorado in Spain. He said he had been there twenty years ago with his first wife, Klara, and was sure Diana would love it. But the holiday Diana had expected to be relaxing and carefree turns into a nightmare of murder and intrigue when they unexpectedly meet Grant Furnival, an old friend they haven't seen for ten years and with whom Diana had once had a brief affair.

Books by Stella Allan
Published by The House of Ulverscroft:

A DEAD GIVEAWAY
ARROW IN THE DARK
A MORTAL AFFAIR

STELLA ALLAN

NO MARKS FOR TRYING

Complete and Unabridged

ULVERSCROFT
Leicester

First published in Great Britain

First Large Print Edition
published 1999

British Library CIP Data

Allan, Stella
No marks for trying.—Large print ed.—
Ulverscroft large print series: mystery
1. Detective and mystery stories
2. Large type books
I. Title
823.9'14 [F]

ISBN 0–7089–4093–5

Published by
F. A. Thorpe (Publishing) Ltd.
Anstey, Leicestershire

Set by Words & Graphics Ltd.
Anstey, Leicestershire
Printed and bound in Great Britain by
T. J. International Ltd., Padstow, Cornwall

This book is printed on acid-free paper

For Pat, because I love him.

1

Coming up out of the hotel annexe, Diana paused on the dusty path to inhale deep gulps of the slight breeze that was blowing from the sea. It was hot enough here, but it still afforded a cooler respite from the oven-like humidity of the bedroom below and she stood and enjoyed the sensuous pleasure of the movement of air between her bare skin and the cotton beach dress which had been sticking to her back. Beneath her, away to the right, some late bathers were collecting their towels and beach bags from the slab and, as she watched, several small boats arrived at the concrete platform, disgorging their passengers who alighted amid cries of pleasure and gratitude, weighed down with fishing tackle, water skis, spear guns and snorkeling equipment. Immediately below her the yachts rose and fell gently on the water of the man-made marina which had been cleverly incorporated into a natural reef of rock formation, fragments of which pointed out to sea.

Lewis hadn't told her about the marina because it hadn't been there last time he had visited the bay twenty years ago with Klara, nor had the swimming pool, and the hotel itself had expanded, but everything else was just as he had described it to her.

'I want to go back to Bahia Dorada,' he had said as they were discussing holiday plans. 'Why don't we? You'd really like it there. It is fantastically beautiful and I'd enjoy showing it to you.'

She'd been surprised because she knew he'd been there with Klara and even after being married to him all this time they still avoided mention of her name.

'What does it mean?' she'd asked.

'Bahia Dorada? It's Catalan for Golden Bay — and that's what it is, a kind of earthly paradise.'

He was right of course. Lewis was always right but it wasn't usually his nature to wax poetic about anything. The more deeply he felt an emotion, the more likely he was to bottle it up. Showing one's feelings was hardly good form and now and again Diana wondered whether there were any real feelings to show.

He had promised her a kind of Spanish Garden of Eden and she had smiled indulgently, taking the buildup with a pinch of salt, so she had been unprepared for the lurch of excitement in her stomach as the car had climbed the final rise out of Bagur and topped the mountain, preparatory to descending the zig-zag route which plunged down among the pine-clad slopes to the azure bay with its creeks and inlets and the majestic promontory of timeless rock which bounded it on its southern side. From the peak where the car had rested, on a clear day you could see as far as Palamos over lesser hills carpeted in bright green.

'I can't get over the trees,' Diana said. 'I always thought of Spain as barren and dry but these trees are so incredibly green and they grow straight out of the rocks. There are forests of them all over the mountains.'

'It's more humid here than further south,' Lewis replied. 'And up here you get a lot of damp mist, rather like living on the Peak.'

It was funny he'd said that because Diana had just been thinking that she had only seen one panorama more unbelievably moving than this one and that had been in Hong Kong. She remembered dining with a young married couple who lived in a luxurious flat several feet above the last stop of the Peak railway and after dinner she had gone out on to the veranda and had walked into fairyland looking down on the myriad lights in the harbour below.

The sandy beach across the water beyond the slab was now deserted and in shadow as the sun sank behind the mountain. House martins swooped and returned to their home under the red-tiled eaves of the annexe and the small brown Spanish sparrows repaired to their nests in the forest. When darkness fell the bats would come out. Diana looked at her watch. Half past six. Three hours to dinner. She turned and walked leisurely up the hill to join Lewis on the terrace for a drink.

The main part of the hotel overlooked the annexe across a tiny creek which housed a dozen fishermen's boats, an old boathouse and a cottage. As Diana went through the front door she could hear the noise of the mechanical winch hauling a boat up the beach. There was no one in the foyer and the dining and grill rooms were silent and unlit as she passed along the marble-tiled passage, through the empty lounge and out on to the terrace. It was the time of day when people retired to their rooms to sit on their balconies or sleep for an hour or two or make love, before bathing and changing for dinner and whatever evening's entertainment they were going to pursue. There were a number of people on the terrace and Diana looked about for Lewis, not noticing him instantly because he wasn't alone. When he caught sight of her she waved but he didn't get up or make any reciprocal gesture and went on talking to his companion as she approached feeling slightly deflated. When she reached their table Lewis turned, as if in surprise, although she knew he'd seen her the first time.

'Diana darling.' He hardly ever called her darling — he was evidently out to impress. 'Here you are at last. The most astonishing thing has happened. Look who's here. You remember Grant — Grant Furnival. It must be what — ten, twelve years?'

The man at the table turned and rose to face Diana, holding out his right hand which she took as she arranged her features into an expression of pleasure and surprise.

'At least ten years,' she said. 'How lovely to see you, Grant, after all this time. What are you doing in Bahia Dorada? Are you on holiday? Are you staying here?'

'He lives here,' Lewis broke in. He was signalling for a waiter and when one appeared and had taken their order, Lewis sat back, beaming at them both as if he had single-handedly produced a rabbit from a hat. 'Yes, sir! You'll never believe it but Grant's your actual local GP.'

'Should I believe it? Is it true and, if so,

5

what became of those dreams of a plushy consultancy in Harley Street with a clientèle composed of sexually unsatisfied neurotics and overfed dowagers?'

Diana was laughing and Grant thought it suddenly made her look younger than her forty-two years and as if she had changed less over the years than had been his first impression on seeing her again. She was as tall as he had remembered, still slim but less bonily so, her neck and shoulders, bare above the sun dress, were smooth and firm, their earlier stringiness and the salt cellars magically filled out. Her hair was different, longer and brushed smoothly back from her forehead and over the crown to turn under in a page-boy style on the nape of her neck. The enormous, widely-set grey eyes were as clear and bright as ever but there were crows'-feet at their corners and the skin underneath was looser and faintly shadowed. Two sharp lines ran from her patrician nose to the edges of her mouth which was startlingly wide and full, out of proportion to her other features.

He smiled. 'It eventually palled,' he said. 'I was incapable of satisfying them all, so I decided it would be better to get out than go under, figuratively speaking of course. Besides, tax was becoming a problem and I thought it might be a good idea to put down a few roots in the place where I hoped to retire. A number of other people had had the same idea so that, when I came here, there was a ready-made English community to form the nucleus of my practice. Since then, of course, I've learned Spanish and my patients now come from both nationalities. It's worked very well. It's a far cry from being an over-worked, underpaid GP in our glorious Welfare State.'

'I can tell that.' Diana grinned. 'You look extremely prosperous.'

Lounging back in the white wrought-iron garden chair, surveying her over a brandy sour, and wearing a self-striped yellow hand-made shirt and toning mustard linen trousers, he looked as smoothly complacent and selfconsciously attractive as ever. Too bloody complacent, Diana reflected and irrationally, as of old, she found herself longing to be in a position to place a metaphorical kick in the seat of those immaculate trousers. If ever anyone had typified the flourishing green bay tree it surely must have been Grant Furnival. He always had been slightly larger than life, with a line in conversation that you derided more often than not as line-shooting, to discover later that he had been speaking the truth. He had a careless disregard for the rules, preferring to

7

make his own which others then followed because in his presence they, like the chameleon, were obliged temporarily to adopt something of his colour, his concepts, even though those concepts might be directly at variance with their own characters. Once or twice in the past he had sailed pretty close to the wind but had never failed in any transaction to carry the day with his customary flair and élan.

'At least, the ones we hear about,' Lewis had muttered darkly. 'There must be plenty that don't come off so well but he doesn't talk about those. He can't win all the time.'

Diana was not so sure. Unfair though it seemed, Grant, however unworthy, was undoubtedly a winner, whereas Lewis, straight, dependable and zealous, simply hadn't got what it took. But then life is an unfair business and only children and fools expect otherwise.

★ ★ ★

He was asking Lewis about his work and Lewis was answering seriously, intently, going into a great deal of meticulous detail.

'A fair amount of it can be done at home,' he was saying. 'I spend most of my time writing books — oh, not novels,' he hurriedly added as Grant raised his eyebrows and started to show a certain amount of interest and surprise. 'Technical stuff, case histories, criminal records, crime analyses, that sort of thing. In fact, I've been thinking of becoming self-employed for some time and particularly now circumstances would seem to favour a change of this nature.'

'How's that then?' Grant tossed his head back to swallow the last of his drink and Diana watched the contraction of muscles in the strong brown throat, her eyes following it down to the beginnings of a bronzed chest lightly covered with dark hair which two open shirt buttons revealed. He was square and stocky rather than immensely tall and she noticed that, sitting down, a slight incipient paunch, that would be invisible when he stood up, swelled above his waistband. The dark curly hair was now flecked with grey but his eyebrows were bushy and black and the skin was still taut on the strong-boned face which had as yet no sign of a jowl. She answered his question.

'My parents died a little while ago and, although it's taken ages, their estate is now all settled and rather to my surprise I find I've come out of it with quite a sum of money. I knew they had a reasonable amount of course, but these days, with death duties twice over, I didn't imagine there would be anything like the sum I eventually got. Father had evidently availed himself of every tax loophole, which in itself is staggering since he had such very upright and inflexible principles and was such a pillar of the Presbyterian Church.'

'Very lucky for you he managed to reconcile his conscience. We ought to drink to him.' Grant ordered another round. When it came he raised his glass and gave a toast.

'Here's to your father, Diana, and to all tax dodgers everywhere. They deserve to prosper. So I suppose, Lewis, this means you can retire and live a life of idle luxury?'

'Well, I wouldn't put it quite like that.' Lewis's colour heightened. 'I could hardly have it said I was living off my wife, but it does enable me to pursue my writing in a much freer way and it also means we can live wherever we like. I think we're both rather tired of London.'

'What better place than here, old boy?' Grant leaned forward enthusiastically. 'Lovely climate, beautiful scenery, cheap booze, no tax problems and, believe me, if Diana's as well off as you say, your worries in that direction are only just beginning if you live in the UK. Unearned income's the very devil.'

Lewis looked confused. 'I hadn't really

thought about it,' he began, 'at least, not seriously. We had discussed the possibility of Malta or perhaps Switzerland in a desultory sort of way but I'm afraid we might find it rather parochial and it's not always easy to find a comparable property to what we have at home.'

'Think about it now, old chap. Think about it now. What's more, I've got the perfect house for you.'

'You have? You mean you know of one that's for sale?' In spite of herself Diana was becoming interested. The state of euphoria induced by three brandies may have been responsible.

'I do,' he said. 'Mine!'

'Yours? But what about you and Hilary? And how is she, Grant? How dreadful of me not to ask before!'

Something flickered behind the tawny, cinnamon-coloured eyes. Somewhere a shutter clamped down and the light went out, but his facial muscles didn't move and his expression remained the same. After an infinitesimal pause he said flatly, 'She's dead.'

He deliberately held Diana's glance as if he were issuing some kind of challenge and she went on looking at him but not seeing him. In her mind's eye the dancing figure of Hilary, effervescent, warm and gay, sympathetic, generous and, above all, so alive, swam into focus, defying attempts at obliteration. She managed to stop herself repeating incredulously the two words he had spoken, which had been her first appalled reaction. She knew she should be expressing regret but to say 'I'm sorry' seemed inadequate after the bald, flat statement. To ask 'How?' or 'Why?' would show an indecent curiosity but that's what she clamoured to know. She sat in shocked silence and looked to Lewis for help.

Grant swilled the ice round in his glass. 'I'm sorry,' he said. 'That was clumsy. I should have prepared you but it's still fairly recent and I can't talk about it much. She was killed in an accident. No one else was hurt.'

Lewis said gruffly, 'That's all right. We're dreadfully sorry. It's devilish bad luck.'

Unreasonably the cliché jarred and Diana experienced the familiar, impotent irritation with her husband. 'Devilish bad luck' — the phrase could cover any number of contingencies in Lewis's day-to-day existence from backing a loser or missing a sitting putt, to having your wife tragically and suddenly killed in an accident.

Grant was speaking. 'Anyway, to get back to what I was saying . . . now that there's only me, the house is far too big and I was thinking of going into something smaller. If you think any more about the idea and you want to see it or buy it, you can have first refusal.'

'Where is it?' Diana asked.

'Beyond the promontory on the southern side and further along towards Tamariu. It's right on the mountain and has a superb view as well as a private beach. I'll tell you what: I'm having a few friends in for drinks on Wednesday evening. Why don't you come and see for yourselves? You can also meet some of the local expatriots.'

'Is that what they call themselves?' Diana laughed, happy to be on lighter ground.

Grant was himself again. 'Must stick together and show the flag, you know. We have quite a colony of writers and artists, retired Service people and stock-brokers — all very proud of their British origins.'

'That sounds rather hypocritical to me,' said Diana. 'They're proud of being British but not too proud to opt out for tax purposes, and having accepted the hospitality of another country, they band together as ex-patriots and become positively jingoistic.'

Grant smiled. 'Come off your smug little Presbyterian conscience, my dear Diana, and make an allowance or two for the frailty of human nature. We can't all live up to such exalted standards. Some of us find the altitude at that height too rarefied.' He spoke in gentle fun, teasing with his eyes, but he wasn't prepared for the sudden ugly flush as if she had been struck or the instant gathering of bright, unshed tears before she lowered her gaze.

She controlled her voice as she spoke more quietly.

'All the same, if I were to come and live here I should want to make some effort to meet and make friends with the people of the country.'

'And you couldn't do that without learning the lingo,' said Lewis. 'You speak Spanish, Grant. How long did it take you to learn?'

'Oh, I don't know. A few months. It's not a bad occupation for that first year when you're prohibited from returning to Britain. Time can lie heavy when you're a bit homesick: just because you can't go back for twelve months is enough to make you long to.'

'But after that you can?'

'Oh, after that you can go back for two or three months a year. I can give you all the gen if you want it. If it makes you feel better, it's only a two-hour hop from Gerona by plane and not excessively expensive.'

'Diana won't fly.' Lewis made it sound like an indictment.

'Why not?' said Grant, addressing her. 'Are you afraid?'

'Terrified, and don't start telling me that I've more chance of being killed in the street or blind me with crash statistics. It doesn't make any difference. It isn't as if I haven't flown, either. I have, tanked up each time with a double brandy, but it gets worse rather than better.'

'What are you afraid of?'

She thought for a moment, then said slowly, 'Of being afraid, of behaving badly in a crisis, I suppose. When those doors close and the engines rev. up and you know you can't run screaming down the aisle to ask to be let out but have got to sit and bear it — that's the worst part. Sometimes I wake up at night as much as three months before I have to fly, having dreamed of that very sensation. I'm not a very brave person. It's very inconvenient and I'd do anything to overcome it if I knew what.'

'You could take pills — tranquillizers.'

She smiled. 'I suppose it's silly but I call that the weak way out. I want a cure, not a temporary panacea.'

Grant was silent for a moment, then he said, 'I could cure you.'

She was surprised. 'You could? How?'

'By hypnotism.'

'Hypnotism? Would it work?'

'Nine times out of ten it does, but you'd

15

have to want it yourself. It wouldn't be any good resisting.'

She considered him seriously. 'I don't know that I'd like to put myself into somebody else's power completely. It's like surrendering one's whole personality.'

'That's why you'd have to trust me. I couldn't make you do anything that was directly contrary to your ethics: it doesn't work that way. I am qualified to do this sort of thing, you know, and I have treated other people with the same phobia.'

'Successfully?'

He nodded.

'I'd forgotten you were a bit of a head-shrinker, Grant,' Lewis said. 'It's worth considering, old girl. My God, I don't look forward to repeating the journey we had to get here! We put the car on the night train from Boulogne and had couchettes in a six-berth compartment which we shared with a French couple and their son, none of whom believed in fresh air. Diana can *parlez-vous* a bit but these frogs spoke a kind of *patois* she couldn't recognize and every time I opened the window during the night the woman's husband was made to shut it. The stench of humanity was abominable and I created hell with the Inspector, I can tell you. *Wagon-Lit* is expensive and driving all the way is a hell of a flog. No, flying's the answer.'

Diana sat back and half listened to him droning on. It was getting dark and lights were going on one by one in the hotel windows and shaded lamps were glowing softly on the terrace. The moon had risen over the mountain and, down in the cove, the water lapped gently while the sound of crockery being stacked and laid came from the dining-room. It would soon be time to go and change.

Lewis was entertaining Grant to a blow-by-blow description of an encounter with the Spanish police at the frontier when a bloody wog had rammed his car, when José appeared at his elbow and coughed discreetly. José had been at Bahia Dorada for twenty-eight years and, apart from being the hotel's senior waiter, he had a son who worked in the bar and a daughter in Reception who was married to the chef. He was short and plump with dark curly hair, and a face that creased readily into smiles. Diana could smell fresh soap and pomade as he bent over her and kissed her hand in mock gallantry and with his hand on his heart declared that she was looking beautiful. She knew that Lewis didn't approve of what he called horse-play from the waiters. He thought it bred undue familiarity

17

and he frowned on her encouragement of it. He didn't see it as 'all a bit of fun' as she did and wouldn't admit she was right when she pointed out that they never over-stepped the mark — that indefinable mark which meant so much to Lewis and conveniently for him slotted people into their appropriate niches.

'It is about your boat, señor. The man from Palafrugell rings now. He would like to speak to you.'

Lewis thanked him and, rising from the table, said: 'I'm afraid I'll have to go. I'm trying to hire a boat and it should have been here today but you know what these people are. It's always *mañana*. One grouses about inefficiency at home but — my God! — we could teach them a thing or two when it comes to organization.' He held out his hand to Grant. 'Until Wednesday, Grant. We'd love to come and I'll think about what you said about the house. Coming, Diana?'

'In a moment. I haven't quite finished my drink.'

'Right.' He strode off purposefully and Diana and Grant sat chatting until their glasses were empty.

'Where's your car?' Diana asked. Grant nodded towards the lower car park. 'I'll come with you,' she said. 'It's on my way to the annexe if I go through the garden.'

Crossing the terrace they went down a flight of steps where, in a square concrete well, a noisy gang of ten- and twelve-year olds were playing American table tennis. At the bottom of a further flight was the lobster tank, a circular pool with a glass top, kept at a constant temperature and floodlit by night. Grant stopped to watch its ungainly black occupants lumbering clumsily over small rocks and each other, but Diana hated looking at them and was secretly relieved that the *à la carte* price of lobster precluded Lewis and her from indulging in this delicacy. It was somehow different ordering Lobster Thermidor in London from choosing your prey here in cold blood and having a small Spaniard fish it out with a net and despatch it for your sole pleasure. She would have felt like a murderess.

'Poor buggers!' Grant commented.

Beyond the lobsters a line of cars was parked among a few intermittent pines. Here and there a lantern gleamed in the darkness amongst the shrubs along a grass verge. Grant made for a white Lamborghini and unlocked the door. Nobody was about.

Diana said, 'Nice car — it's like you. Fast, brash and confident.' She made a sound as if she were laughing but when he put his hands on her arms and drew her against him and laid his face against hers before kissing her, he felt the tears wet on his cheek.

'It's been a long time,' he said roughly.

2

Lewis Holt's mother had been reared from birth to accept and believe absolutely in the fundamental superiority of the male species. To her, Women's Lib. would have appeared totally incomprehensible. It was a woman's place to minister to the menfolk in her family, to wash, cook and clean, run errands and see that their passage through this world was eased. Men must be protected from the more mundane realities in order to be spared for the nobler things of life. Professor Holt, a gentle intellectual, and Lewis, even as a boy, were accustomed to take it for granted that Mrs Holt and Mary, Lewis's sister, should wait on them hand, foot and finger, even to cleaning their shoes and valeting their clothes, filling coke hods and hauling in replenished scuttles from the outside coal cellar. To Lewis that was what women were for.

His mother was the backbone of their family, holding all the threads in her blunt, capable, work-worn hands. She was practical, sensible and immensely house-proud, completely unselfish, desiring nothing for herself in the way of a new dress, a visit to the hairdresser, furs, jewels or the luxuries coveted by other women. Her husband could and would have furnished her needs had she voiced them but she would have considered it importunate to do so. Self-pride was a sin and anyway she never went anywhere to warrant a new dress.

Lewis had been a moody child, given to long periods of sulking and silence when things didn't go his way. Where another boy would have thrown a fit of temper, Lewis shut himself in his room for hours on end, talking to no one and answering none of his mother's anxious questions shouted through the keyhole. In other ways his conduct was more than exemplary. He was an apt, avid scholar at school and later at college, conscientiously devoting himself to the surmounting of each examination hurdle and diligently applying himself to the task with a mind that delighted in meticulous, detailed precision where facts were concerned. Amongst his school fellows he was accepted indulgently as a dull swot but a good sort, though many secretly envied his dedicated academic prowess. They could afford to be magnanimous since this was still the era of the games player, when getting your blue was adequate justification for a public school and university education, and the most damning thing that could be said of a man's character was that he played no sport. Lewis loathed games, considering them a waste of time. He took a lot of knowing and therefore had few real friends, but to those who took the trouble to get to know him, he showed an unsuspected humanity and now and then the rarest glimpse of a sense of profound inadequacy. He had a strong sense of values and exacted too high a standard so that he was constantly being disappointed by people. Lewis made no allowances for others and did not expect any to be made for himself.

At home few sons were more dutiful or considerate but sometimes in the night his mother lay dry-eyed beside the snoring professor, staring into the darkness, wondering where she had failed. Every self-sacrificing gesture she made proclaimed the warmth of her love for them all and her husband was a kindly, affectionate man, but where was the spark of warmth in her son? She comforted herself by believing that, when the right girl came along, the spark would kindle. It was a long wait. Lewis was thirty-six when he met Klara Tolstrup in a bar opposite the Players' Theatre near Charing Cross.

It was a rough dive and the stench of humanity and beer was as thick upon the air as the tobacco smoke that hit him as he opened the glass-topped swing door. It was the sort of place he had frequented during his early days in the police force in search of a nark or a suspected tip-off. Navvies with their sleeves rolled up swilled overflowing pints, beads of froth dripping down the fronts of sweat-stained shirts. Their womenfolk lined the benches along the walls, incongruously dressed as for an evening out, clutching large handbags and sipping sherry and port and lemon, looking, Lewis thought, as he often did when he saw ordinary people *en masse*, so commonplace, with no particular characteristic one would be able to describe at a later date. No wonder policemen were habitually frustrated by contradictory and muddled descriptions of witnesses when so many thousands of faces were so indescribably commonplace.

He was on leave, it being his first visit to London for some years and he had stepped into 'The Fiddler's Bitch' on an impulse to see whether Arnold Rigby was still behind the bar. In the midst of the *mêlée*, sticking out like a sore thumb, was a group of four people in evening dress. The men were in dinner jackets, the two girls in long dresses which covered shoulders and arms, although, when the girl Lewis took to be the younger of the two turned round, he could see that her bodice plunged to a deep V, which was being

24

fully appreciated by the general assembly. As he pushed his way through the scrum towards the bar a hand fell on his shoulder and he turned to find himself face to face with a large man with untidy red hair and protruding startled-looking eyes.

'Lewis Holt, as I live and breathe! What's a nice guy like you doing in a joint like this?'

'Andy! I might ask you the same question. I suppose you're working incognito in that rig or is it some kind of new cover?'

Andrew Dalton laughed and keeping his hand on Lewis's back, he turned to present him to the others.

'Klara, Maggie, meet Lewis Holt. Lewis, this is Jim Ellis, he's C.I.D. — after your time. Lewis and I used to bash a beat together in the old days before he opted for serving the cause of British Justice in the far-flung outposts of the Empire. Look, we can't talk here. Can you manoeuvre over into the corner? There's a free table there now, the people have just left. What are you drinking?'

Andy moved towards the bar while Lewis, Jim and the girls wove their way to the vacant table. He joined them some minutes later with a whisky and soda which he placed in front of Lewis.

'I suppose we do look pretty out of place,' he said with a grin, 'but Jim and I have been

25

showing the girls the sights and we've got a particularly tight schedule with no time to change en route. This evening included a trip down to Putney and back on the river, taking in a visit to a back-street London pub, on to the theatre, and then we're dining at the Savoy because the girls have heard about it. I've warned them there are more exciting places but in Denmark they say everybody knows the Savoy.'

'Is that where you come from?' Lewis asked Klara. She was the girl with the plunging neck-line and, as she sat beside him now, he kept his eyes politely riveted on her face, painfully aware of the comments being bandied between two men who were standing behind her. It was a face worth looking at, almost childish in its innocence with wide, china-blue eyes fringed with dark lashes. She had dark brows too and a short pert nose and rounded high cheek-bones. Her hair was pale gold and fell from a side parting quite straight to her shoulders where it turned slightly upwards at the ends. She had an untouched, virginal expression which contrasted strikingly with the voluptuous curves of the slim body emphasized by the clinging material of the blue dress she wore. She spoke good English but with a faintly broken accent. She nodded now in answer to his question.

'From Funen — do you know it?'

'No,' he said. 'I've never been to Denmark, but I'd like to. Were you there all through the war?'

'Yes.' She looked serious.

'Was it bad?'

'We were lucky. It was bad for some, worse in Copenhagen and the big towns than on our island. And what about you? You too were in the war?'

'Not really,' said Lewis. 'I was in Kenya when it began and they made me stay there. After my leave I'm to be sent to Hong Kong. That's in four months' time.'

'You're a policeman like Andy?'

'We started together as flat-foots and now he's a superintendent and I'm a deputy.'

'Flat foot?' She creased her brows. 'What is that?' She looked delightful, like a puzzled child, and Lewis could not help smiling at her.

'It's a slang expression for a policeman on the beat. So much walking is meant to give him big flat feet. Are you going to be in England long?'

'That depends on whether we can get a permit to work here,' she replied. 'Maggie is a nurse and would like to work at one of the big teaching hospitals here in London. At home I am a speech therapist. I was working with

27

deaf children and people who had to learn to speak again after accidents to their vocal chords — that kind of thing.'

Lewis was surprised. She hardly looked old enough to have left school and he told her so.

'I'm twenty-six. Not so young.'

'Still ten years younger than I am,' said Lewis, and wondered why he had voiced that. After all, it was just a casual encounter in a pub, their paths were hardly likely to overlap again. The thought crossed his mind at the same moment as Andy looked at his watch and exclaimed that they must all drink up or they'd be late for the show. 'Sorry, Lewis, I wish it could have been longer. I haven't heard any of your news. Hey, wait a minute. Why don't you join us after the theatre? Are you staying close enough to go and change? We could meet you at the Savoy at, say, ten-thirty and go on the town afterwards. What do you say?'

Lewis was staying with his parents in Blackheath but three hours would give him plenty of time to get home, put on a dinner jacket and get back in time to meet them. He didn't often do things on the spur of the moment but he had no better arrangement for the evening. So why not?

'I'd like to, but are you sure I shan't be butting in on a foursome?'

Andrew brushed the suggestion aside as nonsense and both girls insisted he would be welcome. Klara looked at him with her wide-eyed, baby-doll gaze and said, 'Please come,' and that clinched it.

★　★　★

Lewis Holt's sexual experience could be summed up by saying that, although he had attained the age of thirty-six, he was still psychologically, if not technically, a virgin. His encounters with the opposite sex had been brief and purely — if you could use the word in such a context — businesslike. From time to time he required sexual release in the same way that he felt hunger or thirst, and in precisely the same way that he would have gratified the two latter basic instincts, he discreetly arranged for the satisfaction of the other, reimbursing the lady in question and never seeking solace twice in the same arms. It was easy enough to organize, particularly abroad, and it had the advantage that he never became involved emotionally or laid himself open to any of the ugly little scenes in which many of his contemporaries became embroiled, playing on home ground and messing around with the bored wives of their fellow officers who got their kicks from liaisons of that kind. That sort of thing could lead to trouble career-wise and in the police force you had to keep your nose clean.

What Lewis called the act of love had little or nothing to do with his heart. He had had no time to think of marriage in his early days in the Force and by the time he was working abroad the most obvious need for a wife had been eliminated by a houseful of servants, supplied by the Service, who waited upon and anticipated his every whim. His house-boy even filled his cigarette lighter and, from the point of view of efficient comfort, the presence of a woman could hardly have improved the existing order of his life.

★ ★ ★

Now as the train trundled across London Bridge and through New Cross, he was disturbed to find himself thinking of the girl he had just met. Klara. Thinking of her reminded him that it was six months since he had had a woman. He speculated upon her possible relationship with Andy. It was obvious even from so short a meeting that the other two he had met — Maggie and Jim — were more than just good friends, or at any rate would like to be. He was trained to recognize the nuances, but he had detected no such feeling between Klara and Andy. Her innocence and the simple straightforward way she spoke gave her the air of a girl unawakened, although his experience told him that, at twenty-six, this was unlikely. Lewis was in no mood this particular evening to listen to the voice of experience.

Once home, his mother bustled around, producing a clean evening shirt from the airing cupboard, his dinner jacket neatly pressed, and took his black patent shoes to the kitchen to wipe away a few imaginary specks of dust. Fastening his gold cuff links and putting the last pearl-topped stud in place, Lewis looked at his reflection in the mirror and tried impossibly to imagine how he would look to someone else seeing him for the first time. He would have liked to have been a little taller than five foot nine and always tried to remember to hold himself very upright to give the impression of greater height. His fair hair was thick and smooth, combed slightly back from a left-hand parting with short back and sides as regulations and the Kenyan climate demanded. Under brows as fair as his hair a pair of shrewd blue eyes were set wide apart in his sun-tanned face. He still looked young enough, he thought complacently. He didn't ask himself for what! They hadn't arrived when he got to the

Savoy Hotel, so he strolled about the foyer, looking at the flower kiosk, reading theatre advertisements, not wanting to sit down and look as if he had been over-anxious and waiting for ages. After about ten minutes, they came in, laughing and talking, and swept him into their midst. After the girls had powdered their noses and left their coats in the cloakroom they went to dine at a table on the dance floor, far enough away from the band for conversation to be audible.

Over the meal the three men reminisced, entertaining the girls with anecdotes of some of the funnier side of police work. Maggie entered into the cut and thrust of the repartee, displaying a sharp wit and a breezy, raucous sense of humour. She was a thin, dark girl, her hair cut severely short in a ragged gamin style which suited her angular, intelligent face. She used her hands a lot, gesticulating to illustrate a story while her dark brown eyes brilliantly mirrored the changing emotions.

By contrast Klara was quiet, but it was far from the dumb blonde brand of quietness. She smiled and talked and was ready to laugh with the others but she was content to let Maggie hold the stage and for that Lewis warmed to her. She could so easily have commanded all the attention for herself with her looks, which knocked spots off poor Maggie who, after all, could be accounted no man's idea of the *Venus de Milo*. As far as he could make out, no particular rapport existed between Klara and Andy, but later when Maggie and Jim were dancing and Klara had gone to the cloakroom, Lewis took the opportunity of asking him outright.

'Good heavens, no! There's no attachment. We hardly know one another. Jim and Maggie have been going out together for some time. He met her in Denmark when he was over there on a job and I was brought in a couple of times over here to make a foursome. No, old boy, the field's clear for you if that's what you want, but I should watch it if I were you. She looks to me as if she might be a bit too hot to handle but no doubt you've got more experience in these matters than I, what with your Eastern women and dusky maidens. I bet they've taught you a thing or two, eh?'

Lewis tightened his mouth and moved beyond range of Andy's leering nudge. He didn't like this kind of talk and it particularly jarred in connection with Klara. She was too fresh and sweet and direct to be smeared by suggestion or filthy inference, and as for being too hot to handle, she had struck Lewis by her cool unawareness of her own sexual attraction. It was her very innocence that had

had such a devastating effect on him and he was now prepared to admit to himself that devastating was not too strong an adjective. He wanted her — but not like any other woman he had had. He wanted to know her, to teach her, to see her flower under his tuition. She would become a woman the possession of whom any man would envy. It was totally out of character for him to feel so strongly on the strength of an evening's acquaintance, so he deliberately made himself wait until late in the evening before asking her to dance.

He put out his arms to hold her stiffly and formally in the conventional way he had been taught and was faintly embarrassed when she moved naturally into a closer position with her face against his and the rest of her body pressing gently against his chest, stomach and thigh. The effect this produced on him was getting decidedly more unconventional every second. When over her shoulder he saw other couples dancing in the same style, he relaxed and began to enjoy himself. The music stopped but she didn't draw away from him and when it started again the tempo was different and they both started off on different feet and she stepped on his toe. He was instantly apologetic.

'Oh no.' She was laughing. 'It was my fault.

It is now I who am the flat foot.'

They resumed their dancing position and Lewis, with his mouth close to her ear, said boldly, 'There is very little about you, Klara, that could possibly be described as flat.' It was his first attempt at dalliance.

He got quite good at it during the next few weeks and sometimes surprised himself with a brand of flirtatious repartee which would have equally astounded the circles in which he was known, where he was reputedly short on a sense of humour. He liked to make Klara laugh, which he found he could do quite easily, although not always intentionally. It appeared there was much about him she found amusing and it could be disconcerting to discover that a great many things he held sacred came into that category. She teased him about his orderliness and precise punctuality. It was nothing for her to be as much as half an hour late for their dates and her happy-go-lucky attitude to life shocked him as much as her stout refusal to acknowledge his ingrained acceptance of the English class strata. His explanation of the public school system and the reverential nostalgic tones in which he recalled his own schooldays met with incredulous mirth and he wished he had never mentioned cold showers and cross-country runs, the purpose of which had been to produce a *mens sana in corpore sano*. He was fully conscious that she knew all too well what she did to his *corpore sano* just by leaning against him in his arms on the dance floor or looking up at him over the rim of her glass with her huge cornflower blue eyes, and as for his mind, he chided himself that some of his thoughts were distinctly unhealthy.

He had kissed her good night on occasions, when he left her outside the door of the flat she was sharing with Maggie, but he hadn't been invited inside and he told himself, and made himself believe it, that he was glad he hadn't. He knew that Maggie entertained Jim there on occasions and the fact that Klara did nothing to encourage him over the threshold demonstrated more clearly than words that she wasn't that kind of a girl. All the same, Lewis was finding it increasingly frustrating that there was nowhere where they could be alone. His desire and his urgency for her increased, and for the first time in his life thoughts of marriage entered his head, and, once conceived, could not be banished. He wanted her more than any woman he had ever seen.

On previous occasions it had been sufficient to work off a passing passion by a discreetly arranged visit to a third party, but now it was Klara he wanted and the only way he could get her would be by marriage. Her sweetness and goodness were touching and he enjoyed the role of instructor and guide as he took her to the Tate Gallery and Syon House, Hampton Court, Windsor and Woburn, The Old Vic and Festival Hall and, on her insistence, Madame Tussaud's and Battersea Fun Fair. At the latter he had put his arm round her shoulders and held her tightly against him for safety in the Dive Bomber as the abominable machine started to wheel and gather momentum, spinning them high at first then suddenly and perilously close to the ground. Klara threw back her head, alternately laughing and shrieking while Lewis was glad that there was no one in the crowd below he knew to witness her extrovert exhibition or his distinct pallor and unsteady gait on alighting. Part of her attraction for him was her uninhibited enjoyment of everything they saw and did together. Illogically, it was the same exuberance that during their marriage embarrassed and irritated him intolerably — when she laughed at some joke in the theatre before the rest of the audience or carried on a conversation with him in a railway carriage without appreciably lowering her voice.

Finally Lewis took her to Blackheath to

meet his parents, making the announcement of his intentions to them deliberately casual to prevent his mother from making preparations on too frenzied a scale or jumping to matrimonial conclusions and bombarding him with veiled hints and discreet questions. As he had known she would, she found it necessary to spring-clean the entire house, already immaculate, in Klara's honour, as well as cooking a three-course lunch and baking her own particular recipe for shortbread and rich fruit tea loaf.

'I wish you wouldn't, Mother,' said Lewis, finding her polishing the brass stair-rods late after supper. 'It's all quite unnecessary. She'll never notice those and they're clean anyway.'

'We don't want her to think you live in a pigsty, do we, or that your mother's a slut and doesn't know how to keep a house?' she retorted, and when Lewis said: 'She's hardly likely to think that and, in any case, does it matter what she thinks?' she shot him a knowing look and replied: 'Doesn't it?'

Mrs Holt was still polishing furniture when Lewis brought Klara up the steps and through the front door and it wasn't until months later, during the course of one of their increasingly bitter quarrels, that Klara told Lewis that on first meeting his mother she had mistaken her for the char. It was hard to equate this drab, wispy woman, in carpet slippers and a stained apron over her shabby grey dress, with the careful, clean, conservative attention Lewis gave to his own appearance. At least the sense of shock was mutual. Klara in her bright cyclamen suit, her flaxen hair shining, her hands white and delicate with nails painted to match her outfit and revealing unashamedly, as the conversation progressed, her profound disinterest in all subjects domestic, was a far cry from the homely, capable daughter-in-law of Mrs Holt's imagination, and watching Lewis's behaviour she had no doubt that this was to be Klara's role. The girl had Professor Holt eating out of her hand in no time and when later in bed his wife voiced some of her misgivings, all he replied was, 'She's very decorative. I didn't think Lewis had it in him to choose a girl like that.'

'That's what I mean,' she emphasized but he only smiled fatuously and said Lewis was old enough to know what he was doing.

3

They married in December, ten days before
Christmas, with the Holts, Jim, Andy and
Maggie and Lewis's sister Mary, as witnesses.
Lewis was relieved to be spared the
commotion of a big wedding. All he wanted
was Klara, and now she was his, standing
beside him looking like something out of a
fairy tale in a nut-brown suit trimmed with
chocolate coloured fur and a fur beret on her
gleaming head. He took her to Bahia Dorada
where the hotel was then one of the few
buildings on the mountainside, and in a
bedroom overlooking the bay, Lewis discovered he had made his first mistake.

★   ★   ★

They had taken a night flight to Barcelona
and hired a car from there, arriving at the
hotel in the early hours of the morning
exhausted from the journey and the
emotional excitement of the preceding day.
He sent Klara up to their room with the
night porter and her luggage and went out
to take his own cases out of the car and to

find a parking space.

She wasn't in the bedroom when he opened the door but her clothes lay in a heap on the double bed and the sound of running water came from an adjoining bathroom, the door of which was slightly ajar. He dumped his case on the rack provided and, opening it, began to unpack and put his clothes away tidily in the drawers. He took off his suit jacket and hung it in the cupboard, then stood irresolute, holding his electric razor and washing bag, wondering whether to put them in the bathroom or wait until Klara appeared. He didn't want to embarrass her. He intended to initiate her tenderly and carefully and he didn't want her to think that, because they were alone at last, he couldn't wait a few hours more, until she was rested and refreshed, before consummating their marriage. As he stood there, the water was turned off and he moved about the bedroom, humming quietly beneath his breath to let her know he was there.

'Lewis, is that you?'

'Yes. I'm just unpacking.' He tried to keep his voice casual.

'Come in here and look at this funny little bath. It must have been made for a dwarf.'

Tentatively, he pushed the door further open and stepped into the bathroom. Klara was sitting doubled up in a square hip-bath, her knees drawn up to her chin and her feet resting on a porcelain step half-way up the bath. Her hair was pulled up on top of her head in a knot with wisps hanging down on either side of her face and she was laughing. Without make-up and devoid of her sophisticated clothes she looked like a mischievous child, until she stood up, as she now did unconcernedly, facing him as she reached for the towel hanging on the shower curtain above her head. Any fatigue Lewis had felt disappeared promptly.

He hadn't believed anyone's skin could be so smooth and creamy. The beads of water slid over her shoulders and down the deep hollow between her high, full breasts which swung gently as she towelled her back vigorously. Her stomach was flat and taut below a narrow waist and her hips had a promising voluptuous swell, tapering down to lean, smooth flanks and thighs. She was watching him and he tried to look away but in the end she said, 'For God's sake put those things down and come here.'

He did as he was told and she reached up to put both her arms around his neck, dropping the towel as she did so and it fell back into the water. She was still standing in the bath which made her taller than Lewis and brought his face on a level with her breasts and he felt faintly ridiculous and at a disadvantage, being held against her wet body and feeling the dampness penetrate his shirt.

'My clothes,' he protested, half-heartedly.

'Take them off then.' And to his surprise and further embarrassment he felt her undoing the waistband and flies of his trousers which fell ludicrously around his feet, making him feel even more like a character out of a Brian Rix farce. By the time he had stepped out of them she had unbuttoned his shirt and renewed her embrace and the touch of her naked flesh against his suddenly turned him to fire and he discarded the rest of his clothes in a fever of impatience.

'That's better. Come on in, the water's lovely,' she teased him with her eyes and hands.

Without thinking, he stepped over the rim of the bath to bring himself up to her level and, pulling her roughly to him, he kissed her, slowly at first, holding back his urgency as best he could, meaning to initiate her slowly step by step. Somewhere along the line he lost the initiative and she had taken over. Her tongue was in his mouth, tasting, searching, probing, devouring, while her hands moved down his back and her fingers dug painfully into his buttocks, pressing their limbs together while she moaned and twisted in a frenzy of desire. Forgetting his original intention, too far gone to remember anything except the agony of wanting her, he pushed her back against the tiled wall behind the bath and straddled her. For a split second he opened his eyes and looked into her face, the virginal, untouched face of the innocent girl he had married, now swollen with desire, the beautiful blue eyes glazed with passion, the slack, wet mouth slurring words of urgent pleading, 'Yes, yes — go on — please go on.' He recalled her deliberately provocative posing, the practised gestures, the hungry appetite that would have allowed him, wanted him, to take her here, standing against the bathroom wall like a common whore, and his hands fell from her. It wasn't going right, not the way he had planned it. Sensing his withdrawal, she clung to him and whimpered.

'I can't. Not here,' he said and she allowed him to lift her from the bath and carry her to the bed and there the last of Lewis's illusions disintegrated.

The behaviour of his bride could hardly be termed remotely virginal in the battle that ensued. Indeed it was Lewis who felt himself to be increasingly at a disadvantage when what advances he was allowed to make appeared amateur in comparison with her expertise. He found himself in the hands of a practised operator and although he had secretly read about some of the moves in the ecstatic *pas-de-deux* in which he found himself a partner, part of him was shocked and appalled to be participating in such deviations, while his senses were so unbearably stimulated and excited that he couldn't have stopped what was happening had he wanted to.

When the world finally stopped spinning and his brain cleared, his first emotion was one of self-disgust. He couldn't bear to open his eyes and read in hers the knowledge of the degradations to which he had been willing to sink with her. He kept them closed and turned from her to face the wall, his head buried on his arm. He lay like that for what seemed like hours. Klara slept. He could hear her soft, regular breathing, and when, much later, he turned to look at her, her face was young and untouched, faintly flushed like an infant's, pure and serene, with her lashes dipping in half-moons on her cheeks. It was hard to believe she was the same woman he had taken to bed, the instrument of such intense pleasure and the pitiless mental torment he now endured. He put on his dressing-gown and went to sit on the balcony to smoke a cigarette and watch the dawn come up.

At six o'clock the fishing boats put out and some time later a spartan couple passed silently down the steps to the slab for an early morning swim. The sun had risen by the time he heard Klara's voice call him from the bedroom. He didn't answer and in a few moments she came out to join him, wearing a blue towelling robe.

'Good morning, darling.' She put her arms around his hunched shoulders but he shrugged them away and she drew back, puzzled and hurt.

'Is anything wrong?'

He remained silent and she pulled a chair nearer to him so that she could see his face. 'Something is wrong. What is it? Tell me.'

Then he looked at her. She was genuinely worried and he was thunderstruck that she had to ask. A thought occurred to her.

'Last night. You were disappointed? Wasn't it good?'

He couldn't help himself. 'I'm sure you're the best judge of that,' he said bitterly. 'I'd say you'd had infinitely more varied experience than I, wouldn't you?'

She looked at him hard and long without flushing, then she lowered her eyes to her hands clasped between her knees and rocked her chair slowly backwards and forwards. After a short silence she said, 'I never pretended to be a virgin. I would have told you if you had asked.'

'I don't make a habit of asking girls that sort of thing,' Lewis said savagely.

'Which is perhaps a pity since it obviously matters so much to you. I'm sorry.' There was nothing abject about the apology and Lewis experienced a primitive desire to hurt her.

'How many were there?' he asked roughly.

She looked at him enquiringly.

'How many men? Do I have to spell it out?'

She looked at him steadily. 'Several, four or five. I didn't count. That sort of thing is not so important in Denmark. What matters is, there won't be any more now. I didn't marry them. I married you.'

'My God!' He put his head in his hands. 'You don't have to remind me. And to think I thought I couldn't have you any other way. A trollop like you. I actually respected you.'

Her expression didn't change but the blue of her eyes deepened and she put her hand to her face as if he had struck her. She said quietly, 'I love you, Lewis.'

His eyes were like stones. 'You disgust me.'

She got up and went to look over the balcony, her hands on the rail and, without turning round, she spoke with a tinge of mockery.

'Why? Because I know how to use my body to give you pleasure? And it did give you pleasure. Didn't it, Lewis? I was pleased it did. Admit it. You enjoyed it. You loved me last night.'

She turned to face him and he felt uncomfortable. It was true but she was too brazen. People's wives didn't talk like this.

'That wasn't love, that was lust,' he spluttered.

She raised an eyebrow. 'No? But still a lot of fun, eh, darling?'

'Fun!' He spat out the word contemptuously. 'It isn't meant . . .'

Comprehension dawned teasingly in her eyes.

'Oh, I see. It isn't meant to be fun — is that what you were taught? Or perhaps fun for you but not for me. Is that it? Not nice for me to admit it.' She suddenly became serious. 'What a bloody hypocrite you are, my darling. In just the same way I should have pretended to be a virgin, but I had more respect for you. In spite of my respect, Lewis, I didn't expect you to be a virgin.'

'It's different for men,' he said, and when he had said that she thought he had said it all.

'Why should it be?'

'Because it just is, it always has been. The way you behaved last night, it — shamed me.' Unexpectedly his voice broke on the last two words and she was horrified to see him put up his hand to brush it across his eyes. Forgetting her own hurt, she moved forward swiftly to kneel by his chair and take his hands in hers.

'There was nothing shameful to me,' she said gently. 'Nothing can shame two people when they love one another and what they do together pleases them. I wanted to please you, Lewis. I say again, I love you.'

He allowed her to draw his head down against her shoulder and they stayed like that for a while without speaking. She felt the tension gradually leave him and presently he raised his face and looked at her. He put his hand against her cheek, studying her features intently and after a time what he read in her eyes must have reassured him because he smiled.

'Come and get some rest, you haven't slept at all.' She led him back into the bedroom and they lay down side by side, not touching. When she felt his hand loosen the belt of her robe she lay quite still and remained passive and acquiescent. He took her in five minutes flat, then rolled off her and went to sleep with a satisfied grunt. She wasn't at all convinced

49

she was going to enjoy behaving like an English lady.

After that she took good care never to be the one to make sexual overtures, which meant that, once the honeymoon was over, she would often wait three or four weeks before Lewis, preparing for bed, might say to her, incidentally, while cleaning his teeth, 'Isn't it about time we made love?' That was the signal for her cold-bloodedly to take her precautions in the bathroom before joining him in the bed, where he spent a cursory two minutes fondling her breasts before getting on with the task in hand. Whether he was afraid of kindling the demon he feared and which he knew she harboured or whether he was just selfish, she never knew. They didn't talk about it and knowing Lewis, as by this time she did, she judged it was his own reactions he distrusted. If he ignored them they would go away.

That alone might not have caused the break-up of their marriage, but there were so many other areas in which he made her feel inadequate.

★ ★ ★

When they returned from Spain there were still two months of leave left to Lewis, and for

50

this period they rented a furnished flat in Barnes. It was right on the river and Klara took a delight in the water traffic that passed continuously under their sitting-room windows. She had had no experience of housekeeping or cooking and instead of being able to evolve a routine by trial and error while he was at the office, Lewis was under her feet all day, criticizing her methods, showing impatience with her culinary failures, staggered by her inability to budget and contemptuous of her excuses. She became hamfisted and clumsy, dropping things and trying all the time to hide the evidence of her inefficiencies from his dissecting eye. On the first occasion he brought two pairs of his walking shoes into the kitchen and placed them on the table for her to clean, she made the mistake of accusing him of joking.

'You don't expect me to clean those, do you?' she'd laughed. 'Have you suddenly been struck with paralysis in your own hands?'

'My mother always cleaned Dad's shoes and mine,' he'd replied as if it were something to be proud of.

'More fool her,' said Klara bluntly. 'I certainly shan't as long as you're able-bodied,' and so Lewis had to clean his own shoes.

It wasn't the only field in which she was

51

measured against Mrs Holt senior and found wanting.

'At least no one will ever mistake me for the char,' she had shouted at him, goaded beyond endurance on one occasion. 'You don't want a wife at all — just a robot housekeeper — so much more satisfactory than a human being.'

It was virtually impossible to get him to answer back. Instead, he would withdraw into sulks for days while they went about their everyday business in complete silence. During these periods he would still expect to make love to her, something that utterly defied Klara's comprehension and when she expostulated he broke his self-imposed muteness so far as to assert that it was his right!

She comforted herself with the thought that things would be better in Hong Kong. Lewis had shown her pictures of the house they were to have and there would be servants and time perhaps for a baby, though she seriously doubted whether she would make much of motherhood, being such a dismal failure as a wife. It was all so much more complicated than she had been led to believe.

It was easier in the Far East. The bungalow supplied by the Force was roomy, airy and cool with two extra guest suites besides their own, a parquet-floored veranda-ed drawing-room, dining-room and study as well as the separate servants' quarters, housing cookie, an amah and a gardener. The latter three were related and there was always an endless stream of hangers-on in their cemented patio near the wash-room, and although Klara suspected that she and Lewis fed them, she was too timid to make an issue of it. The house was half-way up the Peak and it had a garden in which Klara spent much of her time, discovering an unexpected enthusiasm for working with the living plants and communing with Nature. She had no duties in the house. Amah kept it spotless and did the washing and Cookie suggested menus to her for which her sole responsibility was the shopping, and he did the rest. It was a pleasant, easy-going life, but after a time it palled and Klara was bored. She broached the subject of taking up her job again but Lewis couldn't understand her wanting to work when there was no financial necessity for her to do so.

'Besides,' he made the excuse, 'it's tricky getting work permits for wives nowadays when there aren't enough jobs for all the Chinese. You've got plenty to do arranging the guest lists for your dinner parties and don't forget I want cookie to prepare something special in the way of a hamper for Sunday's launch picnic.'

Lewis's department had a boat at its disposal which could be booked for week-end jaunts around the islands, and a picnic organized in this manner was an ideal way in which to entertain VIPs or guests to the Colony.

She renewed her request for a baby, pleading that there'd never be a better time to have one. If indeed they were to have a family they had better start now on account of Lewis's age, but although he half-heartedly agreed and she stopped taking precautions, nothing happened. She wondered if it was her fault because she felt little or nothing during their love-making. It was a long time since he had cared whether it was a satisfying experience for her — if ever — since that first time and yet she told herself she loved him.

★   ★   ★

The first time Klara was unfaithful was the Chinese New Year two years after her marriage. The servants had gone off to celebrate and Lewis was on duty. There was always a certain amount of trouble in the City at this time with fires caused by Chinese crackers and inebriated revellers getting out of hand. The bungalow lay in the depressing, swirling mist that enveloped the Peak for two thirds of the year, so that when the doorbell rang and one of Lewis's junior officers was revealed standing on the doorstep, Klara viewed his advent as a small reprieve from loneliness. He'd come to give Lewis a message but didn't seem in any hurry to catch up with him. It was a short distance from the door to the living-room and a drink, and from thence to the bed. Afterwards, as she re-arranged her hair and put more perfume behind her ears, Klara noticed she had more colour in her cheeks and she felt more alive than she had for two years. In her heightened awareness she began to look around and suddenly there seemed to be no dearth of eligible young men waiting upon her favours. To start with, she was discreet, but as the rift between her and Lewis widened, she stopped bothering to be careful and grabbed at every opportunity, like a woman long starved and never able to be satiated.

Hong Kong is a small place and it wasn't long before the whispers started going round and everyone sat back in pleasurable anticipation to see what Lewis was going to do. But he did nothing for the simple reason that, like the proverbial husband, he was going to be the last to know. But if Duncan Rossiter had anything to do with it, he was going to help Lewis stop the rot before Klara raised a stink in the Colony that could be carried on the winds back to London.

Duncan was Lewis's Chief and it had been at his instigation that Lewis had landed the Hong Kong job. They had known one another for a good many years and the Commissioner had watched the younger man's career with interest and respect, and having found himself in a position to give that promising career a leg-up, had been happy to do so. He would be disappointed to see Lewis's potential jeopardized by his wife's behaviour.

Now, as he sat in his stifling office overlooking Queen's Road, mopping his neck inside his collar with a handkerchief, he wondered what the hell he was going to say to his friend. He knew Klara and he couldn't think of anyone he would have been less likely to choose as a partner for Lewis, although he wasn't fool enough to imagine the situation was entirely of her making. He'd seen this sort of thing happen too often in the East. A bored, lonely wife with no children, a husband making his mark by working all the hours God sent and the ever ready army of grass widowers, whose wives were keeping houses warm at home, not to mention a plentiful supply of bachelors. He sighed and went over to where he could stand looking down at the hubbub of traffic, cars, trams and trishaws, and find a momentary relief from the all-enveloping humidity under the ceiling fan. He was a big man, both in stature and character, and he was tired. In two years' time he would be going home to retirement. Today it seemed a long time to wait.

'Ah, Lewis.' He turned as a corporal ushered in his visitor. 'Come in and sit down. It's a long time since we had a chat. Cigarette?' He proffered a case while Lewis lowered himself into the chair on the other side of the desk and put his cap and cane on a nearby table. 'How are things going?'

'Well enough, sir. We had a spot of bother getting that chap suspected of running those guns out to Macao, but we managed to run him to earth eventually and we're getting the case together for a preliminary hearing next week. I thought he'd slipped through our fingers.'

'Well done,' said Duncan absently as he cast about in his mind for a likely opening.

There was a short silence then Lewis asked, 'Was there something special you wanted to see me about?'

'Not particularly. I was going over the records and noticed you were due for a spot of leave. You didn't take your last entitlement and I don't like my men not to take what's due to them. This bloody heat saps one's strength and everyone needs a rest and a change.'

'I feel perfectly fit, sir. There are one or two matters coming to a head I must be in on. I'll probably take a week in the New Year, if that's convenient when the time comes.'

Duncan turned over one or two files on his desk. 'You may feel you don't need it but what about Klara?' he asked.

Lewis looked puzzled. 'What about her?'

'She'd like a holiday no doubt. Why not take her up to Japan? She told me a long time ago she'd very much like to see it.'

Lewis narrowed his eyes and looked straight at Duncan. 'What is this? Has Klara complained about leave to you?'

'No,' said Duncan carefully, 'she hasn't said anything, but I think she's looking tired and you forget she's young and sometimes rather lonely while you're absorbed in your work. She hasn't the interest of a family, while most of her contemporaries are kept busy with theirs. Of course it's not my business . . . ' he tailed off, seeing Lewis tighten the corners of his mouth.

'No, it's not,' he said shortly, 'but since you obviously want to know why we have no children, let me assure you that we have tried.'

'I'm sorry.' Duncan decided to try another tack. 'Look here, Lewis, we're old friends and I didn't mean to pry or poke my nose into your affairs, but I do think Klara feels a bit out on a limb. She hasn't enough to occupy her. Why don't you suggest she enquires about taking up her speech therapy at the hospital? I could probably wangle the necessary permit and they'd certainly welcome her with open arms.'

But Lewis was not fooled. 'How did we come to be discussing Klara?' he asked. 'I thought we were talking about leave, or is there an ulterior motive and that's the excuse?'

Duncan sighed. 'I'm just saying,' he said, 'as a friend, that in my opinion Klara needs a change as much as you. Take my advice. Take that trip, make it into a kind of second honeymoon. You won't regret it.'

Lewis said nothing for a moment while he pulled a case from his pocket and selected another cigarette. He delayed lighting up until Duncan had gestured his permission and then carefully extinguished his lighter, weighing it in his hand before he said quietly,

'What have you heard?'

Duncan feigned surprised innocence.

Lewis spoke again impatiently. 'You've heard something, you know something. I know your methods well enough to realize that. I want to know what's behind this apparent concern for Klara and me, why you think it would be better if we were away from the Colony for a few weeks when this is going be my busiest time.'

Duncan got up and went over to a blackwood cabinet in the corner from which he produced a bottle of Scotch and two glasses. He pressed a bell and when the corporal re-appeared ordered some ice. 'Drink?'

Lewis shook his head. He smelt a rat and he wasn't in the mood for pacification. When Duncan had fixed his drink according to his liking, he resumed his seat behind his desk and, facing Lewis, squarely said, 'I was hoping I wasn't going to have to tell you this, but since you ask, Lewis, there's been some talk about Klara and I think it would be best for you both to take some time off together and give it a chance to blow over. You know how quickly these things brew up and die down in a tight little community like this.' He looked up. Lewis's expression was politely tight.

'What sort of talk?' he asked icily.

Duncan cleared his throat. 'It seems she's been flirting around a bit. I don't suppose it's anything serious but I don't have to remind you that any wife of an officer of your status needs to keep her reputation more unsullied than that of Caesar's spouse. It could make your own position vulnerable. Our Red friends are always on the look-out for suitable material for blackmail and so forth, corruption in places of authority — you know what I mean?'

'Yes, sir, I know what you mean. Will that be all now, sir?'

'I think so, thank you, Lewis,' said Duncan uncomfortably. His visitor rose, collected his belongings, then stepped back smartly from the desk and saluted formally. After he'd gone Duncan poured himself another drink and cursed the bloody heat.

At tea time Klara had just got off the bed from her siesta when she heard the front door open and close and her husband's step in the hall. He came straight through the drawing-room and down the passage to their room and, as soon as she saw him, she knew something was wrong. And she was afraid of him. There had been other occasions during their marriage when she had known he had been on the verge of striking her but he had always controlled himself. Now he hit her, soundlessly, without a word, which made it so much more horrifying than if he had been cursing and shouting at her, and she bore the blows in silence and with no apparent surprise, only trying to protect herself from whichever direction they came.

The room was filled with the sound of the smack of the flat of his hand meeting the side of her face and the duller, sickening thud of his clenched fist beating her breast, her neck and finally her stomach, a blow that knocked her back on to the bed, her arms out loosely at her sides, her legs spread-eagled, the perspiration shining on her body clothed in her bra and pants. Her mouth was bleeding and swollen but she didn't cry and her eyes looked up at him through the curtain of her sweat-streaked hair. He stood over her, breathing very hard but otherwise looking remarkably cool.

'You bloody slut!' he said distinctly. 'You bloody, fucking slut!' The word on his lips was almost more shocking to her than the actions that had preceded it. Lewis habitually used 'bloody' as an adjective but anything more Anglo-Saxon was abhorrent to him and he had often sanctimoniously expressed the view that such language merely degraded the user. He read the surprise in her expression and laughed savagely. 'That shocks you, doesn't it, my dear? At least you can be shocked at something! Not half as shocking though as being told by your Commissioner that it's common knowledge your wife's being laid by all and sundry while you're at work and that, if you don't do something about it, you're for the chop. A second honeymoon, that's what he prescribed. What do you say, my darling, seeing that the first one was such a roaring success? However, it did teach me a thing or two I have to admit I didn't know before and I suppose for that I must thank you. Get up!'

He bent down and got hold of her arms which hung slackly in his grasp and yanked her to her feet. She stumbled against him, then regained her balance to stand silently before him, her hand going involuntarily to her stomach where a purple bruise had begun to swell over the top of her pants.

'That's better.' Lewis's voice was dangerously honeyed. 'I'm sure you don't want to take this lying down, even though that may be your habitual position.' Taking her free arm he twisted it up behind her back so that she gasped and with his mouth close to her ear, said conversationally, 'Now tell me, my dear, who were they?'

She bit her lip, unable to answer for the pain and he gave her arm another wrench.

'Who were they? Damn you! I want to know and I will if I have to beat it out of you.'

Without warning she kicked out backwards and brought the back of her heel up into his crutch. The movement was so swift and so agonizing that Lewis released his hold and by the time the pain had receded she was over the other side of the bed, facing him in an attitude poised to spring to either side like a matador facing the bull. For the first time, she spoke.

'Lewis, please, wait a moment. Do anything you like with me, but please listen to me first.' She waited warily to detect his reaction and when he made no move she hurried on, the words stumbling out as if she feared he wouldn't give her enough time to say everything that had to be said.

'Darling, you're right, I am a tramp and I have behaved badly. I've been unfaithful. I deserve anything you do but, darling, please try to understand. I've been terribly lonely and miserable. I thought you didn't love me. I know it's not been the same for you as for me — you never want to make love to me and, when you do, it's as if I was a thing, not me at all. I couldn't help wanting you and then when you didn't want me I had to prove to myself that I was attractive and not completely useless. If I'd had something to do here, running the house, a part-time job, anything, but you wouldn't let me. Can you imagine how boring and frustrating it can be? And then people came along and made me feel wanted and not so silly. You always made me feel so inadequate I got to the point where I didn't believe in myself any more. I shan't blame you for not believing it, but I do still love you.'

She searched his eyes for any answering compassion in vain, then as if the effort of her speech had exhausted her, slumped down on the edge of the bed and put her head in her hands. For the brief moment before he reminded himself she had made him a laughing stock, Lewis felt something akin to pity stir in him, but it vanished in the white heat of self-righteous rage.

'If I made you feel inadequate,' he hissed, 'it's because you were. You talk of running a house . . . why, you weren't even fit for that. You can't even control the servants when you've got nothing to do but sit on your backside all day. When I think of the sort of life you've been able to lead in comparison with my mother, plenty of leisure, money, all the clothes you needed, and what have you given in return? Why, you couldn't even have a baby!'

He paused, shocked to the core that he had

been capable of this ultimate barbarity. He didn't recognize himself. He watched her back, turned towards him, stiffen, her shoulders squared as if to brace herself against the blow. But he had to go on, he had to get under her guard. So far she'd uttered no word of real contrition. He wanted to make her beg for mercy, to show her who was master.

'No, Klara. I fear you possess only one talent and one that I'm sorry to hear you feel I don't share. According to you I've not been appreciative enough. Well, I'm giving you a chance now to show me what you've learned from the rest of the more critical connoisseurs of your talent.'

She whipped round on her guard again but too late. He'd unbuckled his belt and removed his bush jacket while he'd been talking and now he lunged clumsily across the bed and got hold of her shoulders. She fought and kicked, scratched and bit him until his blows finally silenced her and she was mercifully unconscious by the time he was half-way through ravaging her.

It was to be his final memory of Klara. She had refused to see him in the hospital where he had gone to visit her, the remnants of his pride in tatters, to be denied the expiation of apology. It didn't make it any easier knowing that, but for her refusal to bring a case or testify in any way against him, he would now be in gaol on a charge of assault, and it was no credit to him that it hadn't been one of murder. He would have found the torture of remorse easier to bear if she had wanted to punish him, but she had even insisted on being cited as the guilty party in the subsequent divorce as if to heap the final humiliation upon his head.

Duncan had accepted his resignation without demur the morning after the long night Lewis had spent in the cells of his own station after the house-boy had called the police on hearing Klara's screams and finding the bedroom door locked. His career lay in ruins and he couldn't face the questions, the shame and disillusion of his parents and contemporaries at the end of the one-way flight ticket home. He wanted time to think, to get to know the stranger he had discovered within himself, to salvage some relic from his personality on which to reconstruct a future, so although he boarded the plane at Kai Tak, it was on pure impulse that he disembarked four hours later in Singapore.

4

The guest house in Orchard Road lay back down a winding drive. The entrance was concealed between the Tanglin shop fronts so that not many people knew of its existence. If you hadn't known it was there you would have been surprised to discover, at its end, the green serenity of the garden that surrounded Miss Denton's establishment where jacaranda and tulip trees cast a welcome shade as well as vying in colour, when blossoming, with cassia and flame of the forest. To Diana it was an oasis of peaceful cool after the hot, tiring car journey down-country from Kuala Lumpur and the unrelieved monotony of the forests of rubber trees that bordered the road.

The main house was gabled and gaunt with a lot of dark brown wood and peeling cream plaster. It had a ramshackle air and an open veranda ran on three sides of the square building at a raised ground-floor level. A dozen brown wooden steps led to it and the front door. Miss Denton's permanent guests stayed here: Major and Mrs Butters, with a boy of four and a girl of two, who were still waiting to gain eligibility for an Army quarter, Mr and Mrs Gardiner, a retired planter and his wife, and three Red Cross Auxiliaries who worked at the Military Hospital out at Alexandria. They had all been in residence on Diana's last leave and now greeted her like a long-lost friend.

Away from the house, set round a paved terrace with a creepered ceiling from which hung baskets of butterfly orchids were four chalets, each with its bedsitter, bathroom and minute kitchen and it was here that Diana stayed when she came down to Singapore two or three times a year. She preferred the independence of the chalet, where she could please herself as to meal times, getting up or going to bed, and where she could escape from the company of her fellow guests. By coincidence on two previous visits the other three chalets had been vacant, allowing her to enjoy complete privacy, but this time on her arrival one of them was occupied by a man, evidently on his own. Diana didn't want to be unfriendly but she hoped he wasn't the garrulous type. She needed this holiday with peace and quiet in which to unwind. But her neighbour was obviously as anxious as she to keep himself to himself, and after she had been there a week they had only come into contact on one or two occasions either coming in or going out. Such comings and goings on his part, unregulated as they appeared to be by any recognizable working hours, gave rise to a certain amount of conjecture on Mrs Butters' part and she counted it as a personal failure that she had been unable to find out what she called 'our mystery man' did.

'Perhaps he's on holiday,' Diana had suggested when Mrs Butters had been confiding her misgivings over a mid-morning coffee.

'No, no.' Mrs Butters waggled a plump finger from side to side in dissent and leaned closer so that she could whisper to Diana, although there was no one else within earshot. 'He's been here over six months. He came just after you were last here and he's certainly too young to be retired. Besides, he gets a great deal of mail, business stuff, typed, official-looking envelopes and sometimes people come here to see him by appointment. You can tell they're not friends on social visits by the way they behave and call each other 'Mr'. No, whatever he does, I should say he conducts his business from here. He told Miss Denton he would be staying indefinitely, maybe for ever. Isn't it intriguing?'

'There's probably some perfectly simple and rather pedestrian explanation,' said

Diana, leaning forward to pick up the Butters baby who was plump and pleasingly dimpled. 'Perhaps he sells encyclopaedias or works from the chalet as a mail order agent.'

Dorothy Butters laughed in mock exasperation. 'How can you be so prosaic — a girl your age? I don't believe you're even a tiny bit interested. It's not natural. Here you are, Fate has thrown a mysterious young man into your lap, and he's not at all bad looking either and speaks well, and you don't turn a hair! I don't know!'

Diana smiled and rescued her necklace from the baby's inquisitive grasp. 'You ought to know by now, Dot, that I'm a hopeless subject for match-making and as for being a girl, I passed thirty-two last birthday, so I've no illusions on that score. As for your mysterious young man, he won't see forty again unless I'm a monkey's uncle, and I'm not prosaic, just a realist.'

'You don't fool me. Don't tell me you wouldn't like to be settled down with a baby of your own. Look how little Julia adores you. I can't think why you haven't said yes to someone before now.'

'I might if someone asked me,' Diana said lightly. She knew Dot wouldn't believe that nobody ever had and it was her standard answer to the standard question that she got

71

asked more often these days. She felt a pang, holding Julia's chubby body between her hands and feeling the bare, braceleted legs thrusting and jumping against the top of her own.

'Oh God,' she suddenly prayed, 'don't let me end up like Miss Denton.'

Their hostess was a slight, mousy woman in the region of fifty, but it was hard to guess her age because she had gone through so much. First she had witnessed her parents' destruction aboard one of her father's ships in the harbour when the Japanese entered Singapore and had caught them all by surprise, and later as a prisoner for the duration in Changi Gaol. People had still been playing mah-jong at the club when the Japs marched across the Straits at Jahore Bahru and her parents had been entertaining a number of local V.I.Ps on board. She had watched the explosion, seen the brilliant ball of fire and had been allowed to wait until the fragments rested or sank in their millions on the water, in the roads, before her captors carried her away. After the war she had returned to her old home, mercifully preserved, and had turned it into a guest house.

It was here Rajah had been brought to her as a baby, smuggled out of Borneo by sailor contemporaries of her father, who had thought to make a fast buck in one of the world's zoos but who had reckoned without the difficulties attendant on trying to disguise the presence of a three-month old orangutan, already weighing as much as a toddler and twice as boisterous and unpredictable. She had taken him to her heart and tamed him and he was all she had by way of family. He was the child she would never have and she dressed him in T-shirts and cotton shorts, carried him on her hip or wheeled him in a push-chair to shop at the Cold Store and tucked him at night into a dropside cot in her own bedroom. One of the more bizarre elements at the Orchard Road Guest House, and the main reason why it was never full, was the sight of Rajah seated in his high chair, picking his food off the tray and feeding himself at meal times along with the other residents. If you wanted to please Miss Denton you couldn't do better than buy a new toy for Rajah, so long as it was of a reputable British make. She had read about Japanese toys being painted with lead paint which had proved injurious to small children and these were forbidden in Rajah's nursery. Diana had once picked up some sweets from the ground that Julia had let fall from an open packet in her hand and offered them to

Rajah, only to be severely rebuffed.

'You wouldn't allow a child of yours to eat sweets that had been on the ground, would you?' Miss Denton had been highly indignant but Diana hadn't answered. She had turned away, her eyes full of tears for the 'mother'.

Rajah was uncannily human. His mannerisms were those of a little old man at play and he looked harmless enough until he smiled, to reveal great powerful yellow teeth which he gnashed in pleasure or excitement. He would shake hands with you and Miss Denton would urge him to do so. But Diana shuddered to feel the smooth palm and enormously long horny-nailed fingers against hers. Nor could she bear to see him sitting in the garden in his pram, for ever rocking backwards and forwards, backwards and forwards, hitting the back of his head over and over again with the mindless frustrated rocking of an idiot child.

'What's going to happen,' she had asked Dorothy, 'when Rajah gets bigger and older? Surely they get savage then? It's not safe for him to be in her room. He could tear her apart one night with those hands and teeth.'

'She'd never part with him,' Dorothy had said. 'I suppose we must all have something to love.'

Perhaps because of her conversation with

Dorothy, or perhaps it was due to the common but inexplicable coincidence that once a topic has been broached, you find it cropping up again almost immediately, Diana found herself constantly bumping into her mysterious neighbour and two days later was in conversation with him. Psychologists might have said the wish had been father to the thought and in her heightened consciousness of his existence she had set herself upon the course that was to alter her life, but if it were true she was totally unaware of the fact.

She knew that his name was Lewis Holt. It was painted on the lid of a wooden crate which stood in the corner of his veranda adjacent to hers. Sometimes in the evening he sat out there in a rattan chair reading and smoking to keep the mosquitoes away and, if Diana hadn't looked at him before, she did so now. Dorothy was right: he wasn't bad looking. It had been a very long time since she had given up assessing every new male acquaintance as a possible husband or lover. She couldn't remember when she had stopped but she was aware that the practice which commonly ceased on marriage or the relinquishing of hope had played no part in her life for some years, and the reason was not hard to find. It was easier that way: no false hopes, no rebuffs, no disappointments or face-saving operations. In her late teens and early twenties she'd had plenty of men friends but never one on a steady basis and the ones who were interested in her were never those she found fascinating.

'The trouble with you is you're far too choosy,' her friend Eileen Brayshaw would say. 'The chap's only asking you out for the evening, he's not proposing marriage. Why not go and have a good time? I would.'

Eileen would, but then Eileen had sex appeal or what it took to make every man in the room take her telephone number at a party and remember to use it afterwards. She liked to play one off against another and picked them up and put them down entirely to please herself.

'I'm not like you,' Diana complained. 'I've got to be able to talk to them. I can't spend an evening with someone I can't talk to.'

'You're too intelligent. You shouldn't let it show, men hate clever women.' Eileen patted the curls on her own empty head complacently.

Diana was accustomed to being asked out to drinks with a man on a first occasion, dinner on the second, and dropped like a hot potato on the third if she refused bed. Later on, the nature of her work forced her to be extra discriminating in her choice of companion. She had access to more confidential material and the rules stipulated that she should never put herself in a position where she could be compromised with her escort either alone in her own flat or in his. It was practically impossible to carry on any sort of love affair under these circumstances except with someone else in the Foreign Office, but they, for the most part, were already married, or if they weren't, it was because no one else had fancied them and neither did she. Like the song, she knew the lyrics, she knew the tune, but so far she had never sung the song and in moments of despair she doubted if she ever would, but with acceptance of the situation those moments became fewer and farther between.

It had been oppressively humid for days with the lowering threat of a thunderstorm that refused to break, and the smell of the open monsoon drains rose unappetizingly through the open windows of the car as Diana drove back from the Swimming Club along the East Coast road. It was the moment between daylight and darkness and the lights of the animated advertisements jumped into life as she looked at her watch and estimated that she could just make the Cold Store before it closed.

As she emerged with a large carrier bag of

groceries, the first drops of rain fell and she raised her face to feel the refreshing cool of the wind that had whipped up out of nowhere with the coming storm. By the time she reached the guest house it was bucketing down and Orchard Road was already awash. She was drenched as she ran the gauntlet from the car to the chalet door, and was fumbling for her key in the dim light when a tremendous clap of thunder and the sensation of a hand grasping her bare knee nearly made her jump out of her skin. She shrieked and, in jerking away from the unseen hold, dropped the carton of eggs which was resting on top of her packages. The contents broke over and around her feet. She got the key in the door and pushed her way inside, switching on the light in the tiny hallway which shone into the garden, illuminating her would-be attacker. Rajah squatted in the rain licking up the remains of her eggs and in a moment or two the figure of Miss Denton, protected by a paper umbrella, hurried from the next door chalet, followed by Lewis.

'Is anything wrong, Miss Travers?' She saw Rajah and was instantly horrified. 'No, Rajah. No! Not off the ground, baby, that's naughty. You'll get a tummy ache.'

Diana didn't know whether to be exasperated or amused. 'I'm afraid he gave me a fright coming out of the dark like that and grabbing hold of me. I didn't know who it was.'

'Was he afraid of the big bang then?' Miss Denton had picked up the animal and was nuzzling her face against Rajah's cheek while he clutched her shoulder and chattered senselessly. 'I'd better get him back to the house and dry him,' and with that she made off into the garden, leaving Lewis and Diana looking at each other. He raised his eyebrows and they both laughed.

'Are you all right?' His voice was pleasant, politely concerned, and trying to make amends for Miss Denton's obvious indifference to her predicament. Diana suddenly realized he was still standing in the rain, holding the soaked carrier which she had put down to prevent further disaster when she had opened the door. She pushed her wet hair back from her eyes.

'Please come in,' she invited him. 'You'll get soaked. Thank you so much.' She opened the door into the bed sitting room and he went in ahead of her and put the bag down carefully on the table. 'Thank heavens it was only the eggs that got broken. I've a bottle of whisky in there. If that had gone it would have been a real tragedy.'

He stood looking at her in her wet cotton

dress which now clung unbecomingly to her thin body and she shivered.

'You could do with a tot of that now,' he said. 'I'll be going. You'd better get changed or you'll catch cold.'

'Well, thanks again.' Diana opened the door for him and as he shook out his umbrella she said on an impulse, 'Why don't you come back and join me for a drink? Say in about ten minutes?'

He looked at her again in that serious, appraising way and she was beginning to wonder if she'd scared him off when he inclined his head and said gravely, 'Thank you. I'd like to. Ten minutes then.'

Asking him in had seemed a good enough idea at the time but now that he was here in her room with a glass in his hand and being decidedly reticent, leaving her to make all the small talk, Diana began to feel it was all too much trouble. Her conversation began to sound like an interrogation in her attempt to draw him out and his answers, when not monosyllabic, gave her no spring-board from which to launch into any specific subject. He was perfectly relaxed and she found herself gibbering on, more afraid of the silence that would fall if she stopped than of sounding as patently ridiculous as she knew she did.

The storm was passing, the rain much

lighter now and she went to pull up the rattan blind across the veranda door which she had lowered to stop the water beating in. There was a deafening crash of thunder right overhead and a tongue of lightning probed vividly into the room, making her jump and drop her glass. She lowered the blind hurriedly and bent nervously to pick up the fragments. Lewis hadn't moved from his chair.

'That's the second thing I've broken.' She stood up with the pieces in her hand and smiled. 'That'll be the end of the storm now. They usually finish on one monumental bang and five minutes later the sun comes out, only of course it's dark now.'

Lewis allowed himself a smile at this glimpse of the obvious.

'I don't like lightning,' she said defensively.

'I shouldn't have thought there was much that scared you,' he said. 'From what I've seen, you seem to me to be a very self-sufficient young lady.'

With one single remark he had given the conversation a personal turn but at least he'd said something. Surprisingly he had more to offer.

'Lightning, you know, only strikes the nine hundred and ninetieth time and the idea of thunderbolts comes from ancient times when

81

it was thought the Gods were hurling bolts out of the sky in retribution. They're really dart-shaped fossils and rare at that.' He sat back comfortably, his head framed by the domed cane of the chair back, confident he had allayed her fears.

'Do you always manage to rationalize your own fears?' she couldn't resist asking.

He replied equably. 'As a general rule. Any emotion can be rationalized if one cares to do so. Most people don't want to, they enjoy their emotions too much.'

'Most of them perhaps. No one enjoys being afraid.'

'No? That would be too deep to go into now but in any case I'm sure life doesn't hold many terrors for you.' He was stating a fact, not manufacturing an opening for flirtation.

Diana was still holding the broken glass in her hand and she now dropped the pieces into a pedal bin by the gas ring and with her back towards him said, 'That's the second time you've said that. I don't see how you can possibly know what I'm like. We've never spoken to each other before.'

'It's my job. I'm a private detective. Didn't Miss Denton tell you?'

'Why ever should she? I didn't ask.' Because it sounded as if she didn't care either, she said the first thing that came into her head. 'You don't look like a private detective.'

He looked amused. 'Don't I? That's good. What would you say I looked like then?'

He watched her eyes concentrate on his face, seeing him properly for the first time, taking in the neat, fair moustache, the military, precise haircut, square, stubby hands with their scrubbed, tailored nails, the collar and tie in spite of the heat and the informality of their surroundings, the brushed, pressed cavalry twills and polished brown brogues.

'Well?' he prompted her.

'I would say every inch the typical Army officer.' Diana laughed. 'I'm afraid a surfeit of Bogart would have prevented me from ever casting you as a private eye. I'd be fooled by the absence of the raincoat and slouch hat. Do you work for a firm or in connection with the police or what?'

She began to feel more at ease with him and, after refilling both their glasses, sat opposite him and waited for his answer.

'I'm a sort of freelance at the moment. I was up-country for a while when I came down here from Hong Kong — Ipoh and Seremban, then I gradually made my way down here where the pickings are better.'

'And will you stay here permanently?'

'It depends. I haven't decided.' He frowned

and looked down into his drink.

'Are the pickings here then so much better than at home? Forgive me, but it seems strange someone like you doing this sort of job out here. One would imagine you'd have more scope at home.'

He was twisting the stem of his glass round and round and didn't look up at her before replying.

'I don't choose to go home.'

There was an uncomfortable silence and then Diana said, 'I'm sorry. Of course it's nothing to do with me.'

'No, no.' Realizing her discomfiture, he tried to explain. 'I don't choose to go home because there's nothing for me there. I've spent the best part of my life abroad and my parents, who were my only real tie with England, died after I came here, so you see I might as well be here as anywhere. It has a great deal to recommend it and I'm used to the heat. I was once in the Colonial Police.'

That accounted for the military cut of his jib, Diana thought. She had been going to suggest that he was too young to have retired, but sensing she was on thin ice, decided to tread warily and said nothing.

'And you work in the Foreign Office in K.L.' He stated it as a fact and when he saw her raise her eyebrows, admitted that Miss

Denton had vouchsafed him this much. 'Is it interesting?'

'As jobs go — very,' she replied. 'More so in the emergency. We were more confined but you felt what you were doing was important. My tour is nearly finished now. I go home after Christmas.'

'And unlike me you have something or someone to go home to, I presume?'

Diana sighed. 'There are my parents but quite honestly I'm in no hurry to go back to them. They'll regard my return as an excellent opportunity to get me to go back to live with them and then I'll be well and truly trapped. I've no intention of that happening.'

'You don't get on with them?'

'With my father, yes. He's not very broad-minded and he's got decided views on the role of an only daughter which don't include a career in any shape or form, but our lines of communication are open. For years I thought I got on with my mother until I realized that it was only on her terms. She takes a great pride in being unselfish but she takes jolly good care to see that what you want is her idea in the first place. If it isn't, you're not reproached in any way but enduring the brave, martyred smile or the tearful reiterations that she wouldn't do anything to stand in your way, usually have the desired effect. When I was in my teens she used to throw self-induced hysterical faints if she couldn't get her own way. My father used to be demented with worry, trying to get her back to consciousness, listening for her heart and pulse, and so did I at first, until I realized what was going on. He thought me very hard-hearted leaving her on the floor and taking no notice and telling him to do the same. I know perfectly well she could hear what I was saying but she couldn't say anything herself about it afterwards or she'd have given the game away.'

'And that made you feel bitter towards her?'

'Not now, and not then really, because I didn't understand just how much her attitude affected my own life. It was later, when I saw what I had missed through her, that I felt bitter. That's over, but you can see why I can't go back. I've hardened. I've had too long living my own life. Even if I felt I should, it wouldn't work and then I'd have made them more unhappy than if I'd never tried. No. Sometimes it's kinder to recognize one's limitations before rushing in with good intentions.'

He'd been watching her intently as she made what she now realized had been quite a speech. She'd spoken quietly, consideringly, in a matter-of-fact kind of way without emotion. It might have been somebody else's problem dispassionately appraised and that was what he liked about her: her cool, unattached approach to life. He'd watched her since her arrival at Orchard Road and he didn't have to know her well to recognize her competence, a feeling of cool efficiency that emanated from her. She would be good at her job. She had capable hands on which he had noticed she wore no rings.

'There's no one else then waiting at home?' he asked, in spite of himself.

'No man, if that's what you mean,' she said, smiling slightly at having interpreted his glance. 'No, I've had plenty of men friends, but that's what they were — friends. Romance is a complicating factor, particularly in my sort of work and then, I'm not very attractive to men. My friend Eileen says I put them off.'

Another man would have leaped in with a denial but Lewis didn't, and Diana respected him for it. It was therefore absurd also to feel slightly piqued.

'Wouldn't you like to get married?' he asked.

'Not just for the sake of it. Would you?'

He put down his glass carefully on the camphor wood chest beside his chair.

'No, I suppose not,' he said. 'I was married once. It wasn't a success. We were divorced some time ago.'

'I'm sorry.' She sounded as if she was. 'Did you have any children?'

'No. Fortunately, as it turned out.' He saw the grey eyes deepen and wasn't sure if it was because of compassion for him or some private emotion.

'That's what I would want more than anything else. I would want a child,' she said. 'It's very important to a woman.'

He stood up very suddenly. She didn't know what she had said but she sensed the tension that had entered the atmosphere. He took his leave stiffly, seeming indeterminate about whether he should shake hands with her, standing awkwardly by the door until she released him by saying it had been nice of him to come in and thanking him again for helping her in the storm.

5

Lewis had not intended marrying again. The traumatic events which had brought his first excursion into matrimony to a conclusion would have been enough to deter the bravest or most stupid of men from a second attempt, and he was no exception. However, whereas others might have feared making a similar hash of things all over again, Lewis had never accepted the fact that his own particular hash had been at all of his making.

In the immediate days and few weeks following his attack upon Klara he had been devastated by remorse, self-loathing and horror that he had it in him to behave with uncivilized savagery. His only justification for such behaviour was that she had provoked him and, unconditioned as he was from childhood to accepting blame, it wasn't too hard with the passage of time to convince himself that the guilt had all lain at her door. After all, he had come out of the whole encounter much worse than she. Gone was his profession and with it the respect of his colleagues, his means of livelihood and his pension, while all she had endured was a richly deserved beating which had left her bloody but unbowed, as she had proved by her re-marriage at a later date to one of Hong Kong's most affluent business tycoons. From the beginning he had been deceived. She had been nothing but a scheming whore and he was well rid of her, but was unlikely to forget that it was she who had brought him to this pass.

In his present line of work he saw plenty of women like her. Sitting outside houses or apartments, making notes on the time of their arrivals and departures and from time to time intruding into hotel bedrooms in order to catch them in bed in *flagrante delicto*, gave him a perverse pleasure in feeling he was getting a little of his own back at the Klaras of the world in particular, and women in general. By classing them together he could retain his moral superiority.

It was because Diana defied this general classification that she had interested him from the beginning. She didn't attract him physically initially. She was right. She wouldn't appeal to men that way, with her thin sinewy body, to all intents and purposes breastless and with the flat, lean buttocks of a boy, but her face was not unpleasing, the clear-cut square bone formation of jaw and forehead balanced by the softening line of her hair and those peculiarly expressive eyes. She was intelligent too.

Their first conversation was followed by others during evenings spent either on her veranda or his, in comfortable companionship, and Lewis reflected how satisfying it was to be able to conduct a discourse on an intellectual plane with a woman such as Diana, unhampered by sexual undertones or implications normally present in any relationship between a man and a woman, and how rare. Excursions together ensued — to the Buddhist Siang Lim Sian Si temple in Kim Keat Road, to admire the woodcarvings and to wonder at the fifty-foot Buddha at the centre of the Temple of a Thousand Lights at the Skaya Muni Gaya. They fed the capricious monkeys in the Botanical Gardens and gloated over the fabulous jade collection from the Sung to the Chin dynasties housed in what had once been the family mansion of the Aw Boon brothers, who were also responsible for the building of the ultimate vulgarity, the Tiger Balm Gardens. Diana and Lewis strolled companionably through their garish oriental Disneyland, amongst the caves, grottoes and amphitheatres that provided a setting for immense painted concrete statues representing legends from Chinese mythology.

'A pretty gruesome lot,' was Diana's verdict. 'Have you noticed how there seems to be a vein of cruelty, a suggestion of menace, running through all these legends? For instance, back there that huge frog is smiling and looks quite a jolly fellow until you realize he's standing on, and got his claws in, a fish who's looking up in agony as the blood runs luridly down. And there — ' she pointed to a tableau just above them — 'it looks a pretty enough scene, a sailor returned home and sitting by the hearth holding his wife's hand. It's only when you look closely you can see he's pulling her fingernails. Disgusting!'

'I suppose *Three Blind Mice* would look fairly blood-thirsty in this context. Come to that, any of Grimm's fairy stories. And what about Greek mythology? Plenty of blood, thunder and tragedy and violence there. Or real life for that matter? It's all there under the surface.'

Something in his tone compelled her attention and she glanced at him quickly. He was looking at the figures but he had forgotten her. She moved on. 'My God, come and look at this! They must have been perverted or something to dream this up.'

She was standing in another stone alcove and when Lewis caught up with her they were both facing a faithfully lifelike reproduction of a man being disembowelled. The naked figure was cast in cement, roughly three feet high and wearing a painted-on expression of patient resignation while a kneeling figure before him still held aloft the knife with which he had recently slit the stomach of his victim. Graphically painted entrails and blood streamed from the gash and Diana shuddered. On a shelf to her right was another scene, depicted in relief, showing the mutilated bodies of the damned drowning in a molten sea and others being flung from a height to impale themselves horribly on barbed stakes. Their eyes rolled heavenwards and their bodies were garnished with a plethora of red paint.

'How terrible to believe that this is what might be in store for one.'

'Every religion has a built-in insurance policy — a promise or a threat,' Lewis said. 'How else could they ensure discipline? Christians are promised everlasting life and as nobody in their senses wants to die, that keeps them toeing the line. Buddhism preaches the law of Karma — that a man's actions control his destiny after death as inevitably as cause follows effect, so that his future is solely in his own keeping. It accepts the Hindu doctrine of a cycle of lives. Look here. Here's where you go back into the wheel and you might come out again in another existence as a cow or a man, or like those poor devils over there.'

They studied a plaque in the wall representing the wheel of life, the paths of those whose lives were finished woven into the centre and re-appearing in different guise.

'I'll stick to my own beliefs, thank you,' said Diana, shivering. 'I fail too often. At least my conception of a merciful God gives me marks for trying.'

'The road to hell is paved with good intentions,' Lewis said with a smile.

'That's a trite fallacy and I don't believe in hell or punishment — not that kind anyway. You have to believe in punishment, you were a policeman, but don't you think, in moral judgements, it's not always easy to tell who's guilty?'

He regarded her thoughtfully then asked, 'What kind of hell do you believe in then?'

'Certainly not a deliberate retribution. If there is one, it's of our own making — personal type.'

'Heaven too?'

'I imagine so. But it's not a conscious reward. If it does turn out to be reincarnation I hope I come back as a very fat, very sleek Persian cat belonging to somebody as crazy about the feline species as I am. I shall be very pampered.'

Their outings so far had been on an informal sight-seeing basis and although Diana had seen most of the places they visited before, she enjoyed showing them to Lewis and their discussions that arose afterwards. She had put off checking up on him security-wise, her customary enforced procedure with anyone she went out with more than a couple of times. It wasn't until he began taking her out to dinner, and she sensed a possible shift in the depth of their relationship, that she put a call through to her office in K.L. and awaited their reply. Just as well to be prepared although there'd been no definite indication that he thought of her other than purely platonically. He'd made no move to kiss or touch her, although there had been opportunities for him to make a pass had he been inclined, and she hadn't wanted him to. Yet her instinct told her that they were moving towards some kind of understanding and she was content to let events take their course.

There was a lot about him that she liked. He was kind and reliable and, when he talked to her, he did so with a total absence of male patronage to the female and considered her own opinions seriously. If anything, he was a bit too serious, she reflected. Once or twice she'd had to explain something she'd said casually in jest, and with other people he was out of his depth amidst the social banter that passed for conversation at the Club. He was also a 'bit of an old woman', nursing himself with exaggerated care for a sore throat or a bout of Singapore tummy. He would meticulously change from wet swimming trunks to dry on emerging from the water and exhorted Diana not to sit in her damp suit. The simplest expedition couldn't be undertaken without the preliminary mapping-out of a detailed itinerary, taking into account probable timings which subsequently had to be strictly adhered to, for no better reason than that a plan had been made and would otherwise prove obsolete. Lewis never did anything on the spur of the moment. The only occasion he had acted on impulse and out of character had been with Klara, and look where that had got him.

He hadn't told Diana about Klara beyond the fact that he had been married, so that he was surprised when she referred to her in their conversation during dinner one night in the Churchill Room at the Tanglin Club. They had a table near the small dance floor and between courses they watched other couples rotating in time to the music and from time to time made idle comments. As the pace of the music changed from a quickstep to something slow and dreamy, the lights dimmed and the floor cleared, leaving one young pair still dancing. The girl couldn't have been more than eighteen and as she passed their table Diana heard her speak with a low foreign accent. She had short, very blonde hair cropped in a boyish style, big blue eyes and youth and health and cleanliness emanated from her. Diana turned to Lewis whose eyes had followed her.

'Isn't she attractive?'

He nodded.

'She's foreign. Swedish or Danish with that colouring I should say. They've got that wonderfully clean-cut look about them.'

He didn't reply and she knew him well enough by now to realize she'd said something wrong. Because of the atmosphere of the place, the music, the lowered lights and the effects of the pre-dinner martinis and the wine she had drunk so far with the meal, she reached across the table to put her hand on his wrist.

'What is it? Did I say something?'

He shook his head, his eyes still on the dancing girl. Diana suddenly remembered.

'Your wife was a Dane, wasn't she?'

His immediate reaction surprised her. He turned his head to look at her, all his attention now focused on her, at the same time withdrawing his hand into his lap.

'As a matter of fact she was. How did you know?'

It didn't occur to her to prevaricate. 'It was mentioned in the report from Hong Kong.'

He looked nonplussed. 'What report?'

'I had to ask my office to do a check on you. It's routine. They checked you out with Hong Kong.'

He sat icily still, his eyes narrowed, and in the ensuing silence Diana felt increasingly uncomfortable. She hadn't expected him to be angry. He knew she had to be careful about whom she made friends with, particularly men. Damn it all, he'd been in a job himself which involved security. Had the boot been on the other foot she wouldn't have expected him to take her at face value. She tried to behave as naturally as possible.

'Well, we have been seeing quite a lot of each other and you know it's something I have to do. I told you, Lewis.' He remained silent. 'Lewis, you do understand, don't you? I wasn't prying. I wouldn't have told you if I had anything to be ashamed of.'

The waiter came to bring them their next course and by the time their plates had been changed and the vegetables served and they were alone again, the atmosphere had eased slightly. His voice, however, was unfriendly as he cut viciously into his steak as if, Diana thought, he wished it were her neck.

'And what, may I ask, did this report have to say? Are you satisfied with my credentials or is it that, now you know all the gory details, perhaps you'll be having second thoughts about me.'

'Lewis, don't be childish. It wasn't like that. Just a confirmation that you were who you said you were and that you had married a Danish girl and were divorced. I didn't want to know anything more. If I did I'd ask you myself. You know that.'

He looked at her sitting there gravely watching him. She was very striking tonight dressed in a silver-grey brocade cheongsam, the high stiff collar flattering her long neck and the colour of the material reflecting the deep grey of those candid eyes. The Chinese dress suited her. Most European women were not finely built enough. They had too much bottom and bust and not small enough waists to look anything but vulgar in a cheongsam, but on Diana it was simply elegant and her legs were long and shapely enough to get away with the provocative thigh-high slit in the skirt that revealed her leg above the knee as she walked. The anger went out of him.

'I believe you,' he said, then after a

moment, carefully: 'I suppose they told you my reason for resigning — from the Police I mean?'

'Personal reasons.' Diana smiled at him, relieved at the relaxation of tension in him.

'Don't you want to know what they were?'

'Not unless you want to tell me and there's no reason why you should.'

'Suppose there were a reason — a very good one?'

'I can't think of one, can you?'

'If I asked you to marry me, that would be one.'

'Only if I said yes. Even then I wouldn't consider I had a right to know everything that's gone on in your past. Would you expect to know all about mine?'

'Yes. I don't want to make the same mistake again.'

'There's nothing to know. I presume you mean men. I'm a virgin, if that's what you mean.'

Other women would have made the statement defiantly, with bitterness or even made a joke of it. Diana stated a fact. They might have been discussing the price of bacon.

'From choice?'

'Yes — no — I don't know. I've never been in love.'

100

'It's not all it's cracked up to be. I loved my wife and yet I came damn near to killing her. I wanted to hurt her. She loved just about every other man, you see.' He spoke with undisguised rancour, gripping the stem of his glass and Diana thought he was going to break it.

'Do you still love her?'

'No. That's all over, has been for a long time. I hardly ever think of her. Just occasionally I remember that, because of what she did to me, I am what I am. I can't forgive her that. She deceived me.'

'How?'

'She pretended to be something she wasn't. I suppose she tried but I couldn't forget. That's why I said I should want to know all about you. I couldn't go through all that again.'

Her expression didn't change. She sat quietly contemplating him and experiencing a sneaking sympathy for the unknown Klara. He was so unbending, so uncompromising in his condemnation of her. Diana had already discovered that tolerance was not amongst his virtues and Klara had obviously been awarded no marks for trying. He glanced up swiftly, trying to read her thoughts before she had time to change her transparent emotions but she returned his gaze with the same steady regard without asking any further questions or sympathizing with him.

Impulsively he said, 'That's what I like about you, Diana. You don't pretend. You're not afraid of speaking the truth and you don't make a big production of it. You're the most honest person I know. That's why I think we get on so well together, and we do, don't you think so?' He looked at her earnestly.

'Yes, we do.' She waited.

'Well then — ,' as if it proved something and he was feeling for the right words — 'I mentioned marriage earlier on. I shouldn't have brought it up in that way, it's not how I meant to broach the subject, but since I have, how would you feel about it? I'm not young — forty-six — there'd be a big gap, but from what you've told me there's no one else in your life, we seem to like the same things and we have a lot in common. I didn't realize how lonely I'd been until you came along and I think you're lonely too. Am I right?'

'Do you love me?' she asked.

'Not perhaps in the way you mean, but I am very fond of you. I'm being quite truthful because I think you feel the same.' He looked for confirmation. When she inclined her head he hurried on. 'Materially I'm not rich but you would be comfortable and you wouldn't have to worry. They may not be good enough reasons for you. You told me once you didn't want to get married just for the sake of it but you also said you wanted a child. I can't guarantee that latter but . . . ' He trailed off into silence and Diana shocked him slightly by voicing the unspoken thought that had been in his own mind: 'But we could have a jolly good try? It's a point. Supposing I met someone later on and fell in love? Would you be willing to gamble on that?'

He shrugged. 'There's always that possibility but I hope I can make you happy enough to remember where your duty lies. Does that sound incredibly pompous?'

'Incredibly.' She meant it, but he could see she didn't hold it against him.

They'd finished their meal and during the few moments it took for him to get the bill from the waiter and settle it up they sat without speaking. Coming out of the air-conditioned restaurant into the heat of the evening was like entering a Turkish bath. Diana took off her stole and folded it over her arm as they went down into the deserted gardens. Someone was having a midnight swim in the floodlit pool. There were the sounds of subdued laughter, a shriek followed by a loud splash and the slap of wet bare feet running on the tiled surround on the other side of the hedge. In the car Lewis put the key into the ignition but didn't switch on. A constraint had fallen between them and he found it hard to return to the theme of their conversation at the table. He supposed he ought to kiss her but if he did, would it look as if he had taken her answer for granted? And she wasn't helping, just sitting well back in her seat calmly waiting for him to put the car in motion. He turned his head to look at her profile in the dark and put his arm tentatively along the back of her seat. To his surprise, he could feel her faintly trembling which aroused a protective emotion in him.

'Don't be afraid.'

She turned her head sharply and he pulled her closer, raising his other hand to her face, his thumb and forefinger on either side of her chin, and leaned over to put his mouth on hers. Her lips were full and warm and she kissed like a child with them slightly puckered and close together. After a moment they relaxed under his and parted slightly without passion, but the moment was sweet and held an unexpected tenderness which was enough for him for the time being. He withdrew and started up the car.

'Will you think about what I said?' he asked.

'I'll think about it.'

'How much time will you need?'

It would take her a month to work out her notice, settle things up in K.L. and send word to her parents. 'Say a month,' she said.

'Christmas then. Will you come down for it?'

'If the answer's 'yes'.' She knew it would be but there was no harm in letting him wait.

Accustomed as she was to making her decisions independently and intuitively, she experienced now no inclination to talk over her resolution with anyone else. Besides, there was no one in whom she could readily confide, even if she had wanted to. Dot Butters had not been unaware of the way the wind was blowing, and had hinted coyly on more than one occasion that, were it in her power, she'd encourage the breeze into a force eight gale. Eileen would doubtless regard Diana as certifiable if she missed what might be her last chance of matrimony and security. Neither Eileen nor Dot could be relied upon to give an impartial opinion. So Diana was content to keep her own counsel.

On a reasoned basis the arguments Lewis had put forward in mutual favour of their marriage she accepted as valid, besides which she was getting on in terms of motherhood and every year that now passed made the attainment of that goal more unlikely. Ahead stretched the dreary probability of bleak years spent in caring for her parents as they passed from active old age to senility. Only that day she had received from her mother a typical letter full of self-pitying complaint.

'Your father and I have both been rather under the weather,' she had written. 'A touch of flu I think — there has been a lot about and he would insist on sweeping up the leaves in a bitter wind the other day and so caught cold, bringing the germ into the house and passing it on to me. So very selfish because it has been me who has had to look after him, running up and down with trays and bringing in the coal when I have felt ready to drop myself. However, of course I could not retire to bed — too much to be seen to — but never mind, I managed to keep going. That's where Helen and Malcolm are so fortunate in having Jill with them. She is a tower of strength and lately nursed them both through beastly colds. I told Helen 'You don't know how lucky you are having a loving daughter to care for you. . .' '.

There was more in the same vein. Diana had no intention of returning home to become a second Jill Hayter, a fate worse than most, from which Lewis offered immediate and final salvation.

If the arrangement was short on romance, well, what you hadn't known you were unlikely to miss. If she passed him up now, where was any definite promise of that elusive commodity in the future, whereas without its disturbing element she could plainly differentiate between the substance and the shadow? The same applied to sexual attraction. Physically he did not repel her. True, there was no magic, no charisma, nor as far as she could judge was there in a good many marriages of her acquaintance where friendship, companionship and kindliness had to all intents and purposes replaced the first fine careless rapture. His kiss had not been unpleasant. She remembered with what gentleness he had held her face in his hand and had told her not to be afraid. She had tried to imagine what it would be like to go to bed with him but her experience of men was too limited to visualize the act in its entirety. It couldn't be so bad when they had so much else in common. She wasn't shy with him and for his part he might not be in love with her but would he be likely to bring himself to make love to a partner physically repulsive to him?

A week before Christmas she telephoned him to give him her answer and to ask him to start making arrangements for the wedding. Neither of them wanted a lot of fuss and Lewis's divorce precluded a church wedding anyway. On Christmas Eve, after a civil ceremony with strangers as witnesses, they left for a short honeymoon in Penang. The wide platinum engine-turned wedding ring and chunky irregular amethyst set in silver claws that Lewis had given her at the beginning of their four-day engagement sat strangely on Diana's finger, but she herself didn't feel strange. When the clerk had called her 'Mrs Holt' for the first time, it was as if she were already used to her new name and Lewis marvelled at, and was thankful for, her well-bred composure. He couldn't have chosen anyone more diametrically dissimilar to Klara.

6

Contrary to what might have been expected, the marriage was a success. Far from feeling chained by the bonds of wedlock, a familiar cry from her married friends, Diana felt free for the first time in her life. Free to indulge in hobbies and pastimes for which she had hitherto had little time, free to choose and make her own friends unmindful of security and free to run her own home and express her personality in its decoration and furnishings.

The flat off the Bukit Timah road that Lewis had found for them was a source of unending interest and delight to Diana. It was her first real home. Apart from that of her parents she was used to occupying a succession of furnished rooms which stubbornly resisted attempts to make them look more personal. She spent hours tracking down just the right sized dining-table and chairs, curtain fabric to pick out the deeper blue in the mosaic-tiled floor and planning where each piece of furniture should go.

The building consisted of four similar flats and theirs was on the ground floor on the right as you entered the main door. One large, airy room which ran from front to back of the house and looked out on to a square, paved patio with steps leading down into the garden was divided across the middle by a tall farmhouse-style dresser. The patio end of the room they used as their drawing-room, furnishing it with comfortable rattan furniture and bright cushions covered with Sanderson's traditional chintzes. On two sides upholstered benches were fixed to the walls and these were covered in gay rep, picking up one of the predominating colours of the chair covers. There was a glass-fronted waist-high bow-fronted cabinet, an inlaid rosewood desk, one or two small tables and a record player. The other half of the room, overlooking the drive, was the dining-room and at this end there was a door leading into a square modern kitchen and a serving hatch. There were three double bedrooms in the flat, one with its own bathroom, and another shower and lavatory was at the end of the passage. Beyond the kitchen were the servants' quarters, a bedroom, a wash-room, lavatory and recreation area. It was peaceful enough, being far enough away from the busy main road, backing on to the wooded residential Tanglin area, and it was cooler than the town, situated on a slight rise where they caught what breeze there might be.

To Diana it was good at last to belong, to be one of a pair and therefore immediately socially acceptable, although Lewis, before he had met her, had lived somewhat the life of a recluse, neither accepting nor giving hospitality, so that their immediate circle of friends could be counted on the fingers of one hand. Diana proposed to remedy this and Lewis too now seemed more relaxed and had talked of not wanting her to be lonely, so she looked forward to enlarging that circle and started with the other occupants of the flats.

Upstairs both couples were English. The Northcotts were in their forties and had a teenage daughter who was in her last term at boarding school in England and would be joining them for an indefinite holiday at Easter before deciding on what she was going to do with her life. Cyril Northcott was in the Import/Export business and, judging by the number of parties they gave, had done quite well, although Diana couldn't imagine how as he was a lugubrious gentleman over six foot tall, who rarely smiled and wore black alpaca tropical suiting which made him look like an undertaker. He spoke very slowly in a hushed undertone so that his voice, coming as it did from a great height, made the interminable anecdotes to which he was addicted virtually unintelligible. Diana liked his wife Vera, who was plump and smart and rather frightening to meet at first until you discovered her kindness and plain good sense.

The Martins in 3a were Army. He was studious and pale, some kind of a boffin, Lewis had said, but Sally Martin had red hair, a sexy figure which she made the most of in tight, shiny, satin trousers or cheongsams, and had an endless stream of male admirers. She had a job during the day working for a travel agency and Diana, sitting over her second breakfast cup of coffee, would see her flouncing out every morning, trim in a white blouse and buttock-hugging navy skirt, the complete 'Men Only' version of a secretary bird. They had two children, a boy and a girl of seven and nine, who were left to their own devices on week days and whom the amah locked out of the flat between lunch and tea time. Diana got used to patching up their cuts and grazes with Elastoplast, sorting out their minor crises and more often than not taking them with her when she went to the swimming club. Once, when the boy had fallen off a garage roof on to the concrete wash-down and had suffered concussion, she had ridden with him to the hospital in the ambulance and had felt a good deal more worried than if she had been his mother. She couldn't understand Sally Martin having children and not caring about what happened to them.

Their Chinese landlord lived in the other downstairs flat. He was an architect and had been educated in Singapore and at Cambridge, a pattern his thirteen-year old son was to follow. He and his son and daughter of eight spoke good English and, although his wife was less fluent, Diana enjoyed their conversations conducted in a mixture of pidgin English and mime. Mrs Hang was a restful, gentle creature, always deliciously cool-looking in bamboo-patterned silks and voiles, her tiny figure finely boned, her face possessing an oriental imperturbability and serenity which made it impossible for Diana to calculate her age.

Lewis was proud of the capable way in which his wife took charge and their home was run on oiled wheels. It was like the old days in the Force before Klara, but so much better now with Diana's companionship to look forward to at the end of the day and the peaceful communion they shared with none of the vulgar emotional brawls that had beset his first marriage. She didn't fire him sexually as Klara had done, but he had been more than a little ashamed of those baser appetites to which the latter had appealed and he preferred to believe that Diana brought out the best in him. She had been as artless and natural with him on their wedding night as in all her other dealings. There had been no reluctance to fulfil her side of the bargain, physically, no shrinking false modesty, just a simple honest innocence that allowed him to take her in his own way. Afterwards she had gone into the bathroom to wash and when she came back into the bedroom she had leaned over his bed and kissed him lightly before climbing into her own and putting out the light. It had been pleasurable if a little clinical, but more dignified than that night at Bahia and, before Lewis allowed himself to remember, he turned over and went to sleep.

Diana had lain awake for some time. So that's what it was all about, all the love stories, the poems, the great romances that had changed the course of history and continents. Did strong men really become weak, women forsake home and children, hearts break, people commit suicide for what had just passed between her and Lewis? She supposed they must as it was a subject taken so seriously by the human race, but she had found it scarcely serious at all; in fact, at some moments she had found it difficult to control her laughter. When for instance would two people be likely to find themselves in a

114

more comical, ungainly position? All that huffing and puffing and jumping up and down, with the bed creaking unromantically but rhythmically beneath them, must have looked nothing if not humorous, and when Lewis had finally slumped, perspiring and spent like a beached walrus on to her stomach and she had allowed herself the suggestion of a smile, he had construed it as one of content and had answered with one of his own. A feeling of protectiveness had overwhelmed her then. She was the strong one in that moment and a warmth enveloped her in the knowledge that she had given pleasure although she had felt nothing herself. It was little enough for her to give and she was happy to give it if that was what he wanted.

He was sexually demanding and not only wanted but expected it often as his right and Diana was not one to disagree with him, for it was as such that she regarded the act. The idea of refusing him wouldn't have entered her head and she knew she was doing him good, like a bottle of medicine or a nice cup of tea.

Six months after their marriage Lewis changed his job. He was offered the appointment of Chief Security Officer to the Hong Kong and Shanghai Bank, which meant a sizeable increase in his salary and regular hours. The hours had been erratic in his previous occupation. When he told her the news, Diana had never seen him so excited about anything and her pleasure and pride for him were genuine as she took a rare initiative and put her arms around him and her lips to his.

'Hey — steady on.' He laughed uncertainly and stepped back from her. 'Cookie might come in.'

'Would that be so terrible?'

'No — but I mean — there's a time and place.'

'We are married.' All the same she withdrew her arms. His embarrassment at the possibility of being seen by the servants was contagious.

'I thought a celebration was in order so I've reserved a table at the Club and I got on to Grant and Hilary. They're going to join us. Does that appeal?'

'Very much. Oh Lewis, it's a lovely surprise. But heavens — my hair! I'd planned to do it tonight but if we're going out I must wash it now. How long have I got?'

'A couple of hours. I told them we'd meet here for a drink before going on.'

'I must get on then. Come into the bedroom and tell me all about the job while I get ready.'

116

He took off his jacket, trousers and shirt while she was in the bathroom, carefully hanging the first two items on a double hanger and throwing the latter on the floor for Amah to remove for washing, then he lay down on the bed dressed in just his underpants and let the delicious breeze from the ceiling fan play over his body. Presently Diana emerged with her head wrapped in a towel with which she proceeded to rub her hair until it was partially dry. She'd let it grow and, as she combed it, it reached down to a point between her shoulder blades. Lewis liked it as she wore it these days, taken back from her face and arranged in a fat chignon at the back of her head. He called it a bun which made Diana feel school-mistressy but it suited her and had the advantage of being cool.

'You'll get a chill on your tummy lying there in the draught,' she said.

'Do you think so?' He sat up anxiously and pulled a sheet up waist high. Diana plugged in the hair dryer and the hum of the machine made conversation difficult for the next ten minutes. Lewis closed his eyes and drifted out on the tide of sound, half asleep, half awake. When he opened them Diana was lying beside him. The brown skin of her legs, arms and torso contrasted sharply with the white of her bra and pants.

'Who's going to get a chill now?' He put his hand across and placed it on her stomach which was warm and damp with steam and sweat. He crooked his middle finger and let it rest in the indentation of her navel.

'I'm getting fat,' she said.

'Never.' He leaned over to look at her more closely. 'Well, perhaps you've put on a bit but I like it; you were too thin before.'

'Would you mind if I put on some more?'

'A little, not too much.'

'Is pregnant too much?'

He withdrew his hand and sat up, propped on his elbow.

'Are you sure?'

'Quite sure. Are you pleased?'

He took a deep breath. 'Yes,' he said. 'Yes, I am pleased. It's what you wanted.'

'More than anything else in the world. I keep reminding myself you made it possible. Thank you, Lewis.'

She could tell from the look in his eyes that he wanted her and she knew of no better way to show her gratitude. She drew his hand back and placed it on her breast, turning towards him.

'Do you think we ought to? What about the baby? You must take care.'

'It won't hurt the baby, the doctor said.'

118

'Does he know? After all, you're no chicken to be having a first baby.'

She swung her legs over the bed impatiently and stood up. The spell was broken. It wasn't as if she'd particularly wanted it at that moment or at any other for that matter, but he was unaware of the gesture he had rejected. 'For heaven's sake, Lewis. I hope you're not going to coddle me for six months. It's a perfectly natural process and I'm perfectly healthy, even if, as you so elegantly put it, I am a little long in the tooth.'

'Don't be cross,' he said. 'I've never had a baby before.'

'I'm not cross, I just — ' She changed what she had been going to say. 'I just wanted to be sure you're glad.'

He watched her dress and do her face. She looked very stunning tonight in a sleeveless dress of dull gold silk jersey. The bodice was draped, giving more fullness to her bosom, and the waist tightly belted before it flared out into a complete circle, dropping in fluted folds just below her knees. She'd tucked four yellow freesia heads into her chignon and wore a gold watch and the gold snake bracelet he had bought her in Penang. She glanced at the watch now.

'You'd better get dressed. They'll be here in five minutes.'

119

'They're bound to be late. You know Grant, never on time for anything.'

'It's not always his fault. You can't help it if you're a doctor.'

'I suppose not. Go and see the drinks have been set out, there's a dear, and tell Cookie he can put the ice in the bucket.'

Diana went into the sitting-room and opened two tins of salted nuts and some packets of crisps, tipping them into glass dishes which she set about on tables conveniently placed near the chairs. The headlights of a car swept across the window in an arc then flashed through the room a second time as Grant reversed his car back in a semi-circle to draw up neatly in the parking lot, and then the lights went out. Diana waited to hear their footsteps on the gravel drive before going to open the door.

The Furnivals had been Lewis's only close friends since he had been in Singapore. At least he hadn't introduced any others to Diana, and then not until after their marriage. She'd thought it strange that, being such good friends, he had not invited them to the wedding but when she taxed him with this, Lewis had merely said, 'I wanted you to myself. Grant can be a bit overpowering and I'm too old for those old chestnuts about blushing brides and grooms and confetti and tin cans.'

Diana privately feared they might have cause to feel hurt but if they were they didn't show it. She had been interested and a little curious to meet someone who had known Lewis so much longer than she, although from first impressions it was an unlikely alliance. The two men were complete opposites — Grant with his extrovert air, his tall stories and broad humour, never appearing to take anything seriously, possessed more arrogant charm than any law should justly allow. Lewis, in contrast, looked almost colourless and Diana sensed that he was embarrassed by many of Grant's more racy anecdotes, sprinkled as they were with a liberal supply of adjectival 'bloodys' and generally relying on sexual *double entendre* for their point. Lewis didn't think sex was funny nor did he approve of salacious stories, particularly in front of Diana and Hilary.

Hilary was one of the best things that had happened to Diana and right from the start both of them had recognized their common wave-length. She was minute, only about five foot two, with hands and feet in proportion and a fragile, dainty body that possessed the strength of steel and the physical endurance and vigour of a long-distance runner. Her hair was brown with burnished copper lights, cut very short and tumbling over her forehead in a fringe that curled up into corkscrews in the humidity. Her eyes were also brown, velvety and melting like a Jersey cow's and they were magnified behind the lenses of a pair of square-rimmed tortoiseshell glasses, the latter perched on a freckled turned-up nose, and the skin on her cheeks and forehead was pearly and transparent. She was twenty-five, seven years Diana's junior, though beside her Diana often felt gauche and naïve and pitifully lacking in energy and enthusiasm. Hilary brought the full force of her unbounded natural vitality to every undertaking in which she was involved and she was involved in plenty — Chairman of the Hospital Visiting Committee, Secretary of the Blood Donors' Association, Social Secretary for the Cricket Club and a member of the hospital Driving Scheme, activities to fill the void in her life which had opened up that afternoon two years ago when she had run into the garden to look for two-year old James and found him floating face down in the sunken swimming pool. Diana hoped Lewis wouldn't mention the baby. She would tell Hilary in her own way when they were alone together.

'Ah! Queen and huntress chaste and fair — I must say, Diana, my dear, tonight you rival your namesake. Is she not indeed a goddess excellently bright in that most seductive of dresses — eh, Lewis?' Grant took her fingers and kissed them with a mock exaggerated gesture. Diana laughed and, retrieving her hand, greeted Hilary with a kiss and led them into the sitting-room.

'I must apologize for our tardiness but my lady wife was out on one of her errands of mercy and didn't return to the shelter of our connubial roof until well past six.'

Lewis placed a gin and tonic on the table within reach of Hilary.

'It doesn't matter,' he said. 'We're in no hurry. I booked the table for eight-thirty. What was it this time, Hilary? I can't keep up with all your activities.'

'We had a particularly heavy session at the Clinic,' she replied, leaning back and sipping her drink appreciatively. 'Ah, that's what I needed. One can't always be sure one's got the explanation across to these people and it takes time. Today we had a particularly inarticulate lot and we had to be extra patient. Once they think you think they're stupid you've lost their confidence and they won't come back.'

'If the cap fits . . . eh?' Grant grinned, then put up his hands in feigned self-defence. 'Sorry about that irresistibly appalling pun.

123

You're doing stalwart work, my dear, trying to control the population explosion, but you must sometimes get the feeling you're swimming against the tide. Like today for instance.'

'What happened?' Lewis asked, then wished he hadn't.

'Some wretched Malay woman they'd fitted up four months ago came back today pregnant. She'd bored a neat hole in her cap and worn it round her neck as a talisman. She's twenty-eight and got ten kids and was on her knees when she got to the Clinic.'

Lewis frowned. He found this kind of conversation distasteful.

Diana said, 'Poor devil. I don't suppose she found it amusing.'

'It isn't.' Grant lit a cigarette and snapped his lighter shut. He was still smiling. 'Sometimes in this country if you didn't laugh you'd cut your bloody throat. Too often Family Planning means having ten children to be sure of five growing to adulthood. Ignorance, poverty, disease, overcrowding — and it's the relatively intelligent ones that come to the Clinic. It's the others whose need is even greater.'

'No shop tonight.' Hilary reached forward and put her hand on his arm and in the second that he turned to her and smiled, a different smile from the one of a few moments ago, Diana was stabbed by a swift and painful pang of envy. The fleeting gesture and the glance between them conveyed an understanding and union of spirit discernible to a sensitive observer and brought home sharply to Diana, not for the first time, the lack of some elemental force in her own marriage. She couldn't have defined it but she recognized it in them and was jealous.

'I've never seen such a change in a man as that you've wrought in Lewis,' Grant said, smiling into her eyes as they were dancing. 'I congratulate you, Diana. You've been good for him.'

'It's fifty-fifty. He's done a great deal for me. We must be good for each other.'

'No doubt, but then I'm hardly a judge of that, not having known you before. I saw the state Lewis was in when he first came here and, believe me, you wouldn't have recognized him as the same man.'

He gave his attention to piloting Diana through a group of dancers towards a clearer space on the floor and she moved with him easily, enjoying their shared rhythm and responding with pleasure to the music. He was a good dancer, better than Lewis who was inclined to be stiff. They were silent for several minutes. She was afraid he might change the subject when he spoke again but in a moment or two he continued as if there had been no interruption.

'He'd been through a shattering experience. It was bound to leave a mark. But of course you know all about that.'

Diana said nothing, feeling guilty for not dispelling this illusion, her curiosity getting the better of her.

'That's why we were stunned to hear he'd married again. I confess I, if not Hilary, was prepared for the worst.'

'The worst?' Diana raised her eyebrows.

'Feeling as he did about women. It's all tied up with the way he was brought up and a strong guilt complex. I must say meeting you was a tremendous relief. I suppose up till then we'd both felt vaguely responsible for him.'

'He's told me how kind you were. I felt bad that he hadn't told you about us before we were married, but anyway, it's good to know you approve.'

She wasn't flirting, and he coloured.

'I hope I didn't sound patronizing.'

'Not at all. I'd have felt precisely the same about one of my friends. We both needed something. It looks as if it was each other.'

He looked at her thoughtfully, his gaze returned blandly from cool, clear grey eyes.

'We all need love,' he said. 'Particularly Lewis. He threw it away once because he didn't recognize it. I don't imagine he'd be so foolish a second time. Besides, you're not Klara.'

'What was she like?'

'Young, pretty, sexually lax in a Scandinavian way. I never met her. I only know what Lewis has told me. I think she loved him in her way. It wasn't his.'

'He must have loved her very much to have been so distraught and bitter when it ended. He said he could never forgive her.'

'What he couldn't forgive was that she showed him a side of himself he didn't like.'

'Was that why he beat her up?'

He regarded her suspiciously. 'Are you asking me to divulge professional information about my patient, Diana? I thought you said you knew all about it. If you don't, you'll have to ask Lewis. I'm afraid I can't tell you anything.'

'He told me he half-killed her — those were his words. I gathered he meant physically. I think I have a right to know what happened.'

'I can assure you he's not violent, if that's what you're afraid of. You're safe enough, besides you're unlikely — ' He broke off awkwardly.

'I'm unlikely to furnish the same provocation. Is that what you were going to say?' She laughed. It was gratifying to read his discomfiture. You didn't often see Grant at a disadvantage.

'I'll take it as a back-handed compliment. I realize I'm hardly endowed to make strong men weep, nor am I the slightest bit afraid of Lewis manhandling me. He's far too civilized and kind. That's the paramount virtue, genuine kindness. It's fairly rare and I'd trade it for passion any day.'

His smile was quizzical. 'Is that what you did?'

Controlling a primitive urge to bring her knee up sharply into his crutch, she danced on without missing a step. 'Why shouldn't I have settled for both? One doesn't necessarily preclude the other.'

'It needn't, but you forget I'm trained to look beneath the surface and there's something about you, Diana, that's untouched, intact. After six months of marriage it's almost as if you're still virginal, unawakened. You're a woman with a passionate nature but so far passion with a capital P has played no part. Am I right?'

She smiled sweetly up at him as their dance ended. 'If you are, doctor dear, then you've made scientific history, having just diagnosed the second immaculate conception. I know that Lewis would want you to be the first to know that I am pregnant with a capital P.'

She turned and left him standing on the emptying floor, shaking off the hand he had put on her elbow to restrain her. She was furiously angry and hurt. How dare he make snide comments on her relationship with Lewis? What did he know about it or her that gave him the right to pontificate with all that pseudo psychoanalytical clap-trap? He had irritated her before and so had Lewis's deference to his opinions. But for Hilary she would have taken pains to avoid him but she'd take good care in future to give him no opportunity to speak to her in such a manner again.

7

'It was all going to be such marvellous fun, the four of us travelling together,' moaned Hilary. 'It seems ironic that, after planning the trip to coincide with your leave months ago and organizing the passage home so that we could go with you, I should fall into that bloody monsoon drain and break my hip at this precise moment. It's just not fair and — Oh, Diana, I'm going to miss you and all the good times you'll be having on that beastly boat.'

'The good times are purely hypothetical and will depend entirely on what our fellow travellers are like,' said Diana. 'These ships are very small. They only take about twenty passengers and, if the company isn't congenial, one can spend a fairly claustrophobic three weeks, according to all reports. Lucy and Tom Carpenter had a pretty gruesome voyage with a missionary Convention, a Japanese corset salesman and three American dowagers weighted with mink and possessing voices that severed the ship from stem to stern like circular saws, so I'm not sure we shouldn't be envying you your flight in comparative luxury. Besides, it'll be appallingly hot and only my phobia about aeroplanes makes me contemplate it at all. You can think of me lugging Peter up and down to meals in the stifling saloon all through the Red Sea. I hope there'll be some other kids his age on board. Lewis thinks we're quite mad and I feel bad that he's got to suffer for my sake. Perhaps there'll be some super unattached floozy travelling to lighten his burden. Thank heavens, selfishly, he'll have Grant.'

'He will, but I'll need him,' wailed Hilary. 'If only he hadn't had the bright idea of working his passage as ship's locum he could have flown with me but now it's too late to find a substitute.'

Diana had brought Peter up for their daily visit to see the incapacitated Hilary, who was lying on a long sun chair under the shade of a jacaranda. Her right leg and hip were encased from ankle to waist in heavy plaster. Peter, who was nearly three, ran on the lawn, dressed in a diminutive pair of striped bathing trunks, gambolling in and out of range of a garden sprinkler and shrieking with delight when the ice cold droplets fell on his warm, bare skin. His straight, blond hair lay in wet dark streaks over his face and his whole body was nut brown and sturdy, square and compact like Lewis's. He had Lewis's blue eyes, but his mother's mouth and the contours of his face were Diana's. Already he was full of imagination and ideas, sensitive to atmosphere and the reactions of those around him with the promise of an early susceptibility to lame dogs.

★ ★ ★

Lewis's chief aim in life was to make a man of his son and to this end their moments together were more often spent in shadow boxing, pummelling each other and the attacking of miniature assault courses built with enthusiasm by his father and endured by the boy. Lewis had an irritating habit of never leaving the child alone, hoisting him aloft and throwing him up and down when he was smaller, swinging him round by an arm and leg hold, fencing with him with a stick — tapping his right shoulder, his left, the small of his back, until Peter whipped from side to side, bewildered and frustrated but knowing that any display of tears or bad temper would be attributed to bad sportsmanship — the eighth deadly sin according to his father.

'Don't tease him,' Diana would be goaded to exclaim. 'It's not fair. You're much bigger than him and much quicker. Give him a chance.'

'Nonsense. He knows it's a game, don't you, old son? Can't have you growing up namby-pamby and wet. Sticking your nose in a book all day isn't going to toughen you up, is it?'

'What's so great about being tough? You said yourself you weren't any good at games.'

'I wasn't fanciful or sentimental either. I didn't have a night light at his age and I didn't suck my thumb. You kiss and cuddle him too much, Di. It's not good for a boy.'

Diana held the small body to her protectively. 'Little boys need all the loving they can get before they're eight or nine. They have to make a store of it to last them through all the years of school and manhood just because it isn't expected of them to show emotion when they're older. Don't grudge him our love, Lewis. It's a foundation only we can give him.'

She knew from his look that she was speaking a foreign language.

★ ★ ★

'Will you be coming back here after your leave, Di?' Hilary asked.

'I don't know.' Diana sighed. 'It depends

on what we find in England. It's a long time since I've been back and even longer for Lewis. His job's open here but he's heard from an old friend of his, Jim somebody or other, who might have something in view for him and, after all this time, he doesn't feel so shy about looking up old contemporaries from the Force. Also there's Peter's schooling to think about. Lewis wants him to follow in his own footsteps and go to Public school and when the time comes we'll have no relatives where he could go for holidays or who could put him on and collect him off planes, and get his trunk ready for school, even if I could bear to see him only once a year. Settling in England would solve that problem. The fact that you're to be in London is another weighty consideration on the credit side. I shouldn't like it if we couldn't meet and chew the fat sometimes like we do now. What am I going to do if I can't run round to you every time a recipe goes wrong or I want reassurance on the way I'm bringing up Peter?'

Hilary laughed and waved a clutch of magazines which lay on the grass beside her chair. 'You could always write to the magazines. Nowadays they publish everything you want to know from home cooking to information about where to find your erogenous zones in case you don't know!'

'Thanks very much, I do,' Diana said. 'It would be more to the point if they put that sort of thing in the men's magazines. After all, they're meant to be the ones to find them.'

Hilary giggled. 'You could always make a chart and stick it on the ceiling over the bed.'

'Lewis'd probably think it was a map of the golf course!'

'At least he knows where to find the nineteenth hole!'

Diana picked up a paper and threw it at Hilary's head and both collapsed in helpless mirth. It was some moments before they could speak without bursting into fresh peals of laughter.

Grant and Lewis appeared after tea. They came out of the house and across the lawn, Grant stooping to kiss his wife lightly before dropping into a canvas chair beside her.

'You two look beautifully cool here in the shade. It's oppressively sultry in town.'

'I feel a mess.' Hilary pulled herself up and put her hands to her hair. 'I didn't realize it was that time. I meant to tidy up before you came in. We've been gossiping non-stop. It's been hilarious, hasn't it, Di?'

'Mummy and Aunt Hilary couldn't stop laughing,' Peter piped up. 'I didn't see what was funny.'

'Should we?' Grant asked.

'We were talking about erogenous zones,' said Hilary.

'Erog . . . what?' asked Lewis, puzzled.

'He doesn't know what they are. Bad luck, Di.' Hilary was off again.

'No, but what was the word?' Lewis persisted.

'It means erotic,' said Diana, and Lewis said, 'Oh', terminating the subject and the conversation. Diana took pains not to meet Grant's eyes. She knew if she did she would see the laughter behind them.

★ ★ ★

Lewis had made a fuss at first about going home by sea but because it afforded Diana a chance of seeing Colombo, Aden and Gibraltar which would be new to her, and also had the added advantage of enabling them to travel with their heavy baggage, he had allowed himself to be persuaded. Although Diana hadn't committed herself definitely to Hilary, neither she nor Lewis believed they would be returning to Singapore and they packed accordingly, making arrangements for the bulk of their possessions to be shipped with them on the *Orient Star* and anything that was left behind was crated

136

so that it could easily be sent after them. The Purser was an old friend of Lewis's whom Diana and he had often entertained on the *Star's* twenty-four-hour stop-overs between Hong Kong and England. This time she came into Singapore for a brief couple of hours, a week before she would return to pick them up for the homeward journey and Lewis, Grant and Diana were on the quay.

'Just leave everything to me, old boy,' Lewis said to Grant. 'Garson's a friend of mine. He'll fix us a good cabin and I'll make it right with him for you to have the best single now that Hilary isn't coming with us.' They had seen her off some days before and Lewis felt sorry for Grant and wanted to do his best to make his trip a happy one.

The arrangements were duly made over a bottle of whisky in the Purser's cabin. However, in the three days it took to get back from Hong Kong the passengers who had boarded her there had played a game of General Post to suit their own convenience, so that when Lewis and Diana embarked with Peter, they found themselves thrust into a cabin not much bigger than a broom cupboard on top of the water line, and Grant was sharing with an Australian journalist. To add insult to injury, the hold had been overloaded and half their luggage would have been left behind, had not Grant, standing at the rail watching preparations being made to raise the gang plank, caught sight of some familiar crates on the quayside being loaded on to a Lister truck and driven into a nearby Go-down. Shouting and gesticulating to the men at the bottom of the gangway to hold everything, he had been able to retrieve their belongings, which had then been brought on board in literally the last seconds before the *Orient Star* drew away from the shore.

Lewis was properly incensed. 'I shall write a complaint to the directors of the Line and post it as soon as we reach Colombo. It's quite disgraceful, herding passengers like cattle, and the Purser apparently having no control over the passengers taking it upon themselves to reorganize his entire administration. They've had the bloody impudence to tell me the baggage'll have to remain on deck, there's no room in the hold. Another miscalculation it seems. I told them they'd bloody well have to find a tarpaulin and get it covered and battened down or I'll sue them for anything damaged or lost. I can tell you, Di, this is the last time I travel this way. Where have you put my things? Heavens, there's no room here to swing a cat and I didn't reckon on having Peter in with us like this. He'll have to go in the top bunk.'

There were two bunks, one on top of the other, and another separate low one beside them. Diana knew what was in his mind and she wasn't being deliberately awkward.

'Lewis, I can't possibly put him up there. He's too small and he might fall out. Besides it's right on top of the porthole. I'd never have a minute's peace. It's not safe. He'll have to go in one of the lower ones.'

She saw him sulking and tried to make light of the situation.

'Darling, it can't be helped. It's only three weeks.'

There was a knock on the cabin door which had been fastened back into the corridor for coolness and the light curtain that was drawn across the aperture twitched. Grant's head appeared. He had overheard Diana's last words and took in the situation at a glance round the cabin.

'Never mind, old boy. You'll get your oats every morning. Only a British Line in this climate could produce porridge for breakfast. I've just scrutinized the menu.'

Diana could have boxed his ears and Lewis was furious and refused to be placated for the first week of the voyage. He was a bad sailor and for three days took to his bed, not actually being sick but making the most of being afraid he might be. Food was sent away untouched in spite of Diana's reiterated advice that it would be better for him to have something to be sick on, which was intended helpfully but received by Lewis as heartless. It was close enough in the cabin to make anyone feel ill and Diana was thankful to escape up on deck with Peter and where Grant and she amused themselves playing deck quoits or swimming in the ship's salt water pool, or just lying side by side in deck chairs, drowsing or talking. She got to know him better than she had before and for the first time he dropped the superficial flippancy he usually employed with her and showed her a serious side to his nature that she respected. It seemed natural to sit together at the table, where Grant delighted Peter with preposterous stories that masqueraded as true-life experiences, so that the little boy was not sure whether Uncle Grant was a real hero or an arrant liar, but either way he was enormous fun.

On the fourth day Lewis decided to live and emerged to eat his way through a five-course lunch and dinner as well as a heavy breakfast and full tea, a process to be repeated on the two subsequent days, so that by the time they entered Colombo Harbour on the seventh day he was complaining of feeling blown out, bunged up and suffering from constipation. From the pharmacopoeia, without which he would never dream of travelling, he had taken several laxative pills which he now informed Diana gloomily hadn't yet worked and he lay in his bunk, his hands pressing his stomach under a loosened waistband and wondering aloud whether it might be an appendix after all.

'I shan't go ashore,' he said wanly. 'I shouldn't enjoy it like this and besides, if it were more than constipation it might be risky. Get Grant to take you. He's been here before and knows the form. Peter will be all right here with me.'

Diana felt guilty but one look from the porthole at the coconut palms and azure sky and the sense of a new place waiting to be explored convinced her that today she had no vocation for self-sacrifice. She stuffed her bathing things, a camera and a shady hat into a beach hold-all and made the right noises of sympathy as she kissed Lewis on the brow. Then she ran up on to the deck where Grant was waiting.

They disembarked down a ladder on the side of the ship on to a pontoon alongside in the middle of the harbour and from thence into a motor launch which chugged without delay to the jetty. Shading her eyes and looking into the sun, Diana saw Colombo's clock tower coming closer until she could read the figures on its face. There was a small light on its very top and Grant explained that it had been designed by some long repatriated Governor's lady and served a dual purpose as a lighthouse.

'What do you want to do?' he asked, as he helped her alight on to the first firm soil for a week. 'Sight-see, swim, something to drink?'

'Something to drink first,' said Diana. 'I'm parched. Perhaps we could have it in one of the places you think I should see, killing two birds with one stone. You take charge. Could we do a quick look round the town and then go swimming? After the ship it would be heaven to get really cool.'

They took a taxi through the town and out past the Colombo Club, stopping at the swimming club for an iced fresh lemon and a cigarette. There were several people swimming and Grant said, 'Do you want to swim here or the sea?'

Diana took the straw out of her mouth to answer. 'The sea, please. Isn't there a place — Mount Lavinia? Would that be too far?'

'We can keep the taxi,' he said, 'or let him go and get another when you've seen the shops.'

She stretched back in her chair and smiled. 'Are they worth seeing? I haven't any money really but I'd like to have something to remind me of Colombo. Would we have time on our way back?'

'Don't see why not. We haven't got to be back on board till six. If we leave the beach in good time we can do a quick recce in half an hour.'

'Let's then.' She took his hand and they got back into the car and went batting down the Galle road at terrifying speed, avoiding bullock carts and gharis and other traffic coming in the opposite direction more by luck than judgement. The hotel at Mount Lavinia had a deserted air. It was still not ten o'clock and the beach was empty. Diana stood and drew in her breath when she saw the cove with rocks on either side and the huge waves pounding up the beach between, washing up to where they were standing and then receding sharply over the shining, clean sand. The wind blew in from the open sea and after the clammy heat of the ship it was like a douche of cold water.

'It's beautiful. Much better than in the film,' she said.

'The Bridge on the River Kwai?'

She studied him silently.

'What's the matter?' he grinned.

'Nothing. It's good to be with someone you don't have to explain things to. Lewis would have said, 'What film?' '

'Aha, but I promised you a guided tour. I can even show you the exact place where William Holden kissed the girl behind the boat. Yea, this very boat, madam. You can see their indentations in the sand.'

He had pulled her, running, further up the beach away from the hotel where two or three fishing boats were lying. Between them the sand was soft and the wooden hulks afforded some shade. Grant got out a towel from his bag and spread it, inviting her to sit beside him. They staked their claim and went to the hotel changing rooms to put on their swim suits.

It was the most heavenly bathe Diana could remember. She had hardly swum in the sea in Malaya where sea snakes and the muddy colour of the water made sea-bathing unenticing if not dangerous. They threw themselves about in the waves, diving, surfing and eventually exhausted, they sat gasping and laughing.

'Oh, that was good. I feel a new woman.' Diana patted herself dry and raised her hands to her hair to adjust the pins where it was falling down.

'Let it down,' said Grant. He lay, looking up at her and, as she took the rest of the hairpins out of her chignon and the long coil fell, untwisting round her shoulders and down her back, he said, 'That's better.'

She lay down with her body in the sun and her head in the shade and closed her eyes. 'Hilary would have so enjoyed all this,' she said. 'I wish she were here.'

He was silent so long that she wondered if he had heard. 'Don't you?'

She was drifting lazily in the warmth and afterglow of the swim. His voice, when he answered, came from very close to her ear and he said, 'To be honest, no. If she were here I couldn't make love to you very well, could I?'

She opened her eyes. His face was about an inch from her and she was looking straight into his eyes. Tawny eyes, like a big cat.

'And could you do it very well without her?'

He came even closer so that she couldn't focus his face and had to shut her eyes again. Just before his mouth closed on hers he said, 'Very well, thank you, Diana darling.'

It would have looked unsophisticated to struggle. She could imagine how he would tease her if she made too much of a light-hearted kiss between friends. She didn't for a moment imagine he intended more than that. She knew he loved Hilary and she was secure in her marriage with Lewis, and there

145

was Peter. These thoughts went through her mind in the split second before all those other characters became no more than cardboard cutouts in a child's three-dimensional picture book and no one existed but her and Grant.

It was like coming home. All their responses seemed to fit. It wasn't a question of trying to please, she was quite confident that she could, because the things that she wanted to do were unconsciously right and he had the patience and experience to make her want to do them. At some stage she had demurred, but only half-heartedly.

'We can't, Grant. We mustn't. Not here — we might be seen.'

'There isn't a soul in sight and we're hidden by the boats.'

'Lewis says there's a time and place.'

'So there is.' His hands were making her tremble and he was kissing her lightly on her breasts. 'The time is when you want to and as for the place, what's good enough for W. Holden is good enough for me.'

She laughed. 'You're absurd. He had a camera crew.'

He kissed her again on her half-open mouth and she clung to him in a mounting fever of passion, wanting, giving, taking, rolling out with him on a glorious golden sea of desire that broke like the waves on the shimmering sand beyond the boats.

Much later they bathed again. The wind had changed and the sea was calmer and they swam out from the shore to a place where they held one another in the clear water within feet of other more respectable bathers who called out 'good mornings' as they floated by. They didn't go shopping nor did they explore the town. After lunch Grant enquired at the hotel desk if they had a room available where his wife, who was feeling the effects of too much sun, could lie down for the afternoon and they were given the key of a bedroom on the first floor facing the sea, where they spent the rest of their time ashore in bed together.

In the taxi returning to the jetty he had said contritely, 'You wanted to get something to remind you of Colombo and I never showed you the shops. There's no time now. I'm sorry.'

'It doesn't matter.' She smiled. 'And I've seen all I wanted. As for Colombo, it's one place I shall never forget.'

8

Now, standing before an open hotel bedroom window in Bahia Dorada with Lewis in the room behind her dressing for dinner, Diana sharply recalled the old pain — the aching frustration of the rest of the voyage when there had been no opportunity for more than a fleeting touch, a chance kiss between her and Grant. Her newly awakened senses clamoured for more. During polite conversation between the three of them every chance remark now seemed to bear a *double entendre* and Lewis must not guess. Finally, there was the agonizing 'goodbye' bidden hastily in a Customs shed at Southampton at four o'clock in the morning, an hour only romantic if one has stayed up for it but impossibly bathetic to be got up at. She had clung to her correspondence with Hilary as a lifeline to her lover and had waited in vain as the days slipped into weeks, then months and a year, for a sign on his part that their shared experience had meant anything more to him than a pleasant way of passing a day.

'Have I touched your mind at all?' she had asked him on the ship two days before she knew they must part. He hadn't answered directly but had looked at her in what she had then taken to be love and said gently, 'That's a very good question, Diana. What do you think?'

In the beginning the desire to confide her unhappiness to someone was almost overwhelming and more than once the temptation to tell Lewis, which she knew would be merely self-indulgent and cruel, was nearly irresistible. So nearly, but not completely, thank God!

Her mother commented on her abstraction. 'Is anything worrying Diana?' she asked Lewis. 'She seems very quiet and half the time not really with us.'

'I don't think so,' said Lewis equably. 'I hadn't noticed. She's never been noisy, as you know, and she found the journey tiring. She seems quite happy to me.'

Diana, overhearing them from the hall where she was hanging her coat, wondered how he could say such a thing and mean it. How could he live with her and share her bed and be unaware of her present mental turmoil? She would have known had their cases been reversed, but then Lewis wasn't renowned for his perception or his sensitivity.

Certain tunes on the radio were unbearable for the memories they carried of Grant and their hackneyed lyrics were clichés no longer, every word holding a significance for her which brought the ready tears to her eyes. Impulsively she had once said to Lewis, 'If I died, would the music we had enjoyed together make you sad? I wouldn't be able to listen to it for years — if ever, without certain songs affecting me,' and he had patted her head kindly and said, 'What an overdose of imagination you've got.'

There had been no immediate feeling of guilt or real remorse. She was too honest with herself to profess sorrow for an experience she knew she would repeat tomorrow if the chance arose and as for guilt, she had taken from Lewis nothing that he had wanted, namely her passionate physical responses, or he would have taken more trouble to guarantee it for himself. It was at a later date when conscience had reared its disagreeable head as Diana, lying in her husband's arms, had caught herself shutting her eyes and imagining the body, the hands, the mouth, to be those of Grant and when she realized what she was doing, she was ashamed of herself. Lewis might not be the greatest lover since Casanova but he didn't deserve that kind of treachery. Perhaps now that she knew what it should be like, she could make it happen for the two of them and in so doing absolve her guilt and add a new dimension to her marriage. Once after a party, emboldened by alcohol and feeling happy and close to him, she had taken his hands and guided them over her body, moving against him in a way she had learned with Grant, caressing and kissing him and not allowing him to hurry, so that when the final moment came they came for the first time together. If Lewis was aware that they'd made a special kind of history he gave no sign, but for Diana it could have been a turning point. As a physical experience it had been an apple off a different tree from what she had shared with Grant, but it held the promise of something infinitely sweeter if she and Lewis could only take it from there. She was determined to try. They already had so much that was good in their relationship, a mutual respect, companionship and kindness. Love hadn't been in the deal but the possibility was surely there. After that, although there were many times when she didn't make the summit and was left lonely on the far side of the hill, she knew now she could and that was worth working for.

She tried very hard and for a time things went well, but like so many things, success took two and after a while it became apparent she was the only one trying. One night he asked her what she thought she was doing.

'Why? Don't you like it?'

He sat up and lit a cigarette. 'Where did you learn this sort of thing?'

'I read a book,' she lied. 'Does it matter? I realize now how unsatisfactory I was for you before.'

'It's not a woman's place,' he said. 'It's my right. Do you understand?' The words were harsh but he said them gently, almost pleadingly. She sighed and understood.

Diana couldn't remember when she stopped loving Grant. She only knew that a moment arrived when she looked back incredulously at a time when she would have thrown up Lewis and even Peter without a backward glance had he made any sign that he wanted her. She had at least that much to thank him for. There had been no sign and he had saved her from the consequences of her own folly.

★ ★ ★

Diana had never expected to see Grant again. Finding him in Bahia Dorada had been a rude jolt. She had been confident of playing it cool all along the line. She hadn't even liked what she had seen of him and the years had taken more than a certain amount of gilt off the gingerbread. Nevertheless, he had only to

152

open his arms to her and all the old magic had been there. Diana was afraid. She shivered by the open window.

'Cold?' Lewis came up behind her and put his hands on her bare arms.

'No. A ghost walked over my grave.' She took her dress up from the bed and stepped into it, turning her back for Lewis to zip it up.

'Speaking of ghosts,' said Lewis, 'What an extraordinary coincidence running into Grant, here of all places. I'd no idea he was living in Spain. You know, it might not be a bad idea of his, if the house is at all feasible. I'm looking forward to seeing it on Wednesday. It might be just our luck.'

'Do we really have to go?' Diana was arranging her hair as she spoke.

Lewis looked surprised. 'Don't you want to? I thought you were keen. We said we would, we can't very well get out of it now.'

'I suppose not, but don't let's get too involved. Grant has a way of taking over and if we're not careful he'll make our plans for us, especially if he thinks he's got a buyer for his house. You know how managing he can be.'

'I thought you liked him.'

'I do.' Diana was afraid she had protested too much. 'Hilary was really my friend. Oh, Lewis, what a ghastly thing — her being killed. I gather it was a car accident. He didn't say and I couldn't ask, I was so sick with shock. I can't take it in yet.'

'I know.' He was having trouble with his cuff links and was giving them all his attention.

'I wonder when exactly it happened. He said recently. That might mean anything up to a year. He seems to have come to terms with it fairly well — having parties and looking quite cheerful,' Diana mused.

'What else can he do?' asked Lewis. 'It's no good moping for ever. Life goes on.'

'That's the sort of sensible thing people say until it happens to them.' She was nettled by his prosaic approach. 'People have been known to die of grief.'

'Only those with a decided lack of moral fibre. Besides, fat lot of good that would do him.'

'Of course, but what I'm trying to say is that emotion seldom takes logic into account. If you're moping, you're moping. It's no good just telling someone to snap out of it and expecting them to do so. However, luckily it doesn't apply. Grant looks to me as if he has already snapped.'

'Out or in half?' It was an unexpected touch of humour and Diana smiled.

'I'm just sorry he turned up,' she admitted.

'I wanted to enjoy this little holiday with you.'

'Well, I think we ought to be nice to him, my dear. He is an old friend and he must have had a rough time.'

Diana was surprised and not altogether pleased. Only Lewis could have naïvely urged her to 'be nice' to her ex-lover. It was going to be more difficult if he insisted on seeing much of Grant. She wasn't afraid of the latter giving her away to her husband nor did she fear the possibility of having to ward off any unwelcome advances from him. What frightened her was the remembrance of how willingly she had gone into his arms less than an hour ago and, far from being unwelcome, his kiss had been like the slaking of a ten-year thirst.

The boat arrived early the following morning and by the time Diana had dressed and had her breakfast on the terrace, Lewis and the Spaniard who had brought it out from Palafrugell, had assembled and inflated it on the creek below the lobster tank and he was impatient to try it out. It was a grey, rubber, twelve-foot Avon Redshank with a five-horse-power engine which Lewis was tinkering about with, checking it over with a book of words in his hand and muttering about thwarts and toggles and other mysterious nautical terms as unfamiliar to Diana as the rapid Catalan (accompanied by much gesticulation) being spouted by the now departing Spaniard.

'Put your stuff in that green canvas bag and stow it up under the bow dodger,' Lewis instructed her, pointing to what, as far as Diana was concerned, was the sharp end covered by a yellow oilskin sheet, and she did as she was told. The boat was resting on a rubber sausage-shaped roller, making it a relatively simple task for the two of them to run it down and into the water. Diana got in and Lewis followed suit after he had shoved off from the beach. The motor started sweetly and they were away. They spent a happy morning pottering round the bay and getting the feel of the craft, Lewis importantly explaining the various pitfalls to be avoided when handling a boat, as if he'd been messing about in them all his life and this was not his first experience of any kind of maritime navigation. He was feeling rather pleased with himself and the only mishap was, on returning to the shore, when he turned too sharply, and sheared a pin on a rock just below the surface. However, they were in shallow water and he was able to push the boat on to the beach and remedy the defect.

A shadow fell across the sand and Diana straightened her back and looked up. Grant stood there, grinning. 'I shouted to you from the top but you didn't hear me,' he said. 'So this is the boat.'

'It goes jolly well,' said Lewis proudly. 'After lunch I want to take her out further.'

Grant jumped the last two steps hewn in the rock face leading from the path above and landed beside Diana, who suddenly became aware of her dishevelled condition. They had swum from the boat and her hair and bikini were still wet though the salt water had dried in white crystalline marks on her bare skin. In the shelter of the creek the sun beat down hotly and the effort of beaching the boat had brought beads of perspiration to her forehead and on her upper lip. Grant, by contrast, looked cool and immaculate. His blue poplin bathing trunks and open shirt had a freshly laundered appearance and she could smell the spiced perfume of some tangy after-shave lotion as his arm brushed hers. He was wearing dark glasses, the kind you can see out of but not in, and it was disconcerting to meet only her own bedraggled reflection on looking into his face.

'Can I come too?' he asked as eagerly as a schoolboy. 'I'd like to show you something.'

'Great to have you aboard,' Lewis responded heartily. 'Shall we say in an hour? We'll meet you here. Or are you lunching at the hotel, in which case you could join us?'

Diana was relieved to hear Grant say he had to go home but would return in an hour. Lewis seemed almost to welcome his company, which in itself seemed strange. Normally on holiday he was reserved and disliked getting tied up with fellow hotel guests, sometimes resenting Diana's interest in people and her disposition for getting drawn into conversations with strangers. His policy was usually one of total uninvolvement. Conversations led to inclusion in other people's parties and that in its turn often meant you couldn't shake them off on the beach or sit peacefully by the pool when reading the newspaper. Of course Grant was an old friend but Diana hoped Lewis wasn't going to allow him to force his company on them at every opportunity.

The sun was high over the mountain and the bay bathed in a drowsy heat as the three of them chugged slowly from the shore, heading out beyond the slab, the first mass of rocks and round the arm of the headland. Looking back, the white dots of the villas stood out clearly on the mountainside, the hotel slumbered above the creek and water-skiers skimmed across the calm surface of the water, the noise of the speed boats shattering the calm of the siesta hour.

Beyond the promontory the sea grew rougher but the little boat made dogged headway through the swell and they could feel the waves slapping against the floorboards of its flat bottom as they dropped down into the troughs between them. Grant and Lewis sat in the stern and Diana on a thwart in the prow. The weight of the two men at the back forced the nose of the boat higher up out of the water and now and again Lewis teased her by turning their craft broadside into a wave, which sent the cold spray over her and made her shriek with shock and childish enjoyment. The coastline became increasingly rugged and awe-inspiring. Huge walls of rock rose two hundred and fifty feet up sheer faces towering on their right. Now and again the base was cleft and they could see the dim recesses of caves or inlets where the water flattened and gulls were the only sign of life. The cliffs were formed in coloured strata, rather like the glass lighthouses of variegated sand that Diana remembered buying as a child at Alum Bay on the Isle of Wight. In many places gigantic boulders had broken away from the cliff face and lay on other fallen rocks at its foot.

'Some of these falls look quite recent. I suppose bits are coming away all the time,' said Lewis.

'Sometimes in the winter we can get very high seas. A little more falls every year, but you can see, the villas, where there are any, are built very close to the edge so whoever built them must be pretty confident.'

'Or foolhardy,' said Diana.

They had been going for about an hour and had passed on the way a couple of small beaches accessible by road and inhabited by sunbathers and swimmers and here and there amongst the rocks a snorkeler's periscope was visible or the shiny black rubber of his suit or flippers. Just ahead, a line of rocks pointed out into the sea and immediately above, built on a ledge overlapping the top of the cliff, was what looked like a derelict lighthouse. The roof had caved in and a wooden gallery that ran around the wall facing the sea was broken in parts, the dilapidated handrail swinging against its supports where it had completely rotted through.

'That's the old Coastguard's point,' said Grant. 'The new lighthouse is further on round the next corner. Come in closer to the land, Lewis. What I want to show you is here.'

They rounded the finger of rock and Lewis turned the boat into a tiny bay, suddenly revealed. It was no more than a sliver of sand on the left enclosed by a semicircular sweep of the cliff which extended out into the water on the right face where a cleft in the rock formed a natural arch big enough for a boat to pass through. From where they sat they could see a lagoon and the darkness of a cave beyond. High up above the beach a villa perched in the sunlight, the pink roof curved Japanese fashion, white walls, green shutters and a bougainvillea-covered terrace wall facing out to the sea. It was a romantic, enchanting prospect and Diana drew in her breath with the beauty of the scene. There were no other villas in sight.

'Like it?' asked Grant. 'I wanted you to see it first from the sea. It's not a view everyone gets of it, which is a pity as it was designed from this aspect.'

'You mean it's yours? This is the house you've talked about?'

'That's it. *Encantador*. It means enchanted. What do you think?'

'It's fantastic, isn't it, Lewis? Can we get to it from here?'

'We can, but it's quite a steep climb and I don't advise it now if we want to get back before dusk. You can see there are some steps cut into the rock on this side. They go right up to the house but the handrail's a bit dicey.'

Lewis had steered the boat towards the lagoon and they drifted under the rocky arch into dead calm water and the gloom of the opening of the cave. Diana looked up. The light was so bad that at first she couldn't accustom her eyes to it, but when she did she saw that the roof of the cave was covered with millions of tiny bats. The whole ceiling was alive and occasionally one of the creatures moved and flew to a better position. Diana let out an involuntary scream and instinctively covered her bare head with her hands.

Grant laughed. 'They're harmless,' he said.

Diana shuddered. 'I know they've got radar but they give me the creeps. Is that your boat?'

Lying just inside the lagoon and tied to a mooring ring at the bottom of the steps was a red and white gleaming twenty-three foot fibreglass jet-setting Vulcan speed boat, five thousand pounds worth of anybody's money.

'What a beauty! I can see your point. Why bother with Harley Street when you can live like this out here — the car, the villa, the boat — nothing but the best. Isn't she magnificent, Lewis?'

Lewis had been scanning the horizon quietly, resting with his hands clasped loosely on the tiller. He seemed to be a million miles away and Diana repeated her question.

'Mm — what? Oh, the boat. Yes, very nice indeed,' he murmured appreciatively. 'Do you use it a lot?'

'Mostly for ski-ing,' answered Grant. 'She can do up to fifty miles an hour. Have you water-ski-ed, Diana?' And when she shook her head he said, 'Well, I'll have to teach you. It's not hard and you've got good balance. It's very exhilarating. You too, Lewis.'

'Oh, I think I'm a bit old to learn that sort of thing,' deprecated Lewis. 'I've got a back, you know. I have to be careful or the slightest thing triggers it off, but you try Di.'

'I'd love to some time.' She sighed. 'What a heavenly spot and you've got it all to yourself. You haven't any neighbours?'

'Only the lighthouse,' said Lewis. 'I suppose you can see that from the house?'

'Only just, but I'm afraid it can't remain unspoilt for long. I hear the developers are interested in all this part of the coast. It's just a matter of time before the other villas come.'

'Is that why you want to get out?' Lewis picked up his discarded shirt from the bottom of the boat and put it on. They were in shadow in the lagoon and with the sun beyond the cliff it was suddenly chilly.

'Partly that. If I get out now I'll get the price. It also holds a lot of associations for me. I think the time has come when it would be better for me to be free of some of those.'

163

'And by moving you can escape.'

Grant looked at him sharply. 'Escape?'

'Rehabilitate would perhaps be a better word.'

'Oh, I see.' Grant laughed. 'Who knows? Life has to go on.'

Diana pulled her watch out of the waterproof bag and consulted it.

'It's half past four,' she announced. 'Shouldn't we start back? It'll take longer than coming. The sea was running out way in this direction. Shall we drop you here, Grant?'

'No, I'd better come back with you. I left my car at the hotel. You shall see the inside of *Encantador* on Wednesday.'

Diana suddenly shivered. Grant put his hand on her back between her shoulder blades and her skin stood up in goose pimples, but not because she was cold.

'You're frozen,' he said. 'Here, Lewis, let's catch what's left of the sun.'

The engine spluttered into life and the boat took them out into the open sea. Diana looked back at the villa perched serenely in the late afternoon light. There was a man on the terrace watching them. He wore a white jacket and a black bow tie and trousers and held a tray of glasses, like a waiter. Lewis turned round to make some adjustment to the pace of the engine and saw him too. For a second they looked at each other across the widening gap of water before the man lifted his tray and moved back into the house and out of sight.

9

That was on Friday. On Sunday Lewis had tickets for the bull fight in Barcelona and though it was Diana's least idea of fun, he had insisted that having come all this way she must see one, if only to be able to say why she didn't hold with the sport. She couldn't help feeling guiltily relieved when Lewis passed an uneasy Saturday night with repeated trips to the lavatory and by Sunday morning it was apparent he was in the grip of a baddish bout of the local lurgi, running a slight temperature and wanting nothing more than to be left alone to sleep it off.

'Take the tickets out of my wallet and see if you can find someone else in the hotel who'd like to go with you. They could help you at the desk. I'm sorry, I wanted to take you myself.'

Diana's heart smote her. He was really so kind and he looked so wretched, flushed and sweating and bracing himself against the next wave of pain as it ground relentlessly from his lower abdomen up to his chest, then passed until the next time.

'I shan't leave the hotel. I want to be sure

you're all right,' she said.

'I'll be right as rain tomorrow. These pills always do the trick. Don't worry.'

'Well, I'll be down on the slab and I'll come up later to see if you need anything.'

She took her book and a lilo and made her way down to the rocks beside the slab, positioning herself so that she could watch the activity in the bay, and lay down on her stomach with the book propped at an angle in front of her. As time passed she was joined by several others, some waiting for boats to be brought round for them and several settling down to sunbathe or watch the passing parade. It was about eleven when the red and white Vulcan swept into the bay and made for where she lay. Grant was at the wheel and he scanned the sunbathers intently before he saw her and jumped on to the small jetty, holding the boat's painter in one hand.

'Lewis told me where to find you,' he announced. 'He telephoned. Thought you might be lonely. Something about a bull fight.'

Diana's first impression was, what the hell was Lewis playing at? She'd made it clear to him that she wasn't hankering for Grant's company and she certainly wasn't keen on the idea of being forced into a tête-à-tête with him without Lewis being there. Last time that had happened it had taken more than a year to get over it. Diana was one of those rare people who learn by their mistakes. However, they could hardly argue the toss in these circumstances where every word was public property. Another boat drew up to the steps and it was obvious Grant was in the way.

'Hop in,' he ordered. 'Leave your clobber here. It'll be safe enough. Bring a towel and your other costume.'

She obeyed and he reached out an arm to steady her as she stepped down into the boat, then they were off. It was exhilarating and a bit frightening at first. The bay receded in a flash and beyond the rocks he turned left in the opposite direction from the one they had taken in the Red Shank. The coastline was much the same but after a moment they came to a small shingled beach and here Grant dropped anchor just off shore and switched off the engine. The peace and silence after the roar of the motor above which conversation had been impossible was almost tangible. The water was like crystal, so clear Diana could see down to the bottom where the rocks and weed on the sea bed glistened in a myriad of colours.

'Shall we swim in to the beach?' Grant asked, and when she nodded he dived in and made for the shore with a powerful crawl.

Diana lowered herself over the side. The sea was cold and deliciously invigorating and she swam around for a long time, revelling in its freshness and a sense of healthy well-being, turning over on to her back, arms out-stretched, to float and survey the grandeur of the mountain above her. At last she swam slowly to the beach and clambered up to where Grant was sitting in a scooped-out chair of pebbles. He had erected a cairn of flat stones on a boulder a few feet away and was now pounding it with flints aimed from his present position. When Diana positioned herself gingerly beside him he dug out a hollow for her. She lay back and shielded her eyes from the sun with her hands.

'We've left the cigarettes in the boat and I want one.'

'You underestimate me, my dear.' Grant stood up and unzipped a small pocket in his bathing trunks from which he produced a packet of Rothman's and a lighter wrapped in oilskin.

'As ever, prepared for any eventuality,' said Diana wryly.

They lit up and smoked in silence, then Grant said, 'There seems to be something about us and beaches. Were you born under Pisces?' He was running his finger lightly down the inside of her arm as he spoke and she made no move to draw away. 'Lewis's bowels have a good deal to answer for one way and another.'

'I'm not going to have an affair with you this time, Grant, in spite of the other night.'

'A pity. You can't deny you were pleased to see me. You tried to pretend you weren't.'

'I wasn't and I didn't seek this situation. Your appeal for me is purely physical and as such I admit it's dangerous, but I've no intention of becoming infatuated again.'

'It wasn't mere infatuation on my part. I couldn't have made love to you like that if there hadn't been more involved.'

'I suppose that's why I never heard from you, no word, no sign. I waited and hoped for a year and after that I was thankful you'd made me see the whole episode in its true perspective. When I think of what I might have done to Lewis — to Peter — how I could have hurt them . . . well, I suppose I should be thankful to you really.'

He said. 'I was married too.'

'Yes, of course. And now you aren't, is that it?'

He sat up and started throwing stones again. 'That's cruel.'

'Don't say you love me. Spare me that.'

'There are ways of loving. Sometimes two people at the same time. I never forgot you,

Diana. Do you believe me?'

'No.' She blew out some smoke in rings but the breeze broke them up and wafted them away across Grant's back. His shoulders were broadly muscled overlaid with a hint of excess flesh which would have lessened his attraction had it not been tanned to a deep bronze. She shut her eyes quickly before she was tempted to put out a hand just to feel him.

'Did you want to forget me?'

'Yes. I tried.'

'But without success?'

'Complete.'

'You're a bad liar, my dear.'

'Why? Because you're too bloody conceited to believe it could be true?'

The noise of the stones hitting the cairn had ceased and she opened one eye to see what he was doing. He was sitting quite still with his hands clasped loosely on his drawn-up knees, looking out to the horizon with an expression of unguarded sadness. Some sixth sense informed him that she was watching him and he turned to laugh at her and said disarmingly, 'Quite probably. Hilary always said that self-pride was my besetting sin.' He scrutinized her silently then asked: 'Does it embarrass you if I talk about her?'

'Should it?'

'I don't know. Some people are funny.'

'She was my friend. I've often thought of that. I suppose I should be ashamed of what I did to her but I don't think I took anything of hers that really mattered, did I?'

'I loved her,' he said.

'That's what I meant. I used to be jealous of the way you looked at each other, at the rapport between you. Oh, I don't mean jealous because I wanted you. I'd never even thought of you in that way before Colombo. No. There was something I was missing or thought I was. You showed me what it was that day at Mount Lavinia and that's why I don't feel guilty on Lewis's account. You enabled me to give him so much more. He's a good man — unimaginative, a little dull even — but good. We've been happy. I said once before that Passion with a capital P was ephemeral. That was before I knew anything about it. I ached for you, longed for just one letter, would have come crawling over broken glass if you had beckoned, but it passed and I'm so thankful you didn't allow me to be such a fool.'

'And what about now?'

Diana didn't pretend to misunderstand him. 'Nothing about now,' she said decidedly.

Grant contemplated her as she met his gaze with a great deal more outward decision than she felt. He moved towards her and for one frighteningly, ecstatically, anticipatory moment she thought he was going to take her into his arms, but he leaned beyond her to lever himself to his feet with the help of the rock just behind her. She sat up and watched him walk across the shingle to rebuild the cairn. His eyes were downcast, searching for suitable flat stones and every now and again he bent down to pick one up. When he came back to her side he sat down again and resumed his target practice.

After a while he said, 'It's strange. You said you were jealous of us — of Hilary and me. You never guessed how much she envied you and Lewis because you had Peter. It's ironic to think how easy it was to have James. We just decided to have a baby and bingo — that was it. They never could find any reason why there shouldn't be another, but it didn't happen and it broke her down. She wasn't the same person in latter years that you knew, Di. She became bitter and obsessed. She'd been so wonderful when James died but when she didn't start another baby it was as if all the grieving returned. I believe it was purely psychological. She wanted a child, but not a replacement for James. She wanted the impossible: James himself. It was a vicious circle and it made her vicious. Well, not actually vicious, but difficult, cantankerous and depressed. She couldn't let go of her grief. It destroyed her.'

Diana sat in shocked silence trying to equate this description with the Hilary she had known. His last words struck a chill into her stomach.

'You're not saying you think she deliberately . . . '

'They weren't sure. They recorded an open verdict.'

'Oh, my God!' She knelt up and put her arms around his shoulders, drawing his head down to her breast and rocking him slightly as she might have comforted a child. It was a spontaneous gesture of pity devoid of any suggestion of desire. 'Tell me what happened.'

He raised his head and seemed about to speak and at the same moment she was shocked to feel his two hands come strongly up to her waist to hold her immobile while his mouth moved over the naked upper part of her breasts. She let go of her hold of him and tried to push him away ineffectually before his mouth came down on hers, forcing her lips apart, exploring and insistent. After the initial surprise, her main reaction was one of fury. She bit down hard on his questing tongue. He relaxed his grasp and raised a hand to his mouth with an exclamation and in spite of her anger she almost laughed at his horrified expression.

'It's bleeding,' he said accusingly.

'Serves you bloody well right. I wonder if you're capable of one decent, genuine emotion. It was a great performance, enlisting my sympathy. Can anyone believe one word you say?'

'You'll never know and that's part of my mystery.' He prodded his tongue carefully and decided that no lasting damage had been done. 'Well then, you're obviously not going to let me make love to you, so what do we do now? Do you want to go to a bull fight?'

'No — and you're incorrigible.' She couldn't prevent a smile and was exasperated with herself for forgiving him as readily as he had been confident she would. 'I can buy one of those Matador posters at the hotel desk for Peter to stick up in his room. He'll be quite satisfied with that. He asked me to bring him a souvenir if we went to a fight.'

'Young savage! What did he expect — an ear?'

'He's not like that at all.' She rose hastily in the absent Peter's defence. 'He's a very gentle person — too gentle for his own good, I often think. It would have been easier for him if he had been a girl. It doesn't pay to be too sensitive or too tolerant in the present world.'

'I shouldn't have thought there was

anything like enough tolerance in the present world,' said Grant.

'But if you always bend over backwards to find out why people behave as they do and so find excuses for them, then nothing is ever condemned — nothing is wrong. It can lead to an inability ever to come down on one side of the fence or the other on a really serious issue.'

'Things are seldom black or white anyway.'

'I don't believe that. Some things are definitely wrong and should be condemned. The trouble is that the standards of the young today are so different. Imposing mine on him, even if I could do it, could prove only a form of selfishness and God knows mine may not be all that hot. No. One has to bring them up in the knowledge of one's own principles, then they have to decide how they're going to behave and you have to be on the side lines to pick up the pieces if anything goes badly wrong. So long as communications are open between us, that's the most important thing. Our parents were lucky. All they had to worry about in bringing us up was sex and possibly the demon drink, but now there are so many other factors — drugs and violence and the general feeling of the breakdown of law and order that's rife at home. One of the senior boys at Peter's school killed himself riding a motor bike through an eight-foot brick wall while under the influence of LSD. From what they could make out, he apparently imagined he was on a horse and could take the wall, but he went slap through it. Every bone in his body was smashed and he was just eighteen. They couldn't find out where he got the stuff from although the episode uncovered one or two others who were also on drugs and they were expelled. Peter says there's no difficulty getting it if you feel so inclined — and that's a boy of fourteen at a decent public school. It's terrifying. I'd castrate the pushers. Hanging would certainly be too good.'

Grant had moved on to his stomach and his head, turned towards her, rested on his folded arms. 'What does Lewis say about it all?' he asked after a moment.

Diana laughed. 'Oh, darling Lewis! He's a child in many ways. These things happen to other people but not to the Holts. He'd consider Peter's background sufficient guarantee of his moral rectitude. It's only the kids with inadequate parents who go off the rails. Parenthood these days is a losing gamble. One is blamed for everything.'

'He expects a lot.'

'Perhaps it's good for us that he does — I don't know. If you know you're held in esteem, surely you rise to the occasion?'

Grant raised an eyebrow at her and she had the grace to blush, knowing what he was thinking. 'It would depend on how much you valued the person's opinion, I suppose,' he said.

She looked down at him quite seriously. 'Very much. I value Lewis's good opinion of me very much, Grant.'

'Let's hope then he'll never be given cause to revise it.' The words were spoken lightly and at the same moment a cloud passed in front of the sun and a stronger gust of wind drove a big wave further up the shingle to where they lay. Diana rubbed her shoulders and arms with her hands. The brightness had gone out of the day.

'The sea's getting up. Is the boat all right?'

The Vulcan was tugging at her anchor, bobbing and twisting on the increasing swell like an animal anxious to be released from its leash. Grant stood up and looked at the sky.

'She's safe enough, but it looks as if we've had the best of the day. There's a mist rolling over from behind the mountain and when it does that at this hour it usually means the end of the sun.'

'What is the time?'

Grant consulted his wrist watch, an anti-magnetic, self-winding, water- and shock-proof expensive affair strapped to a brown arm on which golden hairs curled strongly. 'Two-fifteen,' he said.

'Heavens! Lewis'll be wondering what's happened to me. I promised to go up at lunch time and see if he wanted anything to eat.'

'Don't panic. You're in Spain and it's only nearing lunch time now. We'll be back in a jiffy. Come on.'

Taking her hand, he pulled her to her feet and would have run with her down the beach if she hadn't howled with agony as the sharp stones pressed into her bare soles. Grant seemed impervious to them and had plunged into the shock-cold water by the time Diana had stumbled to the water's edge. She launched herself thankfully into the waves and swam out for the boat. By the time she reached it, Grant had thrown an aluminium folding ladder over the side and he hauled her up on this.

Lewis had been sleeping and woke only when Diana opened the shutters to go out on to the balcony to spread her bathing things to dry.

'Have a good morning?' he mumbled.

'Great. Grant turned up and we went to the beach.' She was immediately ashamed of herself for giving him the impression they'd gone to the main beach. Why hadn't she mentioned the cove? There was nothing to be ashamed of, no reason to feel guilty. She remembered the kiss and, remembering, recalled that Grant never had answered her question just before he had taken hold of her. She still didn't know exactly how Hilary had died.

10

By Wednesday the mist had enveloped the bay for two whole days, bringing with it an unpleasant, heavy humidity, concealing the rugged beauty of the coastline and giving Diana a depressing sense of being shut in. Every now and again the sun could be seen momentarily shining through a thinning in the cloud but there was no breath of wind upon the dead calm sea to drive the fog away.

Grant had invited them earlier than his other guests so that he could show Diana and Lewis the villa before they arrived and he had drawn a rough sketch map of the tortuous coast road which he had insisted was the easiest and most direct approach to *Encantador*.

As the car climbed up the winding mountain road out of Bahia Dorada they suddenly found themselves in brilliant sunshine. The evening sky was blue and gold and beneath them the mist obscured the hotel and the sea, like a flattened blanket. The green tops of the pines rested on the cloud like verdant islands and Diana opened the car window right down to let in the dry, sweet air against her clammy skin. They took the main road to Palafrugell, a twisting, narrow tarmac-ed affair with an uncertain camber at each edge, just broad enough to take two cars if both drivers negotiated carefully. The Spanish cars they met, apparently indifferent for the safety of life and limb, hurtled round the corners well over the centre of the road, forcing Lewis more than once on to its stony border, giving not a straw for his shaking fist or mouthed English oaths.

Diana, not a happy passenger at the best of times, was thankful when they reached the turn-off, but there was worse to come. The coast road, unsurpassed for beauty, was even narrower and meandered up and down the cliff-sides with nothing between Diana and a sheer drop to the sea. She sat rigid, her body uselessly tensed towards Lewis as if with the weight of it she could incline the car away from the abyss, her right leg jammed to an imaginary brake on the floorboards going downhill. It was just as well that they met no other traffic coming towards them as there was nowhere to pull over to. She wondered about coming home in the dark and Lewis voiced her thoughts.

'If this is the only means of access, no wonder Grant has no neighbours.'

'They'll have to build a better road if

182

they're going to develop along here. Although it seems a shame. There can't be a much more heavenly view left anywhere. Look, Lewis, there's the old lighthouse. We can't be far away now.'

As they approached, the road took a detour so that they passed the coastguard's derelict point within a mile. There was only a rough, overgrown track leading down to the lighthouse and although the building looked picturesque in the setting sun, there was something uninviting and eerie in its desolation. Another five minutes brought *Encantador* into view. They'd lost sight of the sea on their left for the moment and were climbing a steep incline, punctuated by half a dozen murderous hair-pin bends and thickly hemmed in by pines and acacia trees. A final twist and a virtually vertical ascent up a concrete drive brought them into a level, open courtyard behind the house and they found themselves looking across the garden and beyond the villa to an unimpeded view of the sea on all sides which made Diana gasp in sheer admiration.

A flight of steps ran up diagonally across the back of the house to a first floor terrace and Grant had been standing there looking out for them. He now ran lightly down to greet them as Diana emerged from the car, hoping she looked unruffled. She wouldn't have put it past him to have sent them that route deliberately as a kind of test. It would be his idea of fun. She was wearing lilac trousers, tightly fitting to the knee then flaring out widely and a lilac and green silk top with long sleeves and a mandarin collar. A chain necklace and jade ear-rings completed the ensemble and she could tell from the look in Grant's eyes that he liked what he saw. He took her hand and gave her a chaste kiss on her cheek, then turned his attention to Lewis and asked him solicitously if he were better.

'While we're out here would you like to come and have a look at the garden?' Grant waved his hand in a circle to embrace the area where they stood. 'This is the highest point of the property. From here everything runs forward and downward towards the sea so that the main level of the house is from the top of those steps. Underneath are the garages and the garden, as you will see, is terraced on either side. On the lower terrace there's a swimming pool.'

He led them down a grassed walk which broadened into a square lawn edged with pampas grasses and monumental green and yellow cacti, the sort of thing that would envelop and devour a man in *Dr. Who* and which Diana felt looked vaguely sinister. Chairs were set about in the shade of unfamiliar trees which bore a leaf similar to that of the olive but whose fruit hung ungainly from the branches, a sort of cross between a flattened banana and a broad bean. Lewis stopped and pulled one off.

'What are these?' he asked Grant.

'Algarrobo, old boy. They're indigenous. Those bean things turn a sort of chocolate colour and the locals feed them to horses. Very nutritious I believe. That line of White Trees or Alamo Blanco I put in a few years ago to make a screen from the wind and they've grown tremendously.'

They had a bark like silver birch but thicker trunks and their pale green leaves rustled coolly in the slight evening breeze. Geraniums and oleanders jostled with the bougainvillea which cascaded everywhere, and the scent of the flowers rose pungently under the shelter of the sun-warmed walls. A kidney-shaped swimming pool had been cleverly landscaped into the cliff side, overhung by a rockery of millions of multi-coloured plants which was inhabited by lizards that darted in and out of their stony hiding places. There was a blue tiled surround and rustic changing rooms. A great red ball of fire was settling inch by inch into

185

the horizon and in the gathering dusk of the garden the mosquitoes began to hover in droves.

'Come on in,' said Grant. 'We'll get bitten out here. Let's get a drink.'

Diana hesitated, hoping to see the green flash she'd heard was sometimes visible at the moment when the setting sun goes down behind the sea. Lewis didn't believe in such phenomena and would have scoffed, but already Diana felt that here at *Encantador* anything could happen. Nothing did, and she turned to join the others who waited for her. They followed Grant through a labyrinth of twisting gravelled paths overhung with foliage and where the encroachment of bordering shrubs effectively obscured what was left of the daylight. Diana, keeping her eyes trained on Grant's whiter-than-white crisp shirt in front of her, heard Lewis stumble and swear softly when a branch swung back at him as he brought up the rear. The path ended at the top of four shallow paved steps beside the house and as Diana descended these she found herself on the terrace which they had seen from the boat, overlooking the sea. In those few moments the sun had been replaced by a giant mellow moon which was climbing in the sky. Tiny lanterns lit the terrace and more light flooded out of the drawing-room through open french windows behind them.

Grant and Lewis went over and stood close to the wall and when Diana remained where she was Grant looked back and called her over. She was reluctant, afraid of looking over the edge and, sensing her timidity, Grant reached out his hand and invited her to take hold of it. She did so and was drawn to the wall, where she stood looking out to where the moonlight lay in a yellow ribbon-like road to the horizon and down to the beach and the opening of the lagoon, more mysterious than ever in the changing shadows. She remembered the bats and shivered involuntarily. Grant's hand still held hers and she felt it tighten at her movement as if to reassure her that she was safe with him. He wasn't looking at her and was talking casually to Lewis, but she knew that every nerve in his body was aware of her and that he felt her instinctive response.

'I wanted you to see it for the first time in this light,' he was saying. 'In a few days there will be no moon, then we shall have four or five nights without or with it rising too late for a view like this.' He waited for them to make suitable expressions of appreciation and was not disappointed.

'Very beautiful,' Lewis acknowledged. 'Beautiful and romantic — eh, Di?'

He repeated his question when she didn't immediately reply and turned to look at her. Diana felt uncomfortable. She felt sure Lewis must be aware that Grant's thumb was caressing the palm of her hand and she flushed guiltily in the dark. She couldn't pull her hand away without creating an incident. Grant held it firmly between his fingers, talking lightly all the while of the problem of irrigating the garden tiers and how many tons of earth had had to be moved and levelled to accommodate the pool, his thumb carrying on a secret, insistently sensuous commentary of its own. Someone put on a record in the room and the unmistakable tones of Francis Albert Sinatra wafted out to exhort them to *Change Partners*. Grant smiled.

'Corny, I grant you, but I promise, uncontrived,' he murmured so that only Diana could hear.

Lewis said, 'Did you say someone else had arrived?'

Grant let go of her hand to put his arm lightly on Lewis's shoulders.

'I didn't but they will be doing so at any moment. We ought to go in to be ready for them. What'll you have to drink, both of you? Victor has made champagne cocktails but you can have spirits if you prefer.'

He strolled with them through the french

188

windows into a spacious split-level room which ran the width of the house and in which a dining area was divided from the sitting-room by two steps. The floor was black and white marble on which were scattered three or four Afghan rugs and there were white squashy leather chairs and Habitat tables and lamps. The dining table and chairs were white marble, tubular steel and more leather, this time black, and although the general effect was of expensive modernity it was all a little too aseptic and chilling for Diana's taste. So much marble reminded her of a morgue although she'd never actually seen one, and she could detect no sign of Hilary's influence on the décor. Perhaps Grant had made a clean sweep after her death, not being able to bear the associations held for him by the furniture and ornaments he and she had so lovingly collected together. Hilary's taste had run to chintzes and colour, cut glass and glazed porcelain rather than this functional simplicity. The only feeling of warmth in the room was provided by the pictures, a handful of what Lewis would have called 'modern rubbish' executed in vivid reds, oranges, blues and greens, to Diana's unversed eye bearing no resemblance to any recognizable idea or substance, but she was willing to believe they were worth a small fortune before Grant actually told her so.

'Don't go in for this Avant Garde stuff myself,' said Lewis, accepting a bubbling champagne glass from a manservant who was in charge of a table of glassware and an array of bottles. 'I suppose it means something but I'm damned if I can see what the fellow's trying to convey.'

'You'll be able to ask him yourself,' Grant smiled, steering Diana towards the drinks. 'He's coming tonight. He's a friend of mine. Lives just down the coast.'

'Is he Spanish?' Diana asked.

'No. English. He used to paint the sort of stuff you could understand, Lewis. Rather well too. Then he saw what was being exhibited in the Tate on one of his trips back to London so he did a couple of these for the hell of it and — bingo! He's a big success and all the art boys are positively clamouring for more. They don't understand them any more than he does, but he's a commercial property now.'

'I wonder if it satisfied him,' said Diana. 'What a wicked waste of a gift.'

Grant laughed. 'Money is always satisfying, isn't it? I shouldn't shed any tears over him, my dear. The so-called prostitution of his art has kept him laughing all the way to the bank. It's a wicked world, thank goodness! A champagne cocktail for Mrs Holt please, Victor.'

The man at the bar handed her a glass and she recognized him as the man she had seen on the terrace from the boat. He was tall and had a pale complexion for a Spaniard, although his hair was dark and brushed away from his temples and his eyes brown and set unattractively close to a long, patrician nose on whose bridge rested a pair of academic gold-rimmed spectacles. His hands were scrupulously clean and deft and when he handed Diana her glass she caught the fresh scent of oatmeal soap as opposed to the spicy pomades beloved by the waiters at the hotel. On the middle finger of his right hand he wore a curiously shaped gold ring formed like a snake with its head coming almost to the finger joint and a curled tail pointing towards the knuckle.

There were noises off, the sound of new arrivals in the hall, and then the door opened and Grant's other guests advanced like a cavalry charge on a wave of 'Darlings!' and 'Great to see you,' the women kissing each other and the men on both cheeks, like a consortium of Continental Heads of State, while the men grasped hands and slapped each other on the back, greeting one another in mock Spanish. They all seemed to know one another well and while this was going on Lewis and Diana stood on the periphery, feeling somewhat spare, until Grant extricated himself from the mêlée and came over in their direction with a woman and a man whose elbows he grasped and introduced them as Dennis and Thelma before excusing himself to help Victor with the drinks.

The woman wore a wedding ring but, not having been told their surname, Diana didn't know whether to address them as husband and wife and it hardly seemed polite to ask them directly if they were married to each other. They looked an unlikely partnership. Thelma was a large lady on the downhill side of fifty, wearing a sleeveless white linen trouser suit with a loose tunic top and a lot of gold bracelets and bangles all the way up her plump arms. Her hair was black with no trace of grey, long and pulled tightly into a pleat down the back of her head, having the effect of drawing back the skin about her eyelids and cheekbones and giving her an oriental look. Large gold gipsy ear-rings hung from the lobes of her ears and she looked like a very tough cookie indeed. She'd heard from Grant that they were considering living in Spain and she, personally, couldn't imagine anyone in their senses needing to think twice. She had the hard, throaty voice of an inveterate gin-swilling smoker and her eyes, tight and bright behind their mascara-ed curtains, darted like a snake's from Diana's face to Lewis's and across their shoulders, to make sure she was missing nothing of greater importance that might be happening in another part of the room.

Diana made an effort at polite conversation. 'You obviously don't regret your decision to leave England,' she said. 'Is there nothing you miss — your friends or anything about your way of life there?'

'You must be kidding.' Thelma took a swig from the glass in her hand and dragged on a cigarette, throwing her head back to exhale the smoke above their heads. 'Miss that dreary routine? The housework, slaving away cooking and shopping and trying to live on the pittance the tax man saw fit to leave us? When I think of it all, I feel so sorry for you poor dears having to put up with all that. No fun. No sun. As for friends, they all come out to stay with us here and of course we have all these beautiful people living nearby. There's so much to do.'

'Like what?' Diana felt her chauvinistic hackles rising. In any other circumstances she'd be the first to criticize how England was run but to be patronized by this complacent, sneering old bag was something else and brought out a measure of patriotic aggression that she hadn't known she possessed.

'Well . . . ' Thelma waved her hand in the air to illustrate a variety of delightful experiences. 'One gets up late. None of that ghastly six-thirty a.m. routine here. A leisurely breakfast. Down to the café in the village to await the arrival of the papers. There's always someone there you know. A few drinks. Back for lunch. Siesta. Down for the evening papers round about six. More drinks. A late dinner. Bridge and bathing. We go out a lot and have people in. Jack and I have a boat, most people have. He has a launderette business. He goes in most days but he has people to work it for him so that if he wants a day off he just takes it. None of your nine to five commuting here.' She smiled brilliantly at Lewis. He didn't reply. 'Do you commute, Mr Holt, and is that what has made you consider giving up the rat-race back home?'

'Actually I'm self-employed,' said Lewis. 'I can work anywhere.'

'Oh?' If she was waiting for him to elaborate she was disappointed.

'Well, it's a good thing to be. Jack's made a fortune since he's been here. Launderettes hadn't reached this part of the world, so he was in time to jump on the bandwagon. We

194

have a really beautiful villa — larger than this and with all the furniture original Louis Quinze — built in, and three cars. Jack's is air-conditioned. He needs it because he's always rushing off to Paris. He can do it from here in ten hours. It sounds incredible but with a Buick and the motorways it's just possible.'

Lewis said flatly, 'I don't believe it,' which Thelma construed as an exclamation of awe-inspired incredulity rather than that he knew she was a liar, which was what he had meant.

Diana turned hastily to Dennis. 'Do you have a business here?' she asked him. 'You look too young to be retired.'

Dennis raised a limp hand to wipe away a drop of perspiration from his forehead. The room was getting very close and he had managed to empty his third glass of champagne while Thelma had been holding the stage. He was rather a limp young man altogether. He wore beautiful pale blue trousers and shirt, a yellow cravat and brown and white co-respondent shoes that Diana thought had gone out with seventy-eight inch records and Charles Boyer. He was fair with pale lashes and a pointed pale face like a ferret. In answer to her question he said loftily, 'I create.'

There was a stifled silence. Diana felt laughter perilously near the surface and she gave Lewis full marks for asking imperturbably and as if he really wanted to know, 'What sort of thing?'

'Anything,' said Dennis vaguely. 'It's hard to say. Whatever anyone wants. I create — interior design, landscaping, colour schemes. I have a flair.'

Lewis coughed. There didn't seem much else to be said. Thelma had drifted away and a tiny bird-like woman, who had been talking animatedly in a group to their left, now detached herself and came over.

'Hi, there, Dennis!' she cried in a strong American accent and he said, 'Hi there, Lottie,' wanly in his BBC tones, then turned round to catch Victor's eye with the circulating bottle. Lottie was not deterred. She engaged Lewis and Diana.

'Hi, you two. I'm Lottie Floyd. I guess you two must be Grant's friends from Bahia Dorada.'

Diana said that they were and how much they were enjoying their holiday. Lottie waxed enthusiastic.

'Oh gee, I just love to visit your very wunnerful country,' she cried. 'You Britishers are truly wunnerful, wunnerful people and I've met so many over here it's been

196

such a meaningful experience for me. I just love anything British. My sister's husband — that's my sister over there.' She indicated an elegant, angular woman of about thirty, dressed in a black fringed Pucci pyjama outfit, who was talking to a bearded, baby-faced man Diana later discovered to be the launderette king. 'My sister's husband is British. I just love him — in a manner of speaking you understand.' She giggled coyly, rolling her eyes in exaggerated emphasis and placing the forefinger of the hand not holding her drink against her nose. She was very small and brittle, like somebody doing a bad imitation of a drunken sparrow. Diana smiled inanely and asked if she were one of the local inhabitants.

'Gee no, I'm on vacation with Laura. She has the most wunnerful, wunnerful little villa here.' The eyes swivelled heavenwards again as if to express the impossibility of conveying just how wunnerful her sister's house really was. 'But really out of this world. She has two of the most darling children — a boy and a girl and my! but she has such a truly wunnerful and rewarding relationship with them. Do you have any children, Mrs Holt?'

'One boy,' Diana said. 'He's in England at school.'

'My, but that's one thing I can never

understand. How you Britishers can send your children away like that to boarding school. Don't you feel, Mrs Holt, that you're missing a great opportunity for forging a truly meaningful relationship with your boy?'

Diana looked round helplessly. Lewis had escaped from his 'Creator' and was standing momentarily apart from the guests with Victor at the drink table. The latter was replenishing his glass and Diana saw them engaged in a conversation which lasted a moment or two before Lewis turned back towards the party. He caught her eye across the room and grimaced slightly. Diana smiled. He was really behaving very well amongst what she knew he would consider to be a bunch of morons. Serve him right for insisting on coming. She was saved from answering Lottie by Grant bearing down on her with Jack whom he introduced, then he carted Lottie away on his arm to inspect the new barbecue he was having built at the end of the terrace.

Faced with Jack and silence Diana said the first thing that came into her head.

'I've met your wife and she's been telling me all about you.'

'Not all, dear lady, I certainly trust not all,' Jack leered. Above the beard his lips were full and shone pinkly wet and the hand he put on

Diana's back and with which he stroked her from shoulder blade to waist was plump and white and slightly moist. He wore cream shantung trousers and a silk shirt and obviously considered himself no end of a lady-killer.

Remembering Thelma, Diana couldn't restrain a twinge of pity. He was like a bladder of lard, all piss and wind, and it was hardly necessary for her to contribute to their conversation beyond an occasional 'Yes' or 'No' because he was having his favourite time holding forth non-stop about his favourite subject — himself. Every now and again he punctuated an anecdote by clasping her shoulders or drawing her nearer to make himself heard above the rising din, holding the top of her arm so that his fingers once lay against her breast, bending his head to bring those slack, voluptuous lips to within inches of her own. She was thankful when Grant saw her plight and whisked her off to meet a local lion, an unassuming little man who looked as if he had come straight off the beach, in a crumpled towelling T-shirt and salt-stained jeans and who turned out to be script writer of a popular television series. His wife was sandy, freckled, and about Diana's age and it was a relief to meet someone real in a room full of phonies. They probably had more to brag about than anyone there but you'd never have guessed it and both possessed a wry sense of humour that made Diana warm to them.

Grant's painter friend proved to be something of a surprise. There was nothing Bohemian about Kenneth Bunn, who was as down to earth as his name and looked as if he would be more at home laying bricks than painting works of art. He had a coarse, good-humoured face with a broad flat nose which matched his vowels, and no delusions of grandeur, only amusement at those of the self-conscious intellectuals whom he had taken for a ride and who had made it possible for him to escape to this haven and enjoy life as he pleased. He was introduced to Diana but before they had exchanged more than a couple of sentences they were interrupted by a thin, scholastic young man who launched into an earnest discussion of Cubism and its relevance to everyday life, and after a short while Diana swam discreetly away before sinking without trace beneath a sea of meaningless verbiage.

The background music, now only faintly discernible amongst the chatter, changed to something with a more definite beat and several couples started dancing. Grant and Laura made a striking pair moving in a lazy practised fashion in the current disjointed way, facing one another but seemingly disinterested. Diana saw Jack weaving into orbit out of the corner of her eye and turned, seeking a means of escape. The door of the room through which she had seen some of the women guests go during the evening, presumably to powder their noses, was behind her and before Jack could get half-way through the throng in her direction, she turned the handle and slipped into the room beyond. She put her hand up to the light switch then changed her mind in the sudden welcome peace and comparative quiet after the noisy, smoky party.

The moonlight flooded through an open picture window which ran the width of the room facing the sea and which Diana guessed adjoined the french windows of the living-room. It was a bedroom. Two white and gilt-headed beds, a white wood dressing table, built-in cupboards with sliding doors and a white shaggy rug on the tessellated floor were its only furniture, apart from a low white leather button-back chair, into which she now gratefully sank. The new thonged high-heeled sandals she had bought for the holiday were cutting into her bare feet, now slightly swollen from the warmth and hours of standing. Diana leaned forward to loosen her shoes, an action which brought her lowered head close to the sill and the open window. She caught the murmur of voices from the terrace and recognized Lottie's American accent. She sounded very close and Diana remained still, unwilling to be discovered and dragged from her sanctuary yet not wanting to play the role of eavesdropper.

'Gee,' Lottie breathed ecstatically, 'it sure is a wunnerful, wunnerful view with the ocean and all — but kinda scarey too. I wouldn't want to live here for a million bucks. I sure don't know how Grant can stand it. He must be reminded every day of what happened. Was it from here?'

'Just about where you're standing. A little more to the left. You can see the new stones in the wall. The old ones were loosened by the sea winds and spray.' That was Thelma. Diana heard the click of a cigarette lighter and briefly smelt a Gauloise being lit.

'If the stones gave way it must have been an accident,' Lottie mused. 'If she meant to jump she'd have jumped off the top. Say, maybe she walked in her sleep.'

'They examined that theory. It didn't hold up. She'd have had to walk through a couple of doors as well as down the steps in the sitting-room to come from their room on the other side.'

'Yeah, and anyway Grant would have heard her.'

'He wasn't here,' Thelma said. 'He came home and found her down below the steps. It must have been ghastly. Her head was crushed in at the back. She must have hit the rock with tremendous force. It's one hell of a drop.'

'That poor guy!'

There were a few seconds' silence then their footsteps passed close to the window.

'Say, do you suppose I could get a freshener for my drink? I don't know about you but all this talking and dancing's given me a powerful thirst.'

They moved away and for some time Diana remained bent, her hands unconsciously massaging her blistered feet, her brain numb, her thoughts paralysed by what she had heard. Irrelevancies flitted through her mind, absurd snatches of the old music hall jokes.

'My wife's gone to the Bahamas.'

'Jamaica?'

'No, she went of her own accord.'

'Did she fall or was she pushed?'

She fell, but had she fallen of her own accord? Is that what Hilary had done? Diana couldn't believe it. Not the Hilary she had known. But then hadn't Grant said she had been a changed Hilary from the one she had known? Small wonder he hadn't wanted to talk about it. Diana covered her eyes as if to shut out the image conjured up by her too vivid imagination of a broken Hilary lying down on the little beach with her brains and blood spattering the rocks. And Grant? How did one ever get over a thing like that?

Diana suddenly felt desperately tired. Slowly she put on her shoes and went to find Lewis to take her home.

11

Lewis was standing just by the door when she came out of the bedroom and he noticed how pale she was.

'Are you feeling all right?' he asked.

Diana nodded. 'Fine, but I'm tired. Do you think we could possibly slip away?'

He frowned. 'Hardly. I mean, it would be a bit awkward. It looks as if we're expected to stay for supper.' He gestured towards the dining table which had undergone a transformation while she had been out of the room and was now laden with an assortment of cold meats, a variety of colourful salads and a collection of ambitious-looking sweets and presided over by the ubiquitous Victor, who stood with serving spoons at the ready, waiting for his first customer. As Diana assimilated the scene, Grant appeared out of the crowd and, taking her arm and Lewis's, shepherded them through the other guests and up to the table.

'Since you two are my guests of honour this evening, you must be first,' he declared, putting plates, cutlery and a napkin into their hands. 'Come along, everyone. Come and help yourselves.'

There could obviously now be no escape so Diana did as she was bid and when her plate was full Grant guided her to a sofa in an alcove and sat her down with a glass of wine. He lowered himself beside her and silently watched her spread her napkin on her knee and take up her knife and fork.

'Well,' he said, 'what do you think of it all?'

Diana couldn't help laughing. 'Very magnificent,' she said. 'Trust you to be able to organize everything on such a grand scale. You must be very rich.'

The naïveté of her remark amused him. 'How forthright you are, Diana. You haven't changed. I admit I am well enough off but still not very rich, as you put it, though I intend to be. You must remember that money goes a good deal further out here and we're all therefore relatively richer.'

'I'd noticed,' said Diana. 'Everyone here appears to be extremely well heeled — a bit out of our bracket with their three cars and their villas and original built-in Louis Quinze furniture.'

Grant grinned. 'That's naughty. You've been talking to Thelma. Okay, she's vulgar and bourgeois and wouldn't know original Louis Quinze from my arse, but you get plenty of people like that at home as well.

What about the house?'

She hesitated. 'The house is beautiful,' she said truthfully, but refrained from adding that nothing could now induce her to live in it. Although there was nothing inside it to remind her of Hilary, the terrace and the beach would, for Diana, be for ever haunted by her poor dead ghost. She wondered, as had Lottie, how Grant himself could bear it.

'I can see there's a 'but'.' He was determined to pin her down.

'A relevant one. I'm sure we couldn't afford it. Even allowing for tax concessions I don't know how you do, together with all the etceteras, the boat, servants. How do you manage? You never seem to be on duty or have any tiresome surgery hours. What about your patients? They're surely not all wealthy?'

'Most of the practice is private, the sort of people you've met here tonight. I told you. It's lucrative. In addition, I do a couple of clinics, but, generally speaking, what I do can be fitted in so as not to interfere too seriously with my social life. I can see from your face you disapprove of my attitude, but if I've learned anything, my dear, it is that there's no virtue in being overworked and underpaid. As for servants, everyone has those. Labour's cheap enough. I had my last man a year. He was good but he fell out with the cook. Victor now is in a class on his own and although he's been here only three months, I've had to teach him very little. He'd probably stay on with you if you liked him. He's adaptable, intelligent and discreet.'

'I've no doubt he's had to be that,' said Diana dryly.

'Jealous? Would you believe it if I told you that, apart from Hilary, you are the only woman I have loved?'

She was amazed and embarrassed to see that he was serious. She smiled gently. 'No,' she said.

He sighed. 'A pity. I'd like to think of you living here though.'

'Why?'

'So that I could imagine you here.'

'Hasn't it got enough ghosts already?'

He looked at her steadily and she saw that he understood. 'Is that why you don't want to come here?'

'Partly. But I can understand that it could be why you don't want to stay.'

'My time here is just about finished.' He spoke abstractedly as if he were thinking of something else, then when he saw she didn't fully comprehend, he went on: 'It's the end of a chapter. The house is too big, apart from anything else.'

'But you'll stay in this district? What

about your patients?'

'I intend to stay if I can. There's nothing for me anywhere else, particularly if you're here.'

He put his hand on her knee under cover of the plate and the napkin and she gently but firmly removed it with her own. Lewis came up beside them and Diana wasn't sure whether he had seen the gesture.

'Where's your plate?' Grant resumed his duties as host, attempting to press Lewis into having another helping and when the latter remonstrated, patting his stomach and protesting that he had already eaten far more than was good for his hardly recovered digestion, Grant said: 'Your glass then. Victor, more champagne!'

'No, no, really,' Lewis declined, laughing. 'If I've got to navigate that treacherous road back I've got to be sober. Are you sure there isn't a less suicidal route we could take in the dark?'

'There is one but it goes miles inland and adds at least half an hour to the journey. I'll tell you what. Leave the car here and Victor will run you back in the boat if you're nervous. I'll come over tomorrow and get you and then you can drive the car back in daylight.'

Diana was surprised to hear Lewis agree to

the scheme. She had expected him to deride any suggestion of nervousness, especially in front of Grant who patently feared nothing, but at the same time she was greatly relieved to have been spared the mountain road in the dark and she was grateful to Grant for having made the suggestion, she believed for her sake.

Most of the others had departed but a few hung on, dancing and drinking, when Grant saw them off from the top of the terrace with a powerful torch in his hand, lighting their way down the steps and on to the beach. Victor led the way, enjoining them to hold on to the rock face rather than the handrail and in moments they were on the beach and he had unmoored the boat and drawn it close to the square stone that served as a jetty. He helped Diana into her seat and waited for Lewis to take his place before pushing off and starting the motor. He was obviously quite accustomed to handling the Vulcan and it crossed Diana's mind that for a servant he was a man of many parts. There was nothing servile about him. In fact, sitting in the stern in the moonlight, incongruously dressed in his waiter's get-up, he looked more like the owner of such a craft than anyone's hired hand. She made one or two attempts at conversation to which he responded politely but without any of the usual Spanish volubility, and Lewis remained silent, which annoyed her. It was just like him not to bother to talk to Grant's manservant and no doubt he would later take her to task for trying to be too familiar with an inferior. Victor drove deliberately slowly to avoid wetting them with spray but, even so, they had alighted at the slab and he was away across the bay in a fraction of the time it had taken them to accomplish the outward drive.

★ ★ ★

Diana was thoughtful while undressing and Lewis noticed how quiet she was.

'Are you sure you're feeling all right, old girl? You looked as if you had seen a ghost earlier in the evening.'

He came to her and turned her to face him, placing his hands on her shoulders and scrutinizing her face anxiously. She was suddenly aware of his kindness and solidity and felt ashamed of the way Grant could still make her want him. She knew that it was a fire that would have probably burned itself out had they both been free to give it expression and it was unlikely that their relationship could have stood the test of time as hers had with Lewis. There were more

211

things in heaven and earth after all than sexual compatibility, whatever the magazines said, and not for the first time she was overwhelmed with a sense of inferiority when she compared her character with Lewis's. He had given her and Peter everything in his power, everything of any real value, and now she put her arms about his waist and laid her head down on his shoulder, content to be close to him and feeling safe.

'Something is wrong,' Lewis said.

She shrugged. 'I had a shock, that's all, and then all those awful people. It was such a strange mixture of an evening. Comedy and tragedy.'

'Tragedy?'

'I found out what happened to Hilary. It was an accident, or at least they're not sure — but it wasn't a car. She fell from that terrace on to the beach. I was in the bedroom. I went in there to rest my feet and Thelma and that American woman were on the terrace and they were talking about it. They didn't know I was there. It seemed so awful.'

He held her tightly and she couldn't see his expression but she felt his body stiffen and it was a moment before he said anything.

'What do you mean — they're not sure?'

'That's the worst part. They think she

might have jumped. No one saw her go over, you see.'

'You mean these women think she may have jumped. What reason have they for saying that? Did they give one?

'No. There was an open verdict at the inquest. Grant told me the other day. He didn't say how it happened but that there was some doubt. No wonder he wants to get out of that house. Everything about it must be a constant reminder.'

He held her for a moment more, then released her, and she drew away to complete her preparations for bed, feeling slightly better. He emptied his pockets on to the top of the chest of drawers, placing his change in neat piles and lining up his fountain pen and pencil precisely alongside his wallet, watch and penknife.

'They were a pretty odd bunch. I suppose it comes from having nothing much else to do but drink and not a lot to sharpen one's wits on. Of course I'd have my work. That would make a difference and I could certainly make enormous strides with that in this atmosphere and the more peaceful pace of life.'

Diana was incredulous. 'You're not serious. You don't mean you'd contemplate living in Grant's place?'

'Why not? I thought you'd like it perhaps.'

'Well, I do, but it's hardly our scene is it? You saw the people and besides he's probably asking much more than we can afford.'

She was astounded. Lewis seemed to be full of surprises this holiday. She hadn't for a moment imagined that he could be in the slightest attracted to this way of life. Of course he was used to living abroad but that had been different. This lotus-eating environment she had thought would have offended Lewis's ordered view of virtue and purpose. His next remark stunned her even further.

'I'm not being unkind, Di, but don't you think you're being a bit hard on the people? Admit it, you'd made up your mind that they weren't going to add up to much. You were pretty blunt the other day when you were talking to Grant about expatriates. It's only another point of view. One must try to be tolerant.'

She was indignant. 'That's rich coming from you, who can't stand Frogs, Wogs, Wops or Niggers! All your phrases.'

Lewis removed his tie and cuff links. 'That's quite different. These people tonight were British.'

Diana exploded with a howl of mirth. Lewis looked round, surprised.

'You find that funny?'

'Excruciatingly but don't ask me to explain.

Just when I'm sure I understand you, you start behaving out of character and then you say something so reactionary I know that's my boy.' She became serious. 'Do you really mean you want to consider the villa?'

She had hoped that this evening would have put an end to the tentative scheme. It was not only that she did not want to live in Grant's house, it was that, in spite of her efforts, Diana felt they were becoming more and more entangled with Grant and she wanted to put a stop to it now while she still retained some instinct of self-preservation. She made a further attempt.

'I want to spend the rest of our time here with you.'

He patted her backside as he climbed into bed beside her. 'We shall be together. Before we turn the idea down finally, there are one or two possibilities I should like to explore. I must discuss them with Grant. Good night, old thing.'

He turned over and within five minutes was breathing evenly and deeply. Diana sighed, turned on her side and switched out the light.

During the night she woke to hear thunder and lay for some time listening to it rolling round the mountains, sometimes sounding distant and at others coming nearer, though as yet the storm was not overhead. Her neck against the pillow was wet with sweat and the single sheet, which was their only covering on the bed, felt oppressively stifling.

Moving so as not to wake Lewis, Diana slid out of bed and went on to the balcony. A large rat slunk by on the beach below, sniffing out the entrails of gutted fish that had been swilled from the boats. The air was very still and the surrounding hills magnificently and brilliantly lit by sheets of vivid lightning. Somewhere they were getting the hell of a pasting and although she didn't like storms, one now would certainly clear the air and relieve the sweltering humidity.

A sudden breeze ruffled the water in the cove and blew her nightdress against her body, rustling the trees, and it was followed almost immediately by the rain. A flash of lightning that seemed to go right past her and into the bedroom and a tremendous clap of thunder right overhead woke Lewis and brought him out beside her, and together they watched the rain bucketing down in torrents. Within seconds they were soaked and in five minutes the veranda was awash. From balconies below theirs, on ground-floor level, bathing towels and canvas chairs could be seen floating away on a remorseless tide, and shouts of alarm were raised as the water invaded the downstairs rooms and their occupants hastily tried to salvage their belongings before they were saturated. Water cascaded down the mountain, bringing loosened trees and boulders in its wake and the fury of the storm continued unabated until dawn. When it cleared and the cataract gave way to a thin drizzle and then, improbably, to sunshine, only the upper rooms in the hotel had escaped devastation and water, electricity and telephone facilities had been cut off.

Diana and Lewis spent the morning helping in mopping-up operations of those less fortunate than themselves whose rooms had been flooded and offering them drying-out facilities in their own bathrooms. Their own room had escaped damage except for a slight wetting of the area of carpet nearest the veranda doors and which the noonday sun had already dried. Steam rose from the waterlogged ground and balconies were hung with soaked bedding, rugs and clothing.

★ ★ ★

They were discussing the situation with Angelo at the reception desk when Grant came through the foyer looking for them.

'I had a call to make on one of the people

staying in the hotel,' he said, 'so I thought I'd kill two birds with one stone and fetch you at the same time. Do you want to lunch here or come back with me?'

He turned to write out a chit at the desk and then handed it over to Angelo. 'That's for Mr Hardy — his prescription. I told him you'd make arrangements for getting it. Someone's sure to be going into the village. You seem to have had quite a party here last night. We were lucky. We missed it, but then, being on top of the mountain, we've less chance of being flooded if we get one of these freak storms. How much damage is there?'

Angelo spread his hands and raised his shoulders. 'It is hard to say, Dr Furnival. All those occupying downstairs rooms will have to be re-accommodated — how, I do not know as the hotel is full. We shall manage somehow.'

'What about your room?' Grant asked Lewis.

Diana said quickly, 'We were lucky. Ours is all right.' She knew before he spoke what he was going to suggest.

'In the circumstances why don't you pack your things and spend the rest of your holiday with me? It would ease the situation here. Someone could move into your room and it would be one less family to re-house — eh, Angelo?'

'As you say in English, every little helps, Dr Furnival. It would be kind. It would probably be more comfortable for you too, Mr Holt. It will take a day or two to restore the water supply here and mend the electricity, but of course it is up to you entirely.'

'In that case,' said Lewis slowly, 'it would be frightfully kind of you, old chap. Wouldn't it, Di?'

'Frightfully,' agreed Diana, her heart sinking. It was almost as though Lewis were determined to pave her own particular path to hell with his good intentions. If her tone was less than enthusiastic, he seemed not to notice, but Grant, more perceptive, added: 'I promise you you'll be perfectly free to do exactly as you like. There's no need to feel at all tied because you happen to be my guests and equally I'll just go about my business in the normal way.'

'That's very decent of you,' said Lewis, then turning to Angelo, began to make arrangements about getting their bill drawn up. Grant met Diana's eye and smiled conspiratorially. She resented him making fun of Lewis behind his back and even more the suggestion that she was in cahoots with him against her husband. She acknowledged his smile coolly and resolved to stick by Lewis's side day and night while they were at

Encantador. There, on his own ground, it would be all too easy for Grant and the charm of the place to work on her susceptibilities and he would have no scruples about trying to take the cheese from under the mouse's nose. The danger of Lewis's presence would add zest to their intrigue.

They travelled this time by the inland road, Grant driving the white Lamborghini showily fast but Diana had to admit expertly, and she was thankful to be travelling at this pace along the flat, straight country roads and through sleeping, dusty villages deserted at this siesta hour, rather than along the coast road which Grant would have turned into a roller coaster. He'd telephoned Victor on their way through Bagur so that, when they arrived at *Encantador*, their room was ready for them, the beds made up and fresh flowers from the garden arranged in a Cranberry bowl on the dressing-table.

It was the bedroom with which Diana was already familiar except that she hadn't noticed that night the second door leading off and beyond, which was a private bathroom decorated with locally made ceramic tiles and equipped with fluffy pink towels, a glass jar filled with coloured cotton wool balls, soap and expensive scented talc to match and an atomized cologne and deodorant of the same

220

make. Diana wondered how many of Grant's women had slept in this room and whether he chose a different perfume for each.

The windows were open but Victor had drawn the pale blue shutters to keep out the mid-day sun and because they were so high up and immediately over the sea, a cooling breeze filtered into the bedroom contrasting with the flat, dead heat of their room in the annexe. After their broken night and the chaos of the aftermath of the storm, it was heaven to sink into the depths of a scented bath, then lie on the bed and surrender to the utter peace of the place. Diana's thoughts drifted lazily. Here were none of the sounds of Bahia Dorada, no noisy boats, no shouting swimmers, no barking dogs or youths on pepped-up, unsilenced motor cycles. Just the sound of the sea and the occasional rustle of the acacias. In broad daylight it was difficult to acquaint the house with tragedy.

Lewis came out of the bathroom with a towel round his middle and she watched him through half-closed eyes. He stood by the window facing East and raised two slats in the blind so that he could see out.

'What are you looking at?' Diana asked drowsily.

He dropped the blind with a click and turned, startled.

'I thought you were asleep.' He came over to the bed and sat on it.

'I was nearly. I feel deliciously cool and comfortable.'

'You're not sorry we came?'

'Mm, not really. Why?'

'I didn't think you were pleased when I accepted Grant's invitation. At the time it seemed the best way out for everyone. He's a good-hearted chap. We could hardly refuse.'

'Of course,' she said. 'There was nothing else you could do without sounding rude. I expect I let my imagination run away with me because of knowing what happened here. I didn't mean to sound not pleased.'

'I don't think he noticed, I hope not, anyway. He seems quite fond of us.'

She didn't want to talk about Grant. 'Do you love me?' she asked suddenly.

'What's that to do with it? Here, steady on!'

She pulled him down against her on the bed and his towel fell off. She badly needed his comfort and reassurance but was afraid she might give herself away. She felt as if she were being pushed to the edge of a precipice and all her efforts to prevent the inevitable disaster were proving vain.

'Say you love me.'

He pushed himself up from her awkwardly, half slipping and feeling foolish, his legs still hanging over the side of the bed. Regaining his balance, he stood up. He bent over and patted her rump affectionately as he might a dog, retrieved the towel then straightened up creakily, one hand on his back. 'Damn. My disc's playing up again. Must have been getting wet last night.'

'You haven't said it,' she insisted.

'I'm getting too old for that sort of thing.' He smiled at her, padded round to the other twin bed and sank carefully down on to it. 'Forty winks before drinks and dinner.' He closed his eyes and soon slept.

Diana lay wide awake, staring at the shadows of the blind slats on the ceiling.

12

Grant was as good as his word. For the most part he left them to their own devices, being occupied himself with his practice during the day and only joining them for a brief snack at lunch time if they were in and for dinner in the evening, by which time they were ready to enjoy his company. In the face of his ungrudging hospitality, Diana felt ashamed of herself for entertaining her earlier unworthy suspicions of him and as several days passed and he made no attempt to behave towards her in a manner other than friendship of the most platonic, she began to relax and enjoy herself. The run of the villa was theirs and Victor scrupulously attended to their every creature comfort with impassive efficiency.

'There's something a bit chilling about him, don't you think?'

They were enjoying a late breakfast overlooking the sea and Victor had just gone into the house, having deposited orange juice, bacon and eggs, croissants and coffee on the table before them. Lewis was absorbed in yesterday's paper.

'Who?' He was abstracted.

'Victor, of course. I've tried to talk to him, smile, make a little joke but he's not a bit like the waiters at the hotel. To tell you the truth, he makes me feel a bit of a fool.'

'He's most likely reserved. Probably doesn't speak much English.' Lewis opened out the paper and refolded it carefully so that it fell into tidy creases at the page he wanted to peruse.

'No. He speaks quite good English.' She poured the coffee and pushed a cup across to him.

'How do you know that if he doesn't talk to you? Grant always speaks to him in Spanish.'

She wrinkled her brow. 'I don't know. I just had that impression.' She was trying to remember something, a trivial incident tucked away in the back of her mind that had made her so sure that Victor not only understood English but that he was capable of conversing freely in their language. Her face cleared.

'I remember now. You should know. You were talking to him at the party, discussing something quite fluently, and you don't speak Spanish.'

'Asking for another drink's the same in any language. I gave him my glass and he filled it up.' He pulled his chair into the table and began to attack his breakfast. 'I'll say one thing for him. He's an excellent manservant. Personally I prefer them a bit on the silent side. If you ask me, some of those chaps at the hotel are a bit too forthcoming. This one knows his place.'

'Seen and not heard, eh?' Diana was sarcastic.

'Exactly. Now, what are the plans for today?'

Grant had taken them across a couple of days before to retrieve the Redshank from the hotel cove and she was now anchored down in the lagoon beside the Vulcan, where she sat on the water plump and square and grey, like a matronly country cousin beside her more sophisticated, sleekly painted relative.

'Shall we take the boat and explore beyond where we've been that way?' He pointed in the opposite direction from Bahia Dorada. 'We could do some snorkeling en route. Grant offered to lend me his equipment. He's got a proper suit and harpoon gun, etc. I wouldn't mind having a stab at it. Or we could take the car back along the coast road and find one of those deserted little beaches we passed that evening we came here first.'

They decided on the latter course of action and Diana went off to find Victor, to arrange for a packed lunch and to assemble their bathing things into a beach bag, while Lewis finished his breakfast and gathered Grant's skindiving gear from the wooden hut by the swimming pool. Round the other side of the house where they packed up the car, they were sheltered from the sea breeze and the sun already beat down fiercely upon the concrete courtyard, which reflected its glare headachingly. The local storms had brought little relief from the humidity and had only temporarily, however violently, unsettled the weather.

Victor emerged from the house, carrying a small hamper and an insulated picnic bag, which he put into the boot of the car. He stood back as Lewis slammed down the lid and wiped the sweat from his palms and forehead with a handkerchief.

'It's very hot.' Lewis enunciated the words slowly and loudly as if conversing with a deaf mute, clinging to the very British tenet that anything spoken in English with enough clarity becomes instantly intelligible to a foreigner. Victor inclined his head in agreement.

'Very hot.' He shrugged his shoulders, raising the palms of his hands to suggest a possibility. 'Next Thursday perhaps a change. New moon.'

Lewis said, 'Not for the worse, I hope. Thank you, Victor.'

The latter bowed slightly then turned to leave them. Lewis got into the car on the driver's side next to Diana. The upholstery on the seats was already red hot and burned the backs of his bare knees. It was a relief to get going and to feel the car fill with air from the open windows.

★ ★ ★

Diana was to remember it afterwards as the last perfect day together, preferring to forget in later years the fact that, even before it happened, plans for the destruction of her happiness had been carefully laid months ahead. Lewis was particularly light-hearted, humming as they went along and driving slower than usual so as not to alarm her when they came to the tricky plunging cliff road. After about half an hour they wound down to a sandy creek lying in a cleft between two mountains. The water was crystal clear and as blue as the cloudless sky, ideal for swimming nearer the shore while way out the surface was broken by the tops of a reef of rocks which Lewis immediately declared great for snorkeling. They ran the car down to the edge of the sand and struck camp in the shade of the mountain on the left.

'We can move to the other side when the

sun comes over,' said Diana. 'There!' as she finished blowing up her lilo and pushed it into the sun and arranged herself on it with a satisfied sigh. She'd plonked a cotton sun hat over her upturned face to protect it from burning and she didn't see Lewis standing looking down at her, or the expression in his eyes. She wore a brown and white bikini spattered with orange flowers and her body was as slim and angular as it had always been. The silence lengthened and something about its quality stirred Diana from her sun-soaked reverie. She moved the hat to one side and squinted up to see where Lewis was. His eyes were now fixed on the horizon, the harpoon gun in one hand, quietly intent and watching.

His attitude recalled an incident that had happened the night before. She had awoken some time between midnight and dawn and Lewis had been standing by the window. There had been no moon to silhouette him but she had known he was there and not in the bed beside hers. The sky was pitch black. There had been an unaccountable tension and a sense of expectancy in the room and without even being able to see him she knew he was waiting for something. In the distance beyond the garden a lone star flashed on, then was gone. That was nonsense, she told herself drowsily, there were no stars tonight.

It must have been a light shining from the headland. But there was nothing on the headland but the old lighthouse which would have provided the obvious answer except that it was derelict. Fuddled with sleep, she'd put it down to one of his nightmares and had told him to come back to bed.

He often had nightmares. They had started after Hong Kong and when they were first married she had been alarmed. He would wake her from deep slumber with a reiterated demand for her to put on the light. If she were slow to respond or tried to placate him with soothing words, he flew into a temper and cursed her until she roused herself sufficiently to switch on the bedside lamp so that he could see for himself that his fears were groundless. They took a regular form: an intruder was coming through the door from whom he must protect her. In so doing, one night he had fought and wrecked a Chinese porcelain vase belonging to friends with whom they had been staying; on another, he had insisted on stripping back their bed-clothes to stand to hold up the wall behind the bed head that was threatening to fall and crush her! Often in the morning the episode was forgotten like a dream until something recalled it to her memory as now, the sight of him standing, silently watching the sea, recalled him standing by the window with a light behind him.

'Do you remember having a nightmare last night?' she asked.

He turned his head to look at her, puzzled. 'You were asleep. You didn't put the light on.'

'You didn't ask for the light. You got up or — ,' she passed a hand across her brow — 'did I dream it?'

There was a barely perceptible pause before he answered. 'I couldn't sleep. I got up for some air.' He bent down to pick up the black rubber diving suit from the sand and prepared to climb into it.

'There was a light outside,' Diana said inconsequentially. She drew her hand in a lazy arc across the sand, making half circles with her finger-tips, then smoothing them out with her palm on the backward sweep.

'Summer lightning,' said Lewis. 'I was watching it over the sea.' He put first one foot into the suit, then the other, and pulled it on up to his waist. When he'd got his arms in and zipped it up, there was a bulge of loose rubber round his waist. 'It's a bit too big but it'll do.' He pulled the helmet over his head, adjusting the goggles, then picking up the harpoon, floundered into the water and struck out for the reef.

She watched him go and thought how

strange it was that their holiday had turned out this way. If she had expected a ghost at Bahia Dorada it had been that of Klara and it was for Lewis's peace of mind that she had been concerned. Now her own was threatened as each day went by and against her will she was in danger of being drawn into a new proximity with Grant and his affairs. He had given up pestering her, it was true, but every day they spent under his roof put them under a further obligation which she knew Lewis would feel bound to repay at some later date and, far from being able to sever her connection with him, as she had once successfully managed to do, they were being drawn into a closer relationship still.

She purposely put Grant out of her mind and started to think about her son Peter instead. He would have loved this part of Spain and there would have been plenty of young companionship for him at the hotel as well as night life, though Lewis, no doubt, would have considered him much too young to participate in the latter. They would have rowed as they so often did these days. Lewis was incapable of allowing the boy a point of view, let alone respecting it. He was too young to know anything, particularly if what he thought differed from Lewis's own opinions and of course it always did. Too often Diana was torn between the two of them, wanting to encourage Peter to think for himself, yet flinching for Lewis when his son's rational arguments drove him to defend his own prejudices in a display of authoritarian dogmatism, the last refuge of the heavy father. That they enjoyed provoking each other, Diana didn't doubt, but she found it exasperating and wearing trying to keep the peace between them. They'd had a ding-dong the weekend before they'd left for Spain.

'I agree with Enoch Powell,' Lewis had said. 'These black buggers ought to be hung up by their balls and not allowed into this country. Send them back where they came from, we're overcrowded as it is.'

'We gave them British passports, we owe them something,' Peter countered.

'Owe them something, be damned. We owe them nothing. The boot's on the other foot. But for us they'd still be in the jungle swinging from trees. We poured money into their countries, educated them, and what do we get out of it? Not even their gratitude.'

'We did what suited us. We also exploited their countries and them for our own ends.'

Lewis started to lose his temper. Peter's quiet, flat statements were like a red rag to a bull.

'Rubbish. What do you know about it, a

young boy like you? You talk like a blasted Red. I hope that's not the sort of thing they're teaching you at school these days. You should be proud of your country's record. I don't know. Patriotism is out of date, it seems.'

'It's certainly not enough.' Peter smiled but the allusion was lost on Lewis.

'It was for me, my boy, and thousands like me who fought in the war.'

'Oh, the war!' Peter raised his eyes heavenward and further incensed his father.

'Yes, the war! And don't sneer. You wouldn't be here now living the life of Riley if it hadn't been for our sacrifices. Don't forget that.'

'I'm not likely to, but it isn't an argument.'

'Don't be impertinent! Your generation just take, take, take. God help the country if it had to rely on you to fight for it. We'd soon be down the drain!'

Lewis stamped off in a huff and Peter complained to Diana.

'You see! You can't have a proper discussion with him,' and she was left wondering ruefully where she had gone wrong. If she remonstrated with Peter she gave him the impression she was siding with Lewis and if she tried tactfully to soothe her husband he said, 'Go on. You always put me in the wrong. I'm just the provider round here. I'm expected to dish out the necessary cash for everything but otherwise I'm part of the furniture.'

Peter within earshot started whistling 'Hearts and Flowers', playing an imaginary violin which was enough to start the whole cycle again. No. It was probably just as well Peter had his exams coming up and couldn't take time off school. Undoubtedly he would have found Grant attractive. As a little boy he had idolized him and, had he been here now, she could imagine Grant discussing ideas with him that Lewis didn't even know he had, teaching him to water-ski, appealing in a flamboyant way to the ready imagination of a boy of fifteen and alienating the affections of the son in the same way he had those of the wife.

Drops of cold water falling on her sunbaked back woke her out of her reverie and Lewis stood over her brandishing a fish, pathetically impaled on his harpoon and reminding Diana of a wet retriever waiting expectantly for a sign of approval from its owner.

'There were masses out there by the reef,' he said, sitting down on a rock to remove his flippers. 'They look enormous under water and you have to look out for jellyfish. Plenty of sea urchins too.'

'Sounds lots of fun,' said Diana dryly, throwing him a towel.

'It was. Want to try?'

'No, thanks. I'll have a nice gentle swim in the shallows. Is the water cold?'

He sat down on the lilo and put a bare, cool arm across her shoulders.

She shivered. 'You're freezing.'

'No, it's heavenly.' He looked round the cove and up at the sky. 'It really is heavenly,' he repeated. He looked down at her face. 'Happy?'

With a rush of feeling she leaned forward and kissed him. His lips were cold in contrast with the inside of his mouth and tongue and the skin of his face felt taut and fresh.

'Very happy,' she said, and meant it.

He allowed her to drive on the way back, a thing he wouldn't normally have done. When they were together it was taken for granted that he would take the wheel. He didn't like being driven but he'd barked his shin badly against the reef during the afternoon and in spite of a thorough cleansing and an application of antiseptic it was stiff and sore and he was content to rest it in the passenger seat. They hadn't seen a soul all day but now, as they dropped down into the adjacent bay where there were a few flat-roofed hovels, a church and an inn, one or two fishermen were hauling up their boats, a man passed, leading a laden donkey, and a handful of local inhabitants were enjoying a sundowner at tables on the pavement in front of the hostelry. They stopped here and enjoyed a long, cool beer before continuing the switchback which finally brought them on to the level, barren countryside before the last fall and rise approaching *Encantador*.

There were still a couple of hours to go until dinner and on an impulse Diana swung the wheel to the left when they came to the track leading to the lighthouse and, changing down, adjusted her speed to negotiate the potholes and sunbaked ruts of what was barely more than a wide pathway. Once upon a time it had been tarmac-ed. Here and there the crumbled remains of broken asphalt presented an additional hazard, the loose bits flying up against the car's paintwork and one lump larger than the rest hitting the windscreen and causing Lewis to expostulate.

'What the hell do you think you're doing?'

'Let's go down and have a look at it.'

'There's nothing there. Grant told you, it's quite derelict. Christ!' as the car jerked in and out of a particularly deep trough. 'For God's sake, mind the springs! Don't forget you've got to turn round and get back up this so-called road. It gets worse further on. Turn back while you can.'

'Not now. We're nearly there, we must go on. I've got a fancy to explore the place. I'm sure there was a light here last night. Just five minutes to have a peep inside.'

He grumbled but she took no notice and within a few moments she brought the bucking vehicle to a standstill under the walls of the lighthouse and turned off the engine. The silence was complete and the tower rose steeply above them. Moss and a small yellow flower of unknown origin grew in the crevices of the brick which had once been painted a shiny white. Flakes of paint still clung here and there to the sills of windows long since broken and framed with their own jagged glass edges. They were in a small courtyard bounded on three sides by what looked as if they might once have been four bungalows, evidently the dwellings of erstwhile keepers. The yard was cobbled and on its fourth side a hollow had been cut back into the cliff and cemented to make a room as large as a big garage. At one time it had boasted a sliding door of which now nothing was left but the metal runners, and inside an iron apparatus bearing a series of rusty dials was attached to the wall and appeared to be an antiquated pump of some kind. The tower itself was built into one corner of the square.

'Well, there you are. Now you've seen it. I told you there'd be nothing here.'

Lewis had only got out of the car on sufferance. His leg was hurting and he wanted nothing so much as to get back to ease it in a hot bath and to wash the day's salt from his skin, where it prickled on his new sunburn against his shirt. All the cottages were empty. Cupboards and light fittings had been ripped from their fitments and in a couple of cases even the front doors had been looted. Only the cracked and broken tiles on the floor had been left, but Diana was not content until she had inspected the lot and he sat down to wait for her in the garage room out of the sun, perched on an old oil drum. She emerged from the bungalow nearest the tower, dusting herself down and grimacing.

'There are rats in there — plenty of evidence. It looks as if someone may have been sleeping in that one. There's a pile of filthy blankets and an old sleeping bag on the floor.'

'Tramps, I expect.'

She came and inspected the dials on the pump. 'What's this for?'

'I imagine it once pumped oil up for the light.'

'I suppose they're all electric now.'

'Most of them are. I expect the new one is.

239

They're gradually changing over. There are only four oil-powered ones left in the British Isles but no doubt there are many more in Spain.'

It was always a surprise to be reminded how much he knew about everything. 'Wherever did you glean that information and how did you remember it?'

'I suppose I was interested at the time.' He stood up and braced his leg. 'Seen enough?'

'Not quite. Now we're here I want to see the tower. I've never been up a lighthouse before.'

'And you're not going up this one. It can't be safe. Be sensible, Di.'

She was twisting the iron ring on the heavy door and it turned rustily and swung inwards. Diana took a step into the gloom, then called back over her shoulder for Lewis to follow. Reluctantly he limped over to join her where she stood inside, at the foot of a spiral staircase which wound up on to two landings above them and through the centre of which ran a hollow shaft of daylight right up to the sky.

'It's quite empty,' said Diana, disappointed.

'What did you expect? They'd hardly leave all that valuable equipment to rot here. The lens itself is worth thousands of pounds. They'll have dismantled it and removed all the main parts to the new light. Don't go up there — it's dangerous.'

But Diana was already half-way up the staircase and had reached the first landing.

'Keep away from the shaft.' Lewis's voice echoed up to her, magnifying a tinge of alarm and irritation.

'It's all right if you keep to the side and don't look down,' she called to him. On this first landing there was a built-in cupboard with a broken glass front, the remains of a desk and a discoloured jug which, if cleaned, might prove to be either copper or brass. She peered out of the window and saw just below the crumbled ledge and rail that ran round the outside of the tower. The rocks and sea looked a long way down and she tried to imagine what it would be like to be incarcerated for months on end in a lighthouse like this offshore. She hadn't heard Lewis climb up behind her and now he stood, breathing heavily after so many steps and ready to be angry with her at her foolhardiness.

To divert him she said, 'I shouldn't like the job of cleaning these windows. I hear they have to, on the outside. I wonder what went down the shaft.'

'There'd be a tube and weights. The 'bleep' is fixed by a clock which would have been about here, the same principle as a grandfather clock and the weights hang right down to the bottom. The lens would be up there resting on a bath of mercury and the whole thing worked by an oil pump here, say, compressed air driving it up. Every lighthouse has its own distinctive 'bleep' so that mariners can't muddle them up.'

She wasn't listening properly but had moved round to inspect the stairs that led to the top floor. They consisted of little more than a wrought-iron ladder, the spiral becoming closer-wound and the treads narrowing perilously to almost nothing on the inside edge. Lewis thought she was going to try to scale them to the top but to his relief she stopped at the second window to look out.

'I thought so. You get a good view of *Encantador* from here. Come and see.'

They had a perfect bird's eye view of the villa on the edge of the adjacent cliff and beyond it to the open sea. It looked very peaceful in the setting sun and Diana could clearly discern the swimming pool and the windows on the side of the house where their bedroom was.

'Come on. It's getting late.' Lewis started making his way down and Diana came behind, holding on to the wall and negotiating some of the bends sitting down where she felt safer. It was worse going down and she suddenly realized how silly she would have looked if she had gone up alone. Without Lewis in front of her, the descent would have paralysed her knees. It was good to be back on the ground floor and, to cover the fact that her legs were shaking, she sat on a square locker to get her breath. It was an open-fronted affair and pigeonholed. One or two of the compartments that weren't covered over by spiders' webs still contained fragments of triangular cloth in faded colours, signal flags for cases of emergency. Diana pulled one out and held it up, dropping it hastily as a large cockroach ran across the back of the material.

'The whole place is filthy,' said Lewis. 'You'll be covered in dust and muck sitting on that.'

'Everything needs washing anyway.' She jumped down and turned to dust off the seat of her trousers with her hand. In doing so, her foot kicked against the bottom locker and something fell out on to the stone floor with a slight clinking sound. She bent down to pick it up from the dirt.

'Hurry up!' Lewis hadn't waited and she could hear the engine of the car being revved up impatiently, then a couple of blasts on the horn.

The ring she held in the palm of her hand was heavy, a snake fashioned out of one piece of gold, its fanged head and tail pointing in opposite directions, the rest of its body twisted to fit a man's finger. Thoughtfully she put it in her pocket and went out to the waiting car.

13

It was hard to say why she didn't tell Lewis about her discovery straight away. She supposed she wanted time to think about it and its possible implications. Lewis would call her over-imaginative. He had pooh-poohed the idea of her having seen a light from the headland and persisted in his assertion that the lighthouse was deserted, which it patently was. She could almost hear him saying that there was doubtless in existence more than one ring of that particular design and he would probably be right. Equally, it was logical the ring could be Victor's and accepting this premise and remembering the pile of bedding in the keeper's cottage, was it not only possible but most likely that he too had been responsible for the light? It was an ideal trysting place, somewhere to take a girl friend or lover and be sure of not being disturbed. Such a romantic explanation, Diana had to admit, wasn't wholly compatible with her concept of Victor as a rather cold fish, but then you never could tell what people were really like. She put the subject to the back of her mind where it remained until lunch time the next day.

There had been guests with Grant on their return and these had stayed on for a meal followed by a friendly game of bridge. Diana was an indifferent player and now had to be reminded of the rules so that her concentration was wholly employed and it wasn't until just before she fell asleep that she remembered the ring briefly and thought she mustn't forget to remove it from the pocket of her jeans before they went to the wash.

The following day Grant had a free afternoon and he came into the house at mid-day, stripping off his jacket and tie and pouring himself an iced beer before coming to look for them, where they lay down in the garden beside the pool.

'Anyone swimming?' He flopped down in a chair between them, tipping the foot-rest of Diana's chair upwards so that it swung back into a reclining position, taking her off balance and making her drop her book and glasses while she tried clumsily to adjust her centre of gravity.

'I don't swim with overgrown schoolboys.' She was laughing and pretended to scream in mock terror as Grant stood up and leaned over her, threatening to pick her up bodily and dump her in the pool.

'Indeed? We'll see about that.' He bent and lifted her out of her chair, struggling and calling to Lewis to help her, and took her over to the side of the pool where he held her above the water. Diana instinctively clasped both hands behind his neck to hang on to him.

'If I go I'll take you with me.'

Their faces were very close together and as she met his eyes her heart suddenly turned over. For a wild moment she thought he was going to kiss her in spite of Lewis in the background, and treacherously she wished the latter a thousand miles away.

'I wish I thought you meant that.' He spoke softly for her alone, then louder for Lewis's benefit: 'I am prepared to go through hell and high water for you, Goddess, but not in these clothes. Wait five seconds and then the last one in is a cissy.'

He released her and strode off to the changing hut, emerging in striped swimming trunks a moment later.

'Coming in?' he asked Lewis.

'No, I had enough sun yesterday. My back's rather red. I think I'd be wiser to stay in the shade.'

'Very sensible. I prescribe a cooling drink. Ring the hand bell and Victor will bring you one down from the house.'

Diana was already in the water and they swam up and down for a while and played about with a big red and yellow beach ball until they'd both had enough. She dried her arms and legs and vigorously towelled her hair, then spread herself out in the sun with a contented sigh to dry off her bikini.

'This really must be the next best thing to the Garden of Eden. It's heaven here.'

'As secluded too,' laughed Grant. 'You wouldn't even need the fig leaves. No one could see you sunbathing here in the nude.'

'Only someone from the top of the lighthouse,' said Diana, lazily. 'Lewis and I had a perfect view of the garden from there only yesterday. You could see the pool perfectly, so you'd better be careful if you're thinking of having any orgies down here. I hear the Spanish police are pretty hot on that sort of thing.'

Grant didn't smile. 'You mean you actually went up the lighthouse yesterday?' He turned to Lewis. 'You said nothing about it.'

'Never thought any more about it. It was Di's idea. Didn't appeal to me, I can tell you. To tell the truth, I don't think she enjoyed it much but she was determined to have a look.'

'I didn't think you liked heights.' Grant's voice was almost accusing, even angry.

'I don't. I would never have gone up if I'd

known what coming down was going to be like. Anyway, I don't see why you should be so concerned.' His tone had nettled her.

'Don't be a little fool. Of course I'm concerned. It's not safe. Everyone knows that. There are notices to say so.'

'We didn't see any. Anyway, dangerous or not, we're not the only people who've been there recently, are we, Lewis?'

Grant, lighting a cigarette, arrested his hand for an infinitesimal second on its way up to his mouth with his lighter, then completed the action, drawing the smoke into his lungs and clicking the top of his Ronson down to extinguish the flame. Lewis hadn't replied. Instead he hauled himself out of his reclining chair, stretched and sauntered over to the side of the pool.

'Lewis!' Diana insisted.

'What?' He turned round and looked at them enquiringly.

'I said,' said Diana, aggravated at his lack of support, 'that someone else had been there before us.'

'How do you know?' Grant's expression was now purely conversational.

'I saw a light there the other night.'

Lewis spread his hands. 'You thought you saw a light. You were half asleep at the time. You'd have made a good writer, Di. She can make a mystery or a romance out of any given set of circumstances.' He was humouring her.

'What about the blankets? There was a sleeping bag too in one of the bungalows.'

'Probably hippies,' said Grant easily. 'We get a crowd of them along here in the summer. They're discouraged from pitching camp along the beaches and the police pick them up in the resorts. A place like that would be ideal shelter for them and nobody would know they were there.'

Diana was only half-convinced. 'There was no sign of the kind of mess a hippy commune might have left. No food tins or cigarette butts. Everything was quite tidily dusty — if you know what I mean. No, I've got a different theory.'

Grant raised his eyebrows and looked amused. 'You have? Are we to be enlightened?'

'If you treat me seriously. First of all you must tell me something. Has Victor got a girl friend?'

'Victor?' He was plainly puzzled. 'What's Victor got to do with it? I'm afraid I'm not exactly *au fait* with his love life. You'd better ask him yourself. Here he is with the drinks.'

Before Diana could stop him Grant had

called out to his servant, who was approaching, carrying a tray. 'Victor, the *señora* has something to ask you. Fire away, my dear.'

Victor put down the tray, then stood beside her, waiting patiently and politely to hear what she had to say and Diana was left feeling furious with Grant for putting her in this absurd position. She had meant to return the ring privately but the tolerant amusement with which she knew the two men were patronizing her goaded her to prove her point publicly. She reached out for her bag, which was lying beside her chair, and bent her head to delve into its recesses while they waited to see what was coming next.

'I found this. I think it may be yours.'

The ring glinted in the sunlight as it rested on the outstretched palm of the hand she proffered to the Spaniard. His reaction was not the one of immediate pleasure she had anticipated. In fact, she could have sworn that, far from being relieved, a temporary expression of alarm had flitted across those usually impassive features, to be replaced immediately by one of courteous gratitude. His free hand instinctively clasped the naked finger where the ring habitually lived and he bowed slightly to Diana before taking it from her and putting it on.

'*Muchas gracias, señora.*' He allowed

himself a smile in her direction which didn't quite reach his eyes, then inclining his head once more, turned and left them.

'What was all that about?' Grant drawled.

'He never even asked me where I found it. Don't you think that was funny?' Diana said thoughtfully.

Lewis answered with another of his own. 'Well, where did you find it? Why the mystery?' He pulled the ring off the top of an iced can of beer and took up a glass to pour it into.

'It was in the lighthouse. It fell out of one of those pigeon holes in the flag locker.'

She didn't know what she had said but the atmosphere suddenly became electric. Both men went on doing whatever it was they had been doing before she spoke, yet without being able to say why, she knew they were both tensed, expectant and wary.

Lewis's tone was relaxed enough when he spoke. 'You said nothing about it at the time. I didn't see you pick it up.'

'You didn't see it because you were outside blowing your blasted horn and I didn't mention it because I put it in my pocket and forgot about it. Anyway, I can't see that it matters. Victor lost his ring and I found it and that's all there is to it. I don't particularly care how it got there except that it proves he was in the lighthouse, and recently, because I know he was wearing the ring three nights ago. Don't you remember? You asked him to take the picture down from the wall to show me its back and I noticed it then. That means he was probably there either that night or the next, if I really did see a light — and I know I did. I think he's got some woman he goes up there to meet. That would account for the bedding.'

'How would he get there?' Lewis sounded sceptical.

'He has a moped,' Grant said quietly.

'It seems a lot of trouble to go to when he could easily bring a girl back here to his own quarters. They are, after all, much more comfortable and well away from the house, which is an advantage.'

'Perhaps he's kinky — likes doing things the hard way.' Diana laughed. 'I was saying to Lewis, there is something a bit strange about him, something that doesn't quite ring true.'

Grant was pensive, turning his glass, now beaded with condensation, between his hands and catching the drops of water as they ran down with his finger-tip. Lewis watched him and again Diana caught some kind of charge between them as if one were trying to read the mind of the other. Lewis's face was tight and shut, showing no expression, but she felt he was, unfairly, angry with her, but she didn't know why. It was over in seconds, and later over a friendly, relaxed luncheon, with Grant telling some of his most outrageous jokes and even Lewis responding, she chided herself for her overfertile imagination.

★ ★ ★

Lewis was exploring the possibility of making a trip to Barcelona. He'd talked about going there before he and Diana had left England — something to do with his work and the textbook he was preparing on the Extradition Laws of European Countries, and there were records there that he could peruse and which he might not have another opportunity to see. He had an introduction to the necessary authorities, written by Andrew Dalton, now Superintendent Andrew Dalton of the C.I.D., who had been instrumental in getting Lewis established in his new field when he had finally returned to England with Diana after his years in the wilderness. Lewis would never have approached any of his former colleagues off his own bat however bad his prospects, but it had been Andy who had sought him out and subsequently made the suggestion that had led to his present employment, writing up records and case histories, pamphlets and textbooks on criminology, some for his own amusement and others as and when commissioned by Andy's department.

By chance, running an eye down the passenger list of sailing arrivals, Andy had spotted the name of his old friend and had been at Southampton to meet him. After all, he had told Diana between themselves, he felt partially responsible for what had happened. He had introduced Lewis to Klara although it was equally true he had tried to warn him when the affair became serious. Diana, numb in her own private hell of having just parted from Grant, had made the right kind of noises over a coffee cup, at the time not registering the man any more than she cared at that moment whether she lived or died.

Now by chance Lewis had received a letter from Andrew, relayed from Bahia Dorada by Victor, who had taken the boat over for the purpose of collecting any mail that might have accumulated for them there, with the news that Andy himself would be in Barcelona on two specific dates which happened to be the next day and the one following. Lewis was elated.

'I'm passing through on a touring holiday and shall be in Barcelona on the 2nd,' he read out aloud. 'Remembering you said you wanted a peek at the records, perhaps we could collaborate and I might be of some use lingo-wise. Just a thought. If you would like us to meet leave a message at . . . ' Lewis broke off, folding the blue sheet of writing paper and putting it into his pocket. 'He gives a telephone number. That settles it. I must go. Jolly decent of Andy to offer to give up a couple of days of his holiday.'

Diana received this dryly. 'What about yours? Pity you left him your address. Why did you?'

'I left it on the off chance. He said he might be coming through. Don't be puggy about it, Di. He can be of enormous help being here on the spot for my researches. He speaks good Spanish. It'll only mean a couple of nights away — three at the outside.' Their holiday finished at the end of the week and today was Monday.

'I'd have to take the car but you've got Grant's.'

'Aren't I coming with you?'

'I shouldn't. You wouldn't enjoy it. We'll be busy all day and what would you do with yourself in Barcelona once you've seen the shops? It'll be dreadfully hot and sticky, and I'm not staying in one of the best hotels or anything like that. I'll find a little *pension* that'll do for me. Honestly, Di, you'd be bored stiff and lonely. We'll be talking shop all the time. Much better for you to stay here and be comfortable. I should be back by Friday.'

It was plausible and rational and in any other circumstances she wouldn't have relished two days in the city when she could be relaxing, swimming and sunning in her present surroundings, but she was afraid of being left at *Encantador* alone with Grant and the naïveté of Lewis's pathetic trust in them both was irritating, shaming, bordering on the insulting, as he proceeded to put her in Grant's charge as if she were a schoolgirl being put in care of the train guard.

'You don't mind keeping an eye on her, do you, Grant? I know she'll be in good hands.'

'The best.' Grant grinned. He had so far listened to their exchange without comment.

'But I want to see Barcelona,' Diana protested.

'What's the matter? Don't you trust me to look after you?' Grant was teasing. He knew bloody well how far she trusted him.

'He's right you know, Goddess. You're not missing a thing. It's a long, hot ride and Barcelona in this temperature is something to be avoided for comfort.'

She made one last effort in their room that night.

257

'Lewis, take me with you tomorrow. I don't want to stay here.'

They had made love. He had been mechanically efficient and although they lay beside each other, their naked bodies still entwined, in *post coitus tristesse* she felt him spiritually far removed and was overcome with a panic of loneliness and apprehension.

He sighed. 'I thought we'd decided. It's better for me to go alone. It's only two or three days. It's not like you to make a fuss.'

'I don't like this place without you. I keep thinking of Hilary when you're not with me — and then that Victor — there's something wrong somehow, and Grant — ' She broke off.

'Really!' He was getting impatient. 'What about Grant? Don't tell me you find him sinister too! Don't you think you've got it all a bit out of proportion?'

'Why can't I come? I wouldn't be in your way. I promise.'

'It'll cost a lot more if you do. I only meant it to be a quick flip there and back.'

'Does the money matter? It's not as though we haven't got it. You'll spend it anyway, carousing, the two of you. You're bound to go out to dinner, probably on the town.'

He spoke slowly and carefully as if he were trying to din something into a dull child. 'The sole object of the exercise is work. He won't want to hold up his holiday any longer than I shall. We'll get a lot more done if you're not there. I might even get it on expenses this way when I get back.'

Being so intimately close was suddenly almost indecent. She moved away from him to the edge of the bed. It hadn't worked. Well, she'd tried, God knows she'd tried. Nobody could say afterwards that she hadn't. After quite what, she didn't ask herself. Whatever happened now was Lewis's own fault. She got up and lit a cigarette.

'What time do you plan to leave?' she asked.

He was plainly relieved she'd decided to be sensible.

14

Lewis drove steadily for nearly an hour after leaving *Encantador*. Once away from the house he slowed his pace, dawdling along the straight, unevenly surfaced road that ran inland through scorched and barren fields on which the cloudburst of the previous week had made little or no impression. The river beds were still dried up, the corn cobs burned to a deep brownish-black, the grapes already dried and hanging like wizened raisins on the vines. He was in no hurry. The day stretched ahead invitingly with plenty of time to do what he had to do before his return under cover of dark to put his plan into operation. Then would begin the tedious vigil, but now he was free and alone and he meant to savour both liberty and solitude to the full.

It had been touch and go with Diana. He hadn't expected her to be so insistent on going with him but luckily Grant had helped to squash that idea, no doubt for his own purposes, and if Diana had been pretending, she had nearly overplayed her hand. There'd been a moment when he'd very nearly weakened, taken her into his confidence and agreed to her accompanying him. But he had remembered in time the way she had looked at Grant by the swimming pool and reminded himself that nothing had changed. Nothing ever really had. That was the root of the trouble. He'd had the same sort of luck with both the women he had chosen in his life. He smiled wryly to think that he'd gone to some lengths to find someone as dissimilar to Klara as possible and for the second time he had been betrayed. Most women were tramps at heart. He should have learned that from his detective work. Just because Diana had looked different he shouldn't have been fooled. All that talk of loving him, trying to wring protestations of love from him . . . it had all been a sham. He would have known she'd been up to something even without Pamela Calthrop's innuendoes on the ship. Pamela was a particularly odious specimen of the mah-jong-playing bridge set in which Singapore abounded — a woman with time on her hands and nothing to fill it with but the latest poisonous gossip. It was a type he despised and he and Diana had had more than one good laugh at her expense, so it was with resigned exasperation that they had found themselves sharing her table on the voyage home.

'So unfortunate for you, Mr Holt,' she had

coo-ed across the breakfast table the morning after they had left Colombo. 'Not being well enough to go ashore yesterday. If I had known your wife and Dr Furnival were going to visit their old friends at Mount Lavinia they could have shared my car. I have a relative staying there on the same floor. At least they were going into their room when I came out of the lift. I'm sure you were wise to remain on board. One needs a strong stomach for some of these sight-seeing trips, doesn't one? One can so easily be made to feel queasy.'

Her bright eyes feasted avidly upon his discomfiture which he hadn't been adept enough to conceal. She knew she'd caught him off balance and was already looking forward to the story she could make of the incident, suitably embellished, when playing cards after dinner. Diana had not been at the table. He didn't tackle her with his suspicions. He didn't have to. Her behaviour in bed told him all he wanted to know. The next time that he took her she responded with a new knowledge, terrifyingly reminiscent of Klara's. Added to her tentative suggestion of innovations in their love-making and a fresh warmth and radiance that dimmed with their arrival in England, Lewis was capable of the simple calculation that equalled Grant. He was furiously, bitterly angry and disappointed. Nothing he had done could have deserved such degrading treatment once, let alone a second time. He had kept to his side of the bargain, first with Klara, now with Diana, had provided for them and guided them and had been repaid by both with infidelity. There was nothing wrong with him sexually and, anyway, five minutes' pleasure two or three times a week was hardly the be-all and end-all to a woman. It might have occurred to another man to look for the signs of failure in himself, but not Lewis.

His anger he kept under control. He had learned his lesson last time. He wasn't going to lose what he had now simply because Diana had made him a cuckold. An ugly word and one that conjured up a figure of fun. Make a scene now and face a break-up and he could hear the whispers already from people like Pamela Calthrop. And there were plenty of them in the world.

'The second time it's happened, you know. Lightning doesn't usually strike twice in the same place unless . . .'

'There was some scandal years ago. Can be quite violent, so I hear.'

He lay awake at night thinking what he could cheerfully do to Grant, knowing that even if he had the opportunity, in reality

Grant would have reduced him to physical and psychological mincemeat. He had always possessed the capacity for making Lewis feel small — less of a man. In any case, once home they had split up and were separated by whole counties. There was no opportunity for Diana and him to carry on the affair and Lewis derived some satisfaction from knowing that she suffered that first year, until time had blunted the agonies of separation and frustration. Then she had turned to him and he enjoyed telling himself that he had almost forgiven her. Not quite. That would be his privilege and he would never thereafter completely rid himself of his reservations. He had his pride. Grant and Hilary faded from their lives and Lewis sometimes had to remind himself of what had happened, like biting on a painful tooth to see if it still hurt and being glad when a twinge tells you you're not bothering the dentist for nothing.

★ ★ ★

It really was extraordinary just how exceedingly small the mills of God had ground in this instance. When Andrew Dalton had rung Lewis some months ago and asked him if he could find time to pop into his office when he was next in town, little did Lewis dream that

264

the longed-for weapon of revenge was about to be put into his hand.

Andy's room at New Scotland Yard was a far cry from the chocolate and green paint and beeswaxed floors of the old building. He sat behind a sanded pinewood desk of contemporary design in front of a large aluminium-framed picture window and the floor was carpeted wall to wall in a mottled design of blues and blacks. There was an inoffensively modern seascape on one wall — no other pictures. Lewis wondered what had happened to all the mahogany framed ex-Commissioners and other dignitaries that had adorned every vacant space on the walls of the offices and corridors of power that he remembered. After the exchange of pleasantries and a tall girl with a short skirt had brought them a cup of coffee and retreated, Andy pulled a file towards him across the desk and opened it. Lewis waited.

'We've got a bit of a problem here and we think you may be just the person to help us.' He looked straight up at Lewis, who was trying to read the heading on the top page of the file upside down without much success. He gave Andy his attention. The latter went on. 'Did I tell you I'd been temporarily transferred to narcotics?'

Lewis shook his head. There was no reason

why he should know. The two men only met occasionally, when Lewis required some information for a thesis he was writing or Andy's department wanted something written up. The next question surprised him.

'How much do you know about drugs?'

'Not much. I suppose a little about their effects, that's all. Mostly what I've read in the papers.'

He remembered walking from Piccadilly to Leicester Square one evening when it was still light and seeing the bodies lying on the pavement and sitting propped against the curb. There had been a girl, dressed like a red Indian and lying in a shop doorway having a bad trip. She'd been crying and moaning, grovelling hopelessly in an open pouched handbag and when two young men with dirty jeans, bare feet and tangled shoulder-length hair took her by her shoulders and feet and lifted her out to a waiting car, her trousers had fallen down and Lewis could see she'd long since lost any control of her bowels and bladder. Fear had pierced him like a shaft, for Peter. There, but for the Grace of God, went kids like him.

Andy sat back in his chair, making a pyramid of his fingers and looking at Lewis over the top of them.

'The opium poppy's grown in Turkey. It

produces a resin that is sometimes smuggled out as it is, or more usually, is first boiled with water and slaked lime, strained, dried and sent out as a dark powdery substance, a morphine base which, refined, becomes heroin. It finds its way to secret laboratories around Marseilles where it is distilled. From there it goes on to the pushers all over Europe, and to England. We have reason to believe that the head of the ring responsible for smuggling seventy per cent of heroin into Britain is an Englishman living in Spain. We'd like to get our hands on him.'

Lewis was puzzled. 'Very interesting. But I don't see where I come in. Surely it's a matter for the Spanish police?'

'Not entirely. This man has contacts and knowledge of the whole drug network in this country. He'd be an invaluable catch if we could land him and for that reason we don't want him alerted. There are signs he may be going to ground. It may be getting too hot for him or he may have made his packet and now wants to get out. No one retires voluntarily from that racket and remains alive, so when the time comes he'll take his money and disappear. Information from our contact there is that there will be one more drop, possibly two, but we can't count on that. We've got to get him before he scarpers.'

'I still don't see what I can do. I'm not a policeman. I have no authority now. I'm sorry, Andy, I don't want to get mixed up in this kind of cops and robbers lark. Pick someone else.'

There was a pause. Andrew leaned forward to emphasize his point and said quietly, 'There is no one else who knows him as you do.'

He watched it sink in. Lewis looked startled. For a moment he thought Andy was having him on until he explained.

'This man's name is Dr Grant Furnival.'

'Grant?' Lewis said the name more to himself than aloud, plainly incredulous, and Andrew allowed him time to digest this latest piece of information. After the first expression of shocked disbelief, the policeman, watching Lewis's face, saw it change first to bewilderment, then to a dawning credibility, so that it didn't surprise him that after a silence lasting a couple of minutes Lewis said thoughtfully, 'It is possible.'

'Of the man you know?'

Lewis nodded. 'Incredible — extraordinary — but possible. He always was a big shot. Biggest bull-shitter you ever met. I can imagine him getting a kick out of this kind of thing. The danger would be half the fun.'

'The money's not bull-shit either,' said

Andy dryly. 'He had a practice here in Harley Street, middle-aged society women mostly — lonely, bored, nothing wrong with them a good day's work and a dose of salts wouldn't cure but when he sold up and left, the doctor who took them on was alarmed to find how many of them were hooked on varying doses of narcotics. That put us on his scent and we'd have dragged him in before this, but it would be neat if we could wrap up the whole package in one operation. I want you to go down there. Meet your old friend by coincidence. I leave the rest to you. Just so long as you blow him wide open — the supplier — everything.'

Lewis got up and went over to the window. It was raining. The rain smacked down on the tops of cars, bursting like soapy bubbles. It was May but there was no sign of summer and he thought how a spell of Spanish sunshine might not come amiss. He turned.

'What would I get out of it?' Apart from getting even with that smooth bastard, apart from showing him up to Diana and being able to make her sorry, although those were good enough reasons to take the job without any other consideration.

'You'd be looked after. It's too late for us to reinstate you officially but there's your pension. That could be resumed — back-dated.

Trust me. I know it's not a pleasant thing to be asked to do this to a friend, but he's a menace now. You must remember that. It would be a chance for you, Lewis. I'd like to be the one to put it in your way.'

A chance to wipe out the past was what he meant. Lewis cleared his throat. 'Don't think I'm not grateful. You're a good friend, Andy.'

'You'll do it then?'

Lewis smiled. 'I wouldn't say no to a holiday — all paid. Where am I going?'

'You know the place. Bahia Dorada. Furnival's villa is just down the coast. From there you can be sure of running across him, even if you have to invent an illness. You can see now why it had to be you. It's tailor-made.'

'A perfect fit,' said Lewis sourly. 'I can have a second honeymoon.'

'You'd better keep Diana out of this. It'll probably be tough and she might get curious.' Andrew looked doubtful.

'She's more likely to smell a rat if I go off on my own without good reason, especially there. Besides — ' an expression Andy couldn't read crossed his face — 'she could have her uses on this one.'

He sat forward intently. 'Right! Brief me!'

★ ★ ★

He hit the main road round about mid-day and had the choice of turning left and heading for Barcelona or right for Figueras. Midway between the two and the nearer to him than either, lay Gerona, but it might be dangerous to stop there and shop for what he needed. Too many local residents from Bahia Dorada and Tamariu used the place for their weekly shopping sorties for anything more sophisticated than food and it would be just his luck to run into Jack or Thelma or one of their ilk. Barcelona was miles away but Figueras, though it meant back-tracking, was the sort of place English people passed through without stopping, far enough from the coast, on their way to the border. Unlikely to meet any of the locals there and yet a big enough town to provide his requirements. He turned right and joined the main stream of traffic heading for France.

The town, when he made it, was thronged with tourists taking this last opportunity before the frontier to spend or change their pesetas. The shops were ready for them with assorted basket work and plaited ropes of garlic hanging from their awnings, celluloid Spanish dolls in Flamenco costume, toy bullfighters, postcards and castanets.

He parked the car under some trees in the square, locked it and, taking with him a small hold-all, located an insignificant hotel in a side street, in front of which the residents and passers-by sat at tables cooling themselves with beers and watching the world go by. He made for the Gents and was lucky to find he had it to himself. The lightweight town suit considered appropriate for Barcelona was discarded in favour of cotton trousers and a loose open-necked shirt and stowed in the hold-all. Canvas shoes replaced leather and he stepped out into the sunshine again, indistinguishable from a hundred other holidaymakers.

He returned to the car to deposit the bag in the boot, then went in search of what he needed. He found it on a corner of the main square, a shop specializing in camping and sporting gear, where he acquired a sleeping bag, a hurricane lantern, primus stove and billy-can and a frogman's rubber suit. Further down the road a chandler supplied him with two lengths of stout rope, while a delicatessen provided enough basic rations for a couple of days. If his information was correct, the affair should be buttoned up by then and, if not, food would hardly be his main concern. Only one thing remained to be done and he did it, putting through a pre-arranged telephone call to Inspector Salvador at the Gerona Constabulary to confirm that the operation was under way. There was no point in hanging about this place. He filled the car up with petrol then turned back along the way he had come. Some miles down the road he took a right turn, leaving the noisy stream of traffic to roar on relentlessly whilst he meandered through deserted by-roads until he came upon a tiny village at the foot of the Pyrenees. Here he enjoyed a luncheon of veal escalopes and fresh fruit, washed down with Sangria. Later he pulled the car into a grove of trees, opened all the doors and windows and, spreading himself along the back seat, slept.

15

The sun had slid into its downward arc, piercing a clearing in the trees and making the car as hot as an oven when Lewis awoke. He looked at his watch. In three hours it would be dusk and although it wouldn't be wise to arrive at the lighthouse in daylight, he wanted to be able to stow away his equipment and camouflage the car before complete darkness descended. There would be no moon tonight, or for the next two; that's how Andy's contact had been so sure of the date of the delivery. If they ran true to form they would choose one of the three moonless nights in the month. It was just a question of waiting. The man had said Thursday, but Lewis wasn't taking any chances. This opportunity, smacking of Divine retribution, wasn't to be allowed to slip.

He got out of the car and stretched, took a comb from his pocket and straightened his hair then, although there wasn't a soul in sight, disappeared discreetly into the trees to relieve himself. 'Picking flowers' had been his mother's euphemism for this simple act of nature performed in the open air.

'Stop the car, Father, Lewis wants to get out to pick flowers' — on journeys as a boy. He thought of her now as he buttoned his flies, reflecting wryly that there were precious few flowers to pick here in this arid, barren dust.

It was twilight when he reached the lighthouse. Now, at *Encantador*, Grant and Diana would be preparing for dinner, bathing and changing with the night before them. He had little doubt as to how they would spend it. He thought of Diana sitting at the dressing-table in their room making up her face, doing her hair, performing the actions he had watched a thousand times. Perhaps Grant was watching her even now. Tonight they wouldn't bother to dress. He pulled himself up sharply. Wasn't that the way he had arranged it? Had it not been for their mutual attraction the plan would never have succeeded. While she kept Grant occupied and unsuspecting, Lewis could go about his business undisturbed. The storm had been an unexpected stroke of luck. Without it he would have had to find another way of breaching the enemy's defences and installing himself inside the citadel. He'd paved the way by allowing them enough time together to rekindle their old passion without the opportunity to satisfy it.

Except for the morning when he had pretended to be ill, they hadn't been alone together for more than a few minutes and that day they had been under surveillance by Andy's contact. It had given him enough time to make a reconnaissance of his own before returning to his fevered couch, to act out a convincing charade for Diana's benefit. She would never have suspected him of deliberately throwing her into Grant's arms and now that he had her tuned as taut as a bow string with frustration and resentful with him for not taking her with him, Lewis calculated the time was ripe for unconditional surrender.

Let Grant enjoy the fruits of his short-lived victory. It'd be a hell of a long time before he enjoyed another woman where he was going. As for Diana, maybe she'd open her eyes and view them both in a very different light after this, the bitch! A bitch on heat. He savoured the phrase and repeated it to himself in an endeavour to revitalize the acrid resentment that the thought of her infidelity had fanned all these years, but strangely all that now came to mind were the good times they had shared, the serene compatibility without the aching jealousies of passion, the comradeship and honesty of their relationship unclouded by the petty tyrannies of so-called love during their early years together. When this was all over, when she had finally got this fellow out of her system, and Lewis was pretty sure that that would happen when she saw him for what he was, when she had been taught her lesson, then he, Lewis, would be prepared to forgive her.

Putting Diana out of his mind, he switched off the engine and ran the car silently the last few feet down a slight incline and into the courtyard. A couple of bats swooped above his head as he opened the door, got out and looked around. The place was as silent as the grave and after a moment or two spent listening, and having satisfied himself that no one else was here, he went round to the boot and unloaded its contents, which he carried to the derelict cottage nearest the furthest wall. When the car was empty he got back inside, re-started it and drove it back out of the yard and up the track until he came to a clump of scrub and brush near the cliff edge fringed with pines and into the centre of which he ran the car. There was still just enough light to enable him to re-arrange the undergrowth and cover the tracks of the tyres, and when he was satisfied that no one would suspect that anything had been disturbed, he made his way back to the keeper's cottage on foot.

It was dark and the temperature had

dropped like a stone but he didn't dare light more than the small pocket torch that he kept in the car and which he'd brought with him. Anything stronger might be seen from a headland beyond, as had already been proved. The hurricane lamp must be saved until he was underground, which would be any moment now. Thanks to Andy's contact, he knew what to look for and where. Outside in the courtyard, piled against the wall, was a collection of old oil drums. Three or four lay on their sides, the rest stacked haphazardly one on top of the other and jutting out from the wall at a distance of four or five feet. Between the fourth and fifth stack there was a gap at the lowest level, only made visible when he rolled aside a couple of the loose drums in front of it, and kneeling down, Lewis crawled into it and shone his torch along the ground. The beam rested on a round manhole cover, its diameter only slightly wider than that of the drums themselves but big enough, when raised, to reveal a hole that could receive the body of a man. He took hold of the ring and pulled it upwards but it was too heavy, which meant laying down the torch and using two hands. The lid came up silently then and with it a draught of cold, damp air and the sound of water somewhere far beneath.

He shone the torch into the aperture and it showed him the beginnings of a metal ladder fixed against a rock wall and travelling downwards, but the battery wasn't powerful enough to penetrate far into the gloom for him to see more. He knew what to expect when he got to the bottom and had seen for himself the stairway cut into the rock face that ran from the concealed beach beneath, up into the cliff, but it would be as well to satisfy himself that this latter went all the way to meet the other steps before lowering himself into the unknown darkness.

Lewis crawled backwards out of the cave made by the oil-drums and went to get the hurricane lantern and the rope from the cottage. Back in his shelter, he lit the lamp and attached it to one end of the rope. Lying on his stomach over the hole he lowered the light down into the abyss. It swayed gently from side to side but it showed him what he wanted to know. The metal rungs of the ladder ended on a square platform some feet down. He played out the rope until he felt the lamp come to rest on the firm ledge, then looked down. Away to the left he could see the top of a flight of stone steps and it was clear that the tunnel ended here and opened out into a wider dimension, the size of which it was impossible to guess. If his calculations were correct, this was the roof of the cave he had seen only once before, on the day he had borrowed Grant's frogman's suit and gone snorkeling, leaving Diana sunbathing on the beach. He knew it had to exist but it had been a job to find it.

There had been nothing to be seen from the boat when he, Diana and Grant had taken that first trip up the coast in the Redshank. They had been fairly close in to the shore and he had been looking for a cove, somewhere one could have run a small boat into and near enough to the lighthouse to have made a connection between the two a possibility. If he hadn't already been informed that the lighthouse was being used, Grant's behaviour when Diana had mentioned their visit to it and his expression when she had told him of the finding of Victor's ring would have confirmed his own suspicions that it was the obvious place for the drop.

He knew from Andy's contact that the consignment came by sea on one of the moonless nights in each month and a vessel had been observed on three such strategic nights in succession. It had come in close to the foot of the cliff, where it cut its muffled engines and was obscured from the watcher above by an overhang of shale and rock formation. After about ten minutes the motor had started again and the boat slid out into the darkness in the direction from which it had appeared. Just time enough to make the delivery but the question was: how and where?

Lewis's scrutiny of the coastline from the boat had revealed no beach, no cave, not even a plateau of rock where a package could have been hidden in safety from the water or where it could have been easily recoverable except by boat. It would have been easy for Grant to use this method of collection but Lewis didn't think it likely. The Vulcan was too distinctive a craft, drawing attention to its owner and, besides, Grant was too fly to run the risk of the stuff being found aboard his property if suspicions were aroused. Lewis had read a certain amount about the geology and geography of this particular coast and had heard of concealed grottoes lying behind sheer rock faces and running back underground in some cases many yards, several boasting pebbled beaches and lagoons bedded in coloured stones. Without a closer examination of the rock fall in the vicinity of the lighthouse, he was unwilling to reject his theory that such a grotto existed there and if proved correct, then he had the solution to the whole business within his grasp. Making an opportunity for his investigations proved more difficult than he had anticipated.

Since their arrival at *Encantador*, Diana had stuck as close to him as a limpet. It was as if she were afraid to be out of his company for more than a few moments and at one juncture Lewis even wondered whether he hadn't been as clever in concealing his motives as he had thought and that she had her own suspicions that he was up to something. Then she had suggested their picnic and he had seen his chance. The little bay where they had spent their sun-filled day, although some distance from the lighthouse by road which had to negotiate the mountainous cliff sides, by sea as the fish swam was a distance easily traversed by an average swimmer. Wearing Grant's rubber suit and leaving Diana safely drowsing on the beach, he had gained the reef and turned the first jutting headland rock, using an easy crawl. Round the corner he paddled into the shallows, crossed the beach and its opposite side where the rocks shelved flatly down, affording a foothold all the way until they ended at a further point and here he had once more donned his flippers and dropped again into the water.

He could see the lighthouse about fifty yards ahead and, as he neared it, he swam slowly right in against the cliff face, examining it carefully for any sign of a crevice through which a man might be able to squeeze. The water was very deep and still and here and there small reefs stood up in the sea. Judging from the scarred stone strata above these were huge boulders that had at some time broken off from their land mass and were now covered in slimy weed and spiky black sea urchins. He rested against one such rock, getting his breath and scanning the impenetrable wall before him. To his left was the overhang under which the boat had been seen to disappear. He pulled his mask down over his eyes, lying flat on the face of the water, and proceeded along gingerly, propelling himself with motions of his left arm and leg while on his right side he kept close to the precipice. Shoals of tiny fish shimmered this way and that beneath him, then sped away. He watched them, forgetting momentarily his purpose, only wondering at the speed and miraculous colourings of the filtered light playing on their scales and, as he did so, he noticed something that brought him back to reality with a jolt of excitement.

The shoal immediately beneath him had hesitated, almost stationary, then with a concerted twitch of silver-blue tails had darted towards the rock face — and had disappeared. It took a moment for the significance of their flight path to dawn. When it did, he raised his head out of the water, standing upright in the buoyant sea with his hands against the visible cliff base and felt cautiously with his feet along its submerged projection. The tip of his flippers encountered a blank wall and then, as he lowered himself deeper into the water, he felt the front of them disappear, sucked into an unsuspected opening and his weight was thrown backwards and would have been pulled downwards had he not kicked himself away from the suction and surfaced to float on his back.

Amongst the snorkeling equipment in Grant's room by the pool had been a miniature waterproof version of the Davy lamp — a tiny light that could be worn fixed by a band on to the helmet of the rubber suit. Lewis produced it now from a zip pocket and fastened it round his forehead, then, taking a deep breath, he dived down below the surface. Where his feet had been there was a sizeable gap in the rock like the opening of a cave. He had only meant to take a look but the same force that had drawn his feet under and inwards seemed to grasp his whole body once his head was close to the aperture and, before he knew exactly what had happened, he had found himself sucked in under the rock, then released to float upwards. He broke the surface gasping and not a little afraid to find himself swimming in what appeared to be a small lagoon which he realized must be behind the cliff face which he had so recently been searching. After only a few strokes his feet touched shelving ground and he floundered out of the water on to a small shale beach.

He was in a cave. The meagre light showed him that much. At the back the shingle was dry and there must have been ventilation somewhere because the air was fresh and he experienced no difficulty in breathing. He explored the walls which were close in upon him with his hands but he couldn't see the roof in the light afforded by his head lamp. It didn't matter. He had found what he had been looking for. Some steps had been cut into the rock face on the right hand side which, like the ladder in *Jack and the Beanstalk*, reached up into infinity and he knew that he had found Grant's delivery spot. The boat hadn't needed to beach, not even to anchor. It would be a matter of moments only for any frogman familiar with the secret opening of the cave to dive down with his waterproof package, deposit it under the stones near the steps and return through the gap to be hauled up into the waiting vessel.

Getting back through the mouth of the cave required a greater effort than entering it, but Lewis found that by reason of being able to kick off from the sea bed he could propel himself under the rock and within a few seconds later he had bobbed up into that other world of sunlit afternoon. He had been gone three hours by the time he rejoined Diana on their beach.

It had taken him by surprise, her insistence on exploring the lighthouse on their way back. It was almost as if he had communicated to some sixth sense of hers the importance attached to the building by him in his thoughts. He'd sat and waited for her in the courtyard. From the window of the lighthouse he had idly traced a line back from the overhanging cliff, a little to the left and his eye had rested on a stack of rusty oil-drums.

Now, looking down the manhole, Lewis could see that the platform on which the lantern rested was like a small landing approximately six foot square and big enough to stack his equipment on. Once again he repaired to the keeper's cottage and, working by torchlight, undid the sleeping bag and opened it out. Across it he laid the rubber suit, the box containing the small gas primus and as many of the provisions as the bedding roll could accommodate when it was once more wound up into a tight bolster-shaped sausage and secured with string, through which he looped one end of the second length of rope. What remained, a couple of cans of beer and a packet of biscuits, he stuffed into his pockets and carried it all to the top of the ladder. The bedding roll was bulky and heavy but he managed to push it through the hole, then bracing it gently against the metal rungs, lowered it down until it rested beside the lamp. He let go of the rope and sat back on his heels, taking a few deep breaths and making a mental check that he hadn't forgotten anything before pulling the two oil-drums he had previously rolled aside across to cover the gap he was in.

He let himself down backwards into the tunnel, feeling with his toes for the first three rungs of the ladder. When only his head and shoulders were level with the ground, he drew the manhole cover down towards him, where it fell into place with a dull thud, bringing down a cloud of dust and covering his hair and face with a layer of fine dried earth. At the same time there was a rumbling noise like thunder from above and from it Lewis deduced he had dislodged some of the drums which must now have come falling down on top of his means of exit. He pushed with both hands against the trap door but was unable to shift it. He swore. It was a nuisance but with the underwater channel at least he wasn't trapped.

In spite of the chill, dank air, he was sweating when he reached the platform. He was getting a bit old for this kind of thing. If he'd known, when he'd taken it on, that this job was going to involve diving into underwater grottoes or negotiating himself along subterranean tunnels he would have thought of his health. Now all he could think of was the look on Diana's face when she realized just what he had accomplished. No need then to look beyond him for a real man.

Tying one end of the rope on the lantern to the bottom rung of the ladder, he dropped the light over the side of the steps, letting out the line until the lamp hung below against the side of the cavern, illuminating enough of the beach below to allow Lewis to see where he was going. In the same manner he played out the second rope, swinging the rolled sleeping bag and its contents downwards and, when the rope was taut, letting it go so that the bundle dropped on to the shingle with a dull thud. Then, lighting his way down with the pocket torch, he clambered carefully down the stone staircase, half crouching and keeping one hand flat against the wall. The steps narrowed nearer the bottom where they were little more than niches and, to prevent himself slipping, he turned round and came gingerly down backwards, almost on all fours, which meant extinguishing the torch, but from here he could judge vaguely how far he had to go. After what seemed an eternity but was in reality only about ten minutes, his foot touched some water and just beneath it, the beach. He stumbled round to his left.

Where he was he stood in darkness. The lantern swung high up at the back of the cave casting a magic circle of welcoming warmth and light where the ground was dry, but not extending further to embrace the water. Luckily his pack had landed well up and out of the wet. So far, so good! He moved towards the light, rather pleased with himself at having got so far without a hitch, when his feet encountered an obstruction lying across his path and he pitched forwards, managing to save himself with his hands from going completely flat. The sharp stones grazed and cut his palms and, cursing, he fumbled for the torch and shone it down to see what it was that had brought him a cropper.

The surface of the ground was uneven. A small hillock of stones piled across his path had caused his stumble and he made to circumnavigate it when something brought him up in his tracks and made him look closer. Where he had fallen, the pebbles had been displaced and the torchlight glinted on something metallic that shone like gold. He bent to pick it up but it was attached to something. Brushing aside more stones he saw what it was and recoiled, withdrawing his free hand as if it had been stung. A man's finger bearing a heavy gold snake ring protruded from the shingle. After the first horrified shock, it was a matter of moments to uncover the whole body.

Andy's contact lay face down. Lewis didn't have to touch him to know that he was quite dead. There was a neat, black hole at the base of his skull where the bullet had entered the sleek, pomaded head and when Lewis turned the body over, there was a corresponding hole in Victor's forehead to mark the flight passage of the shot that had killed him.

16

His first instinctive reaction was one of irritation rather than alarm. Victor had bungled again and this time Grant had taken no further chances. He'd been suspicious when Diana had mentioned seeing a light from the lighthouse and then there'd been the matter of the ring, proof positive that Victor had been sniffing around up there. Diana's hammering of the point had hardly helped and Lewis could have murdered her for her insistence in front of Grant that Victor had a particular interest in the place. He could have murdered her! His blood ran cold, sickening realization of the danger in which she now was, dawning, followed by a sense of panic about what he should do.

He looked at his watch. It was nearly nine-thirty. Even if he could have raised the trap door and gone to warn her, there wasn't a telephone for miles. And suppose there had been, by the time he had got himself above ground and back to the car, uncovered it and found an instrument, precious time would have elapsed and he might by then have literally missed the boat. If it came tonight, it would be between eleven and two in the morning and if he wasn't here, as arranged as a reception committee for the frogman, all was lost — retribution for the past, plans for the present, vindication and hopes for the future.

In any case, whom could he have rung? Salvador would have left by now for the police launch with its crew. He supposed vaguely their craft would be in radio communication with the station in Gerona, but once embarked, the police chief would serve no useful purpose in cancelling his operation to come here to view a body that would be equally as dead if it waited a few hours for his attention.

He toyed with the idea of the cave's alternative exit. He could use it and then get a message through somehow but if he swam out now in the hopes of locating Salvador's boat, he didn't know precisely where to look for it. The inspector had said it would be in wait but not its exact location and in searching for it, he might easily lose his quarry. By staying where he was and carrying through the plan, he was discharging his orders. These took precedence over any other consideration, including the thought of what harm might befall Diana. He could only warn her at the risk of failing and Lewis had had enough of failure. If the consignment didn't come tonight, then he could contact the police tomorrow.

The confused thoughts raced through his brain and he was still bending over Victor's body, noticing for the first time contusions on the face and hands crusted with congealed blood and how, when raised from the ground, the head fell back at a grotesque angle as if the neck were broken. The injuries were consistent with his having been shot before being dropped from a height and Lewis wondered whether he had been snooping around above ground and had run into Grant, or whether the latter had killed him at *Encantador* and transported him here, to be bundled unceremoniously through the manhole cover.

Lewis had no doubt that Grant was responsible. He wouldn't have risked anyone else knowing about the cave. Victor's cover had been blown — how or when Lewis couldn't imagine now — and if Grant knew about Victor, how much might he know about Lewis himself? His safety and that of the plan depended upon whether Victor had given him away. Not only his safety, but Diana's.

Her safeguard was in her innocence. As long as she remained ignorant of what was happening, Grant would have no need to harm her. But he was ruthless enough to despatch her if she got in his way, as he had despatched Victor and, before him, perhaps even Hilary. They hadn't been able to prove anything at the time but it was on the cards that she had tumbled to what her husband was up to and had had to be silenced. If Grant had murdered her, Salvador had been content to wait to give him enough rope to hang himself and his confederates when the time was ripe. That time could be tonight and agonizing as the realization was, there was nothing that could be done to help Diana until tomorrow.

He knelt down and shovelled a covering of stones once more over the body. His job was to wait for the delivery. If the frogman surfaced and the first thing he saw was Victor he would be alerted and unlikely to leave his package without making a thorough search of the cove. Lewis's whole advantage lay in the old Army principle of warfare of surprise. When the man came up out of the water, he would be ready for him. If all went well, Lewis should be able to dispose of him temporarily in order to be able to slip through the under water opening himself and join the messenger's boat. In the dark one frogman looks much like another and those on board would only see what they were expecting.

After that, it would be up to Salvador. Lewis hoped he wasn't too far away.

He was suddenly and incongruously aware that he hadn't eaten for over seven hours and that he was extremely hungry. It must have been all that extra physical exertion. Diana had never been able to understand how he could retain an appetite under emotional pressure. Under any kind of stress her own bowels turned to water and eating without gagging became a physical impossibility. She had marvelled when she had been told that Lewis had sat down and demolished a huge plate of oxtail, accompanied by carrots, parsnips, celery and all the trimmings on the day that his mother had died. That he had been deeply affected she had no doubt. It had been painful and long drawn-out and a sense of relief for the sufferer was unavoidable, yet death with its customary attendant sense of guilt bequeathed to those left behind and the difficulty in comprehending the finality of so terrible a separation had not deterred Lewis's appetite. It was just one more difference between men and women, she had supposed.

He scrambled up the beach to where the bulky bedding roll lay beneath the cliff. He released the string and straps, unwound the sleeping bag and retrieved the portable primus, a loaf of bread, some tins and a couple of smaller packages. The rubber suit he laid out on the shingle, checking on each piece of equipment. He would need that at the ready for later. It would be wiser to save the tinned stuff for subsequent nights, should it be necessary to extend his vigil beyond this one. He'd make do now with the loaf and the ham, a packet of salami and a can of beer.

He was cold — probably the aftermath of shock and the sweat of his exertions, now dried upon him, and the cave, though dry enough where he was sitting, was full of condensation and a current of air passed across the water coming from some unknown source. He'd had the sense to include a thick pullover in his luggage and this he now donned as well as unzipping the bag and getting into it up to his waist. Sitting there, eating ham sandwiches, was like having breakfast in bed. It had been a strenuous day for someone of his age and he hoped he wasn't going to catch a chill. Normally so solicitous for his own health he had really achieved some spectacular feats during the last week. The over-riding will to make a success of this final assignment had given him the necessary strength.

That, and the overwhelming desire to have proved himself once and for all irretrievably right where Diana was concerned. After the frugal meal he felt better. Out of habit he tidied up its remains, neatly collecting any paper and stuffing it and the beer can into a plastic bag. It seemed rather pointless worrying about litter at such a time when Victor lay dead not more than a few feet from him, but habits and early training die hard and, besides, there was nothing else to do. He wished he'd brought a book. The lantern's light wasn't strong enough to read by but his torch could have been used for the purpose. Better get some rest. They wouldn't be here yet awhile.

He zipped himself back into the bag and lay down, trying to relax each set of muscles consciously, starting at his toes and travelling up through his hips, back and shoulders. He didn't sleep, lying with his eyes open, looking up into the ceiling of the cave but not seeing it.

Images floated before him. Klara, so sweet and pretty on their wedding day, so apparently innocent. Diana with Peter as a baby in her arms, cool and calm and clear-sighted, the sharper planes of virginity rounded by contented motherhood, grey eyes mirroring her innate honesty. Innocence and honesty! It was incredible how he had been taken in with Klara, who had been as innocent as a Piccadilly whore, and honest

Diana who had lived a lie with him for more than half their marriage.

Why couldn't one of them have been at least half-way as good as his mother? She had known how to please a man, waiting on his creature comforts, always there to encourage and champion one. His father had been a fortunate man. Lewis found himself wondering about the sexual side of their relationship and was immediately ashamed of himself as if he had been caught actually (instead of mentally) undressing his own mother. His father had spoken once to him about the facts of life, drawing upon the animal kingdom for some rather obscure analogies in which, as everybody knew from Biology at school, the male was the natural hunter, the female by character submissive.

He must have dozed because, when he next looked at his watch, it was after midnight. He struggled out of the sleeping bag and stretched his legs. It was time to put out the lantern and this he was reluctant to do. The friendly light had helped him to forget the loneliness, not to mention the danger of his position and that, lower down the beach, the innocent-looking mound of stones covered Victor's corpse with a bullet in it. Now, in the dark, sitting waiting, clad in the frogman's suit, the reality and improbability of the situation came rushing in upon him and the cadaver made a macabre companion.

Shortly before two he heard a muffled chugging like the engine of a boat and he stiffened, holding his breath and straining his ears in the darkness. It seemed to approach and then the noise stopped. At the same moment the water in the cave rose with a sudden gush, causing miniature waves to break beside his feet. The muscles in his stomach tautened and a sweat broke out under the rubber. This was it! Up to now he hadn't really believed they would come. He waited.

Five, ten, seconds passed, then a splash, a shout and the sound of the boat's engine again, this time at an increased speed, fading into the distance. Lewis stood irresolute. Something must have gone wrong. The messenger had not appeared and the boat was unlikely to have left without him. Perhaps it had been some other boat or, worse still, he had miscalculated and the delivery had been made in some other place. Had he made a cock of it all? If he had, he couldn't just wait helplessly here. He had to find out.

He pulled down his goggles and adjusted his rubber head-piece, then wading into the water, found the stony shelf with his feet and dived. He felt the rock on either side of the opening with his hands as he swam through, then allowed his body to float to the surface, lungs bursting, apprehension constricting his chest. The night was very dark but, compared with the palpable pitch of the cave, it was like coming up from the grave into twilight.

The first thing he saw was a vessel coming in on him and for a moment he thought it was the smugglers deliberately running him down until he saw the police light on the top of what turned out to be Salvador's launch. They must have been looking for him because they cut their engine immediately and a rope ladder was slung down over the side while two men leaned over the bows and heaved him into the boat. One of them was thin, with a gaunt, cadaverous face on which exaggerated lines were carved running from nose to chin and more were etched beside eyes that pierced Lewis like a bird of prey.

He waited while Lewis removed his goggles and helmet then without preliminaries asked, 'What happened?'

'I was going to ask you the same thing. All I know is I heard a boat and it stopped. I thought our man was coming in and I was ready for him but they seemed to take fright. There were a few shouts then they made off.'

Salvador swore in Spanish. 'They must have seen us. Something alerted them. Are you sure you couldn't have missed him?'

'Impossible.' Lewis shook his head.

'If we've lost him we shan't get a second chance. They must have gone on but how far?'

They looked at each other, the same thought in each man's mind.

Lewis said, 'To *Encantador*? Would they risk it?'

'What would you do, my friend? They know we have seen the boat and will have guessed we have launches up and down the coast ready to pick them up. They must get rid of the stuff before we find them. They have to leave it somewhere. Where else but *Encantador* before we get there? They only have to off-load their man, even if he has to lie low there for a time.'

'My wife is there alone with Furnival.' Lewis suddenly remembered Diana.

'Alone? I thought your man was guarding her.'

'He's dead. I found him in the cave when I got there. He'd been shot.'

Salvador stiffened. 'You are right, *señor*. She is in grave danger. We must hurry.'

He turned and issued some staccato orders and the boat sprang once again into life, turning on her axis and heading out from the rock face. With the initiative taken from him,

Lewis was numb and incapable of coherent thought. All he could think of was that this chance, too, had eluded him. If they escaped, then he had failed through no fault of his own. Salvador's men had not been careful enough. They must have shown themselves too soon and in doing so had ruined the plan's chance of success. Grant would disclaim any knowledge of the cave and, without the evidence of the drugs, no motive could be pinned on him for Victor's murder. Alternatively, if, as he suspected, they made the delivery to *Encantador*, Diana could well see or hear something that would do her no good and, unless they could get there in time, she could be hurt. Either way, he was a loser.

They hugged the coast, their engines muffled, scanning the gloom for any sign of the boat. Just before they came to the beach below the villa, they cut the motor and listened. There was no light in any of the rooms facing the sea and the silence was total. By the jetty the Vulcan bobbed gently on the water that further up lapped the beach. Suddenly the silence was shattered by the roar of a boat's engines going at speed away to their left. Salvador snapped a command and prepared to give chase. Lewis, galvanized out of his lethargy, made up his mind.

'You follow them,' he shouted. 'I'm going in after the other.'

Salvador only hesitated for a second. 'Good luck!' he shouted back. 'I'll send someone to help. Be careful, my friend!'

As he went over the side the boat jerked away and Lewis was left in the cold, unfriendly water.

17

It had been a strange sort of day, Diana reflected, as she stood draped in a towel after her shower in front of the open bedroom window, taking in the beauty of the sloping, terraced garden and the setting sun upon the sea. The ice plants were closing their spiky petals for the night and the scent of hibiscus and oleanders wafted on a movement of air not strong enough to be termed a breeze but sufficient to afford a pleasant alleviation of the flat heat of the day.

Perhaps it was in herself that the strangeness lay. She hadn't thought of Lewis once since his departure this morning. It was as if, with his going without her, a chapter had ended, a decision had been made, or was it that by his defection, he had given her justification in her own conscience to do what she had wanted all along? Had he turned at the final moment and invited her to accompany him, would she truthfully not have been disappointed? This way she could blame him for any consequences.

Which brought her back to the present. At this rate, she had to admit reluctantly, it didn't look as if there were going to be any. It was a bit of an anti-climax to find that, after having decided to abandon her virtue, so far no hint of the sacrifice being demanded had been cast. Grant had been a cheerful enough companion for most of the day, but with no suggestion of anything more intimate. He'd taken her with him on his rounds.

'Nothing much more taxing than bowels, bladders and babies today,' he said cheerfully, swinging his bag over on to the floor and sliding down into the seat beside hers. 'We can dispose of those in a couple of hours.'

He consulted his list. 'Laura Mortimer for coffee, I think, and old General Dennington should be good for a snifter round about noon if we time him right. Nothing wrong with either of them but they consider paying my fee a privilege of which I should be the last to deprive them. Laura's also an old friend. Wipe that expression of shocked morality from your pretty features, Goddess, and don't tell me that your faithful National Health Service retainer back home doesn't take precisely the same view over his private patients.'

'I should hate to think that he did,' said Diana, trying to be severe.

'I'm not saying the treatment's any different but they're paying for his time. Of course he can linger half an hour on their doorsteps or make a special visit to administer a flu injection. It's all the same, only I'm honest about it.'

'You're a cynic.'

'Not according to Wilde's definition. Oh, dear me, no, Goddess. Believe me, I have a very good idea of the value of everything.'

She studied him. 'And everyone — in terms of money?'

He laughed. 'The trouble with you, my darling Diana, is that years of consorting with that boring pillar of moral rectitude, combined with your extremely correct upbringing, are inclined to make you the teeniest bit censorious. Come on, you're with me now and you don't have to pretend. Have you ever met anyone who wouldn't look more attractive if they were rich?'

She opened her mouth indignantly to defend Lewis when she saw him looking sideways at her with a grin that took the sting out of his words and she could only drop her head on to the seat-back and laugh.

'How much does it take to qualify?'

'It depends on existing assets. For instance, for you it wouldn't take so much. You know you already have what I want, without taking into account your parents' money — but you're not in the market, are you?'

306

It wasn't a proper question, more a bland statement of fact and he kept his eyes on the road ahead so that she couldn't tell if he were expecting her to rise. It came as a cold surprise that he had remembered her chance remark about having inherited the sum her father had left her. Not inconsequentially, she recalled that Hilary had been financially independent and, before she could stop herself, found she had made some comment to that effect. Grant wasn't in the least put out.

'I've told you it enhances the attraction. I'm not saying we weren't in love with one another when we married. We were. But I don't deny that marrying a girl with no money at all didn't fit into my scheme of things then.'

'And now?' She could have bitten out her tongue.

'Let's say that marrying at all doesn't fit into my present scheme. Like all men, I'm basically selfish and what I have now and what's to come I can enjoy better fancy free. Perhaps later — who knows? At present I have too much on my plate to get encumbered.'

They had paid a few of his calls and were now ascending a tree-lined hill in a residential district unknown to Diana and Grant swung the car to the right, through a pair of open wrought-iron gates into a garden, where grassy slopes ran down on their either side as they approached the front door of one of the most curious houses she had ever seen. It stood on raised ground and was white and square, except that its corners were rounded, as were the lines of its roof, the windows and the balconies jutting out from the first-floor rooms. Even the roof tiles were circular, lying overlapped and shiny like the scales of a vast herring on a fishmonger's slab.

Diana exclaimed and Grant laughed and said, 'Wait until you see the inside.'

The front door was open and a woman came out on to the steps as she heard the car draw up. She was tall and very thin, with dark hair greying slightly, and she wore a lime green linen dress, immaculately and expensively simple. A green and tangerine scarf was tied with apparently casual effect at her throat and the two ends fastened with a diamond brooch as big as the knob on the top of Grant's gear lever. The rest was informal — bare brown legs and feet thrust into yellow sandals. She wore no other jewellery except for a gold wedding ring. She raised a hand in welcome and came round to the driver's seat. The sun had been against her as she peered through the windscreen so that she didn't realize Diana's presence in the car until she had put her face in at the window to kiss Grant. Diana could see that she was surprised but obviously far from nonplussed, for after a second of initial hesitation she put her fingers under Grant's chin and planted her lips firmly on his mouth. He took her wrist in one hand, turning his head towards Diana.

'This is Mrs Mortimer, Goddess. Laura to her friends. Laura, may I introduce Diana Holt, an old friend?'

The brown eyes took in Diana at a glance then Laura's rather acquiline features slid into a smile. It softened the angularity of her face and Diana found herself liking the woman better than she thought she was going to. She smiled back.

'Laura's always doing her best to get me struck off,' said Grant as they all went inside the house.

'And would have succeeded before this but he's too damn careful to examine me without a chaperon. Aren't you, darling?' She tucked her arm into Grant's on one side and Diana's on the other and drew them with her across the hall to a door on the left.

The hall was completely circular with a broad staircase which followed the wall and curved up out of sight in a grand sweep. Laura ushered them into a large, pretty, chintzy drawing-room with picture windows. The furniture was English and for the most part antique, which was a surprise. It wouldn't have looked right in most of the Spanish houses Diana had seen but somehow seemed to belong in this extraordinary setting. Beyond sliding doors which were open, Diana glimpsed another large room and Laura, seeing her obvious interest, invited her to look over the house.

The salon, as she called it, was another round room furnished with tapestry chairs, Madame Recamier sofas upholstered in deep blue velvet, and it boasted a circular parquet floor, in the middle of which stood an open grand piano. It was easy to imagine ladies of Jane Austen's era taking a turn around such a room after dinner. More sliding doors led into the dining-room, which was exactly the same size and shape as the first drawing-room.

'It amused me as soon as I saw it,' Laura said when Diana expressed her admiration. 'The way all the rooms led out of one another. The bedrooms and bathrooms are all the same. It was built early in the century by some grandee for his mistress and one can imagine the games of round the houses and clicking of castanets that must have gone on during those dirty week-ends. Commonly known hereabouts as *Laura's Folly*, but I adore it.'

Diana could understand it. Bizarre as it was, the house had an air of comfortable luxury and every item of its contents seemed to express a facet of the owner's character. It was a refreshing change from the stark modern décor or determinedly Spanish interior decoration plumped for by most of the British expatriates.

Coffee was brought by a young Spaniard who couldn't have been more than twenty-two years old: Laura called him Jonny and Grant addressed several sentences to him in Spanish to which the boy replied easily, smiling confidently and joking. He wore the customary garb of the Spanish house-boy — black trousers with a ribbon stripe down the side seam, white linen jacket and black bow tie — but his manner, though respectful, was more familiar than any house-boy's, and Diana would have been puzzled as to his exact status had she not caught the unguarded expression in Laura's eyes as she watched Jonny answering Grant.

'So that's the way the land lies,' thought Diana and tried not to be disappointed or shocked. She looked at Grant and was discomfited to know he'd read her mind. He'd be silently calling her bourgeoise and a hypocrite and she recognized the justice of this. Who the hell was she to condemn Laura when, for two pins, she would have jumped into bed with Grant had he wanted her? She wanted him. She admitted that now, sitting in Laura's drawing-room, and she didn't give a damn who made the first move.

Jonny withdrew and Grant looked at his watch.

'It's been so pleasant, Laura, that I'd almost forgotten this was a professional visit. Perhaps we'd better get down to brass tacks. How have you been getting on with those pills?'

Diana rose. 'I'll leave you to it then,' she said.

'No need to go — there's nothing confidential. I'm not taking my clothes off or anything like that. Worse luck, darling.' Laura mocked Grant.

'I want to powder my nose anyway,' Diana insisted. 'Don't get up. I'll find my own way.'

'Upstairs, darling, and first door straight ahead. Use my bedroom. The loo's off it.'

Diana went out into the hall, closing the door behind her. The house was very quiet. She knew there were servants but they must be out in the kitchen quarters. She went upstairs and found Laura's bedroom, a frothy feminine room, all nylon frills and satin valances. She touched up her lipstick in a triple mirror on the kidney-shaped dressing-table. There was a double leather photo frame on the top, holding two pictures. One was of a man with a long face and humorous eyes. He was wearing a dark suit and what looked like some kind of old school tie. In the opposite frame a gap-toothed little boy of about six beamed out irrepressibly. His hair was slicked back neatly behind two big ears that stuck out and he was holding a black and white rabbit. The phone rang. Diana turned towards the white instrument beside the bed. It rang several times and she began to wonder whether she ought to answer it when it gave a ping as if someone had picked up the receiver in the hall. She went to the door and opened it.

Jonny was saying, 'I'll fetch him. Just a moment please.' He put the receiver down on the hall table and disappeared into the drawing-room, returning with Grant who picked it up, dismissing Jonny with a gesture of his hand.

Diana had begun to descend the stairs but was still in the curve where she could hear Grant but not see him. The conversation was curt on his side. Whoever was on the other end was doing most of the talking. Something in his voice arrested her and she stood where she was, listening in spite of herself.

'How did you know where to call me?' He sounded angry and the answer, when it came, was obviously unsatisfactory.

'I told you . . . ' he was cut short and listened for some seconds. When he spoke again his voice was lower and more urgent. 'Are you quite sure? Yes. No, no. Leave it to me. I shall have to think.' A pause. 'Yes, yes of course it'll be safe. I'll see to that. No, nothing will go wrong. There won't be another time, everything is organized for my departure.'

A door banged somewhere in the servants' quarters and the sound of a conversation being carried on in rapid Spanish became audible as the owners of the voices approached. Grant said quickly, almost furtively, 'I can't talk now. Trust me. I'll deal with him,' and rang off.

Diana would have preferred to remain concealed from the hall until he had returned to Laura in the drawing-room, but at that moment Jonny appeared behind her, seemingly from nowhere, and without looking foolish or appearing to be eavesdropping, she could hardly linger on the staircase, so was obliged to descend. Grant looked up and saw her and the same shuttered expression that she had first seen him wear when she had enquired after Hilary on the hotel terrace came into his eyes. For no accountable reason her throat felt dry and her stomach gave an apprehensive lurch. He passed a hand across his brow as if to clear his thoughts and the absent look disappeared as swiftly as it had come.

He said, 'Something's come up. It's a damn nuisance but one of my patients has had an accident and I'll have to go. I'll come back later for you, Di. Laura, is that all right if Diana stays with you until I can fetch her?'

They turned to their hostess, who had by now joined them in the hall.

'Of course, darling.' Laura smiled at Diana. 'Don't hurry back. Diana can have lunch with me and we can have a nice long girlish chat. You're very welcome to stay.'

'Thank you.'

'That's settled then.' Grant picked up his bag and made for the door. On the threshold he turned to give them a wave and a smile which didn't quite reach his eyes.

'He really is worried,' Laura commented as they turned back into the room. 'It must be serious.'

Diana, trying to remember the exact words he had used over the phone, agreed automatically. But it hadn't been the words themselves that made her so sure that the call had had nothing to do with any patient. They had for the most part been compatible with a professional enquiry, with the exception perhaps of the sentence — 'everything is organized for my departure.' The tenor of the exchange had been all wrong. Angry, furtive, even frightened, except that Grant had never been frightened of anything. Then there'd been that look when he'd realized she was on the stairs — surprised, calculating, wondering perhaps how much she might have overheard.

'I'm afraid it's spoiled your day. I hope you won't be too disappointed. Don't look so glum.'

'Was I? I'm sorry. I was thinking. I didn't mean to be rude. It's very kind of you to ask me to stay.' Diana shrugged off her feeling of unease.

Laura said, 'It's a pleasure to meet someone new, especially an old friend of Grant's. Everyone around here is very sweet but one does find it a bit parochial sometimes. So you've known him a long time?'

'Fifteen odd years, but we hadn't met for a long time until we ran into each other here a week or two ago. It was a great surprise to find him here.'

'But a very pleasant one, I'm sure.'

Diana resisted the probe. 'Of course. My

husband and I have always had a soft spot for them both. It was a blow to hear that his wife was dead. She was a special friend of mine.'

While they'd been talking Laura had taken her through to the dining-room where two places had been laid at one end of the gleaming, oval table which was fully extended and could have accommodated fifteen or sixteen people by Diana's calculations.

They ate salmon off Spode and drank Hock from old Waterford goblets while the cutlery was silver with heavily embossed handles, each piece bearing some kind of family crest. They were served unobtrusively by Jonny and Diana found herself relaxing and enjoying the conversation which touched on antiques and pictures, the shows at present running in London, bringing up children in the permissive society, religion and politics. She liked Laura and found her interested for news, sharp and witty with her comments, and they shared many views in common. Diana told her about Peter. Remembering the boy with the rabbit she asked Laura about him.

'He was my son.' She finished peeling a peach with the utmost care. 'He would have been a little younger than your Peter. The other photo was his father. They were both drowned in a boating accident some years ago. I couldn't bear to stay where I was without them. Everything was too painful. Some friends, including Grant, had come to live out here and thought it might be good for me. They finally persuaded me, so here I am. I was very fortunate to have such good friends, particularly Grant. I could never repay him for what he did for me at that time. Did you know that his own little boy was drowned? It was a bond and he was able to understand so well what I had gone through, and then even later when he lost his wife, it was so strange. I like to think I helped him at that time. I'll never forget he was here the night it happened.'

'That must have been grim.'

'It was.' Laura shuddered. 'Though he was terribly brave, poor darling.'

Diana wondered if Laura was in love with Grant. Remembering his comment in the car about the attraction of a rich woman, and Laura had much else to offer physically, apart from her wealth, Diana experienced a pinprick of jealousy. She felt even more uncomfortable a second later when Laura leaned across and patted her hand where it lay on the table.

'You needn't worry, my dear. Fond as I am of Grant, I have no designs on him. That's why we're such good friends. We can enjoy each other's company, knowing there's no danger of demands being made on either side. He knows I have no desire to be hurt again and, as soon as one becomes involved with any other individual, that's inevitable. It probably sounds cowardly to you and perhaps it is, but David and I were so very happy together. What we had in our short time is sometimes not experienced in a lifetime, so I couldn't hope or even to try to repeat that again. I have Jonny — but that's nothing to do with my heart. We fulfil a purely physical need in one another which isn't a betrayal of David, there being no intellect involved. I hope I'm not shocking you.'

Diana shook her head. 'No. Once you might have but I think I can understand very well now. It may sound strange but I think I envy you.'

Laura lit a cigarette. 'Are you in love with him?'

Diana opened her mouth to profess misunderstanding but said instead, 'More than a little. Why? Does it show?'

'To me, but then all women seem to fall in love with Grant. It's nothing new.'

'What about him?'

'He's human. He'll take what's offered.'

'I thought you liked him.'

'I do, but that doesn't prevent me from

seeing him for what he is, and that's ruthless. If you're serious, Diana, you'll be out of your league.'

Even knowing she was right, Diana didn't greatly appreciate her frankness. Laura proceeded with all the subtlety of a sledge hammer.

'Where does your husband fit in to this scene — or is that the trouble, he doesn't? Unbedworthy?'

Diana said, 'Not really. It's the other way round. I don't seem to be much good at it — with him anyway.' The qualification slipped out and wasn't lost on Laura.

'He's not a man you'd talk to about that sort of thing.'

'And of course to Grant you can,' Laura said dryly.

'He's more experienced. He's not a man to seek only his satisfaction.'

Laura threw back her head and laughed aloud and when she'd finished she said, 'That's rich. Grant is the number one egotist of all time, selfish to the core, and if it came down to brass tacks, he'd sell his own grandmother to get something he wanted.'

'You said you were his friend.'

'I am, sweetie, I am. But I'm not blind to his faults. That's what friendship means, being buddies in spite of them. Did you know his wife?'

'Hilary? Yes, she was one of my best friends.'

Laura raised her eyebrows and Diana flushed. 'It wasn't like that. What happened between us was very brief and Hilary wasn't on the scene at the time. It was over a long time ago. It never really began. I doubt if he'd even fancy me now.' It wasn't true but she was afraid she'd already said too much.

'Then you were hardly to blame for her state of mind, for her condition at the end?'

'What was her condition? Grant told me she had changed. That was all.'

'I didn't know her before she came out here so it's difficult for me to say. I'd met Grant some time before that but never Hilary.' Laura pushed her chair back from the table and reached a long arm behind her for an onyx cigarette box on the sideboard. She offered one to Diana who shook her head then took one herself. 'All I can go by is what people said and that was that she was depressed and deteriorating. She never went anywhere and never asked anyone there. I think she was suffering from some kind of depressive illness.'

'So it wouldn't have surprised anyone if she had killed herself?' Diana frowned. 'It doesn't sound at all like Hilary.'

'Doesn't it?' Laura studied the glowing end

of her cigarette. 'I wonder then what triggered it all off. Something must have and it wasn't you and Grant from what you tell me.'

'She wanted another child and couldn't have one. She'd lost James, remember.'

'I guess it takes all sorts but, even when I lost David and Ben, I didn't feel like jumping off a cliff. Does it sound the sort of thing she might do?'

'No, and anyway you're taking it for granted that she did jump. Much more likely she fell.'

'She hadn't any enemies so the alternative would hardly apply.' Laura was deliberately casual.

'Murder?' Diana took the ridiculous suggestion as a joke. 'That's rubbish. Whoever would want to murder Hilary and for what motive?'

'She had money, I believe.'

Diana stared at her as if seeing her for the first time and not liking her as much as she had an hour ago. The conversation she and Grant had had in the car flitted in and out of the corridors of her mind. He had admitted that Hilary's money had enhanced her attraction. What if, when the attraction itself had faded and a depressed, mentally ill, unstable woman had been all that was left of his wife, the cash had seemed to Grant to be

322

the only remaining asset? Was he capable of murder? She knew instantly, had always known, he was capable of anything — anything. That was what she loved about him and found so lacking in Lewis. She dragged herself back to the present moment and sanity.

'You ought to be writing thrillers in your spare time, Laura,' she said lightly. 'You've got enough imagination.'

Laura shrugged and laughed. 'I'm too lazy to get down to it although, believe me, out here we're not short of plots — mainly light-hearted erotica to make your hair, or incidentally anything else, stand on end.'

'You're passing up a fortune then,' said Diana, relieved that they were on less dangerous ground. 'That's the only kind of book a publisher's interested in England today. Don't bother about a story.'

'What about the law of libel? I probably shouldn't have any friends left.'

'No problem if you were rich and successful enough. They'd probably go around bragging they were on page one sixty-eight.'

'Would you?'

'I'd make very dull copy.'

'I've learned not to judge the book by the cover.' Laura looked at her watch. 'Let's have a swim before we lose the best part of the sun. If I know Grant, he'll get hung up for another hour or two. He's too damn conscientious once he gets to that hospital of his amongst what he calls his real patients. He looks on us all as a bunch of pampered hypochondriacs and he's probably right, but we're a necessary evil.'

They went through the drawing-room out on to a patio, below which a circular pool shimmered welcomingly. Cane furniture was arranged under umbrellas and a glass-topped table supported copies of yesterday's *Times* and *Guardian*. In such a world it seemed impossible that anything sinister could exist.

18

Grant came back in the evening. They had swum and talked, enjoyed tea brought out to them by Jonny, swum again and changed and were thinking of having a drink when he emerged on to the patio, looking tired and, Diana thought, rather pale. He declined the pool but accepted a whisky gratefully, then sank down on to a chaise-longue with a sigh of contentment. He emptied half the glass in three quick gulps and relaxed back in the cushions, easing his shoes off his feet with first one big toe, then the other.

'You don't mind, do you, Laura? It's been a pretty gruelling afternoon.'

'Don't apologize. Relax. What happened to the patient?'

'Who?' Grant made a visible effort to collect himself, then said: 'Oh, the patient. He died.' He obviously didn't want to talk about it and to prevent Laura asking any more questions, Diana got up and suggested she help her gather up her things. They left Grant lying in the chair and went indoors to tidy up. Seeing him out there visibly exhausted by the events of his day and obviously disheartened by the loss of his battle for the life of his patient, Diana felt a pang that only a couple of hours ago she had been wondering if he were capable of murder. His job was saving life, not destroying it and she felt unworthy at having been so easily encouraged in such a base suspicion.

They didn't say much on the way back and by the time they entered the drive to *Encantador* the colour had returned to his cheeks and he appeared more relaxed. He ran the car into the garage under the house and together they mounted the steps and went inside. Dusk had fallen and the house was in darkness. There was no sign of Victor or any of the other servants. On the marble dining-table two places were laid. There were candles in a modern three-branched silver candelabra and a bowl of flowers from the garden. Diana was aware of unexpected quiet and peace. Grant went round the room, lighting up the lamps, and it immediately came to life, glowing and comfortable and intimate in a way it hadn't seemed a moment before.

'Where's Victor?' Diana asked.

'Gone off for the night on that motor bike of his. It's some feast day or other — always is in the Catholic Calendar — and I told the cook and the others they could go. You don't

326

mind, do you? It was arranged some days before I knew Lewis wouldn't be here. Good Lord — ' he turned to look at her in the middle of pouring a drink — 'I hope you don't think I've laid on the big seduction scene on purpose!'

'Shouldn't I?'

'Honestly no. This time, not guilty.'

She was disappointed. It was hardly flattering to be told so plainly that he had no intention of trying to seduce her — even if it were true, which she doubted, but now couldn't be sure. It would be ironical, having come so far, to play the evening for 'just good friends' when the setting, the opportunity and the time, was available for so much more.

'How did you get on with Laura?' He took the lid off an insulated container on the drinks trolley and looked inside. 'Damn,' he said. 'No ice. Hang on a second.' Taking the ice bucket he disappeared in the direction of the kitchen while she wandered about the room, running her hand idly along the back of the leather sofa and pressing her fingers into its deeply buttoned upholstery. There was a comforting, sensuous feel about the leather and she remembered hearing somewhere that people with psychological problems were sometimes specially recruited for the manufacture of handbags, the handling of the material being considered therapeutic for such cases.

He came back with the ice, continuing the conversation at the point where they had broken off, but after a moment he realized she wasn't with him.

'I was talking about Laura. Where were you? You'd gone off into another realm.'

She turned and took the proffered drink. 'I was thinking about leather.'

'Leather?' Grant raised his eyebrows. 'Kinky.'

'Is that why you have so much of it about you?' She gestured to the furniture, smiling.

'Probably.' He came round to sit beside her. 'Freud would no doubt ascribe it to some deep sexual principle. I just happen to like it. Do you?'

She nodded and lay her head back against the sofa. The drink and the afternoon's swimming had made her feel delightfully relaxed.

'In fact, I believe I'm beginning to like it all far too much. With very little encouragement I think I could enjoy living here.'

'I'm amazed. I thought you disapproved of us all and our lotus-eating way of life.'

'I suppose I must have sounded intolerably smug.'

He turned his head and looked at her along

the sofa back and his eyes were uncomfortably close to hers and yellow like a tiger's.

'You were perhaps a little uncompromising. Who or what has wrought this change, I wonder?'

She sighed. 'I suppose Laura had something to do with it. I had her mentally labelled in two seconds flat as rich, idle gigolo fodder, empty-headed as all those people at your party. I'm sorry, I know they're your friends. Then after we'd spoken for a while I realized that, far from being shallow, she was a woman of great strength of mind, making the best of life with what has been left her and the devil to what people say.'

'They don't say much — at least not to your face, when you're as rich as Laura.'

She was annoyed. 'Everything comes down to money with you in the end, doesn't it?'

'I was merely pointing out that, with it, one can afford to hold independent views. Anyway, I'm glad you liked her. What did you talk about?'

'She told me about her husband and her little boy, her friendship with you. I wondered if she were in love with you.'

'What did she say?'

'That you were ruthless and selfish. I'm not going to pander to your ego.'

'That's something I'd never expect from

you, Goddess. You've always been too brutally frank. But to go back to what you said earlier, now that you've discovered you can be wrong about people and we're not such a bad bunch, do you really think you might be interested in coming out here? What does Lewis think about the house?'

'Lewis?' She frowned. She had forgotten Lewis. Foolishly she had allowed her imagination to run on the prospect of *Encantador* with Grant. She had forgotten that she was far ahead with plans of which he as yet knew nothing.

He got up to mix another drink.

'Speaking of your absent spouse, wouldn't you like to phone him, or is he going to ring you later?'

She brought herself down to earth with an effort.

'I don't imagine so. It will depend on where he is and whether he's out beating up Barcelona with Andrew. He doesn't usually ring if he's away for less than a week. I can't ring him because I don't know where he's staying. Besides, there's nothing to say. Nothing's happened to tell him.'

Grant stood, swilling a piece of ice round in his glass, and Diana thought again how pale and tired he looked. The afternoon had taken its toll. She got up and gathered up her things.

'I think I'll go and have a bath and a bit of a rest before I get dressed. Why don't you do the same? You look bushed.'

'I think I will. Here, take this with you.' He held out her replenished glass and as she took it from him their fingers met. Impulsively he bent down and kissed her lightly on her forehead.

'You're sweet and very good for me, Goddess,' he said.

In her room she touched her brow where his lips had rested briefly and tried to analyse that kiss. There had been nothing of the lover in it, more the kind of embrace one would have given a child, but the touch of his hand had been different and she was willing to swear that he had been as aware of the current that ran between them at that touch as she was. She knew she was at a cross-roads. She recalled his words — 'Everything is organized for my departure' — innocent enough words which might have meant anything but they had enhanced the intuition that she had that time was running out. It had been born when Lewis flatly refused to take her to Barcelona and everything that had happened since had made her feel she was running full tilt towards some kind of climax.

She had a bath, then lay on her bed,

watching the light dying from the sky and listening to the movement of the birds in the silent garden. The house was hushed and this evening no sound came from the water. She drowsed and woke much later to hear a telephone ringing. Someone, Grant, answered it but she couldn't hear what he was saying, then some moments later he tapped lightly at her door.

'Yes?' She sat up and pulled the bedcover around her, unsure whether he'd take it as an invitation to come in, but he just called through the door.

'Scoff will be up in about half an hour. Don't dress up as there's only us two.'

She took him at his word, climbing into a comfortable pair of pale blue jeans and a clean blue denim shirt. Her face was tanned, needing little make-up, apart from lipstick and a touch of eye shadow. She combed back her hair, allowing it to fall loose, pencilled in her brows and gave herself a liberal dash of perfume on neck and arms. He heard her open her door and called to her from the kitchen, where she found him heating up a saucepan of soup.

'Would you like to make the salad? It's all washed. Just sling it about in a bowl and make a dressing, will you?'

She complied, finding what she needed in

the cupboard and, when they were ready, they carried the food through to the table, where a platter of carved chicken and salami and a bottle of wine awaited them.

'Isn't this cosy?' Grant held out her chair for her and settled her into the table before seating himself. 'I rather enjoy the nights I play house for myself. I suppose it's hardly a novelty for you but now and again it's good to have the house to oneself.'

Diana reached for the salt. 'I don't suppose you ever get lonely?'

'Too busy.' He munched in silence for a few seconds. 'Do you object to onions?'

She shook her head and he helped himself to half a dozen spring onions, dipping them in the salt on his plate and eating them with his fingers.

'Have some?'

'No thanks.'

He smiled. 'Not even as insurance?'

'No thanks.' She returned to her theme. 'Wasn't it lonely here for Hilary? You're out a lot. It's pretty isolated alone. Laura said she hardly ever went out.'

He shrugged. 'Needn't have been. She could have made a lot of friends but she didn't seem to want to. People tried to be kind and take an interest but they got fed up in the end. It wasn't easy.'

'Did she ever have psychiatric treatment?'

'I wanted her to but she could be very stubborn. She used to get terribly worked up if I suggested it. Accused me of saying she was mental, trying to get her certified. I don't know. One lives with someone, a situation, and doesn't always realize how far gone they are. It's so gradual a process.'

'Even you with your psychiatric training?'

'Yes, even me. I wasn't her doctor, only her husband and as such hardly more perceptive than the average husband.'

'Is there such a thing? Isn't it a meaningless expression like 'the man in the street' or 'your typical housewife'? How does one average character? Intelligence, business acumen, brains, yes — but personality, definitely no.'

'You can add up the separate totals and make a whole.'

'Still can't calculate on basic — for want of a better word — soul.'

'You believe in that then?'

'Certainly. Don't you?'

'As a doctor I've seen too many people die. I don't know. It has uncomfortable implications of retribution and reward.'

Diana laughed. 'You must have a guilty conscience. I had this conversation once with Lewis.'

'And?'

'He wasn't convinced there were going to be marks for trying.'

'And you?'

'I hope so. We've got very profound. Can I have some coffee?'

'You'll have to come and make it and it'll only be Instant.'

They cleared the dishes off the table, then sat and talked but Diana knew they were both filling in time though Grant seemed superficially at ease, but she could sense in him an edgy tension that matched her own. It was less surprising than inevitable when he finally put down his coffee cup and said, 'Well, Goddess, have you made up your mind yet what's going to happen about us?'

She didn't bother to prevaricate coyly. 'That depends upon whether one is taking a long or short term view.'

'Which are you offering? I must warn you I may not have much time for the latter.'

'You are leaving then?'

He looked at her sharply. 'What do you mean?'

'I heard you say something about leaving — about your departure being arranged, on the phone at Laura's.'

He frowned. 'What else did you hear?'

'Nothing that mattered. I wasn't listening,' she hastened to justify herself. 'I was coming

335

downstairs and heard you speaking.'

His brow cleared and he said, 'Of course not. Well, it's true. I am leaving. You know I've had enough of this place, that's why I want to sell, but an opportunity has come up for me elsewhere sooner than I expected. If you want to come with me, Goddess, now's the time to say so.'

'I thought you said you didn't want to get encumbered. Where should we go?'

'South America, to start with, anyway. As for encumbrances, I don't intend to let you be one. What do you say?'

She thought about it. It was more like discussing the plans for a day's outing to the sea than an elopement scheme. There had been no declaration of love on either side, no physical contact, not even a kiss.

'Do you want me?'

'I've always wanted you. And that's another reason. Any other woman would have said, 'Do you love me?' '

She said slowly, 'I don't ask more from you than I can give and I don't know whether what I feel for you is love. I know you can give me what I want. If you'll have me on those terms I'll come.'

'What about Lewis?'

She sighed. 'He's had his chance. I can't go on trying all the rest of my life when he

336

doesn't even notice. I'll hurt him, I suppose, and I'm sorry for that. Of course he'll do his best to cut me off from Peter.' Her eyes darkened and filled with tears. 'But in another few years he'll be old enough to lead his own life. But if I lose you again now I'll never get another chance. Does it sound dreadfully selfish?'

He got up and came to sit beside her on the sofa. His hand reached out behind her to turn off the lamp and the room was lit only by the light from the open doorway to the passage and one of the flickering lanterns from the terrace.

'Dreadfully selfish but terribly human. Which is why I think I love you. I know that, under all that conventional propriety, you're not at all like your mythological name-sake, who turned into a tree when she was pursued by a man.'

His hands were undoing the buttons of her shirt and she sat immobile, waiting, remembering their feel as they slid round to unclasp her bra and caress her breasts. His eyes hadn't left her face and she could feel his breath on her cheeks as her head fell back against the leather upholstery.

'I knew you'd be sorry you didn't eat those onions,' he said.

She opened her mouth and arched up

towards him, drowning in the luxury and savagery of the kiss she had dreamed of since Colombo. The leather under them squeaked and rubbed against their bare skin emitting noises like the unsuppressed breaking of wind. Diana went limp against him and, when he looked down at her, he was momentarily disconcerted to see she had dissolved into helpless laughter.

'I'm sorry. I can't be serious on this farting sofa. It's like when you rub your patent leather shoes together under somebody's dinner table and they make a rude noise and you do it again on purpose to show everyone that you haven't let off.'

He rolled off her on to the floor and stood up, pulling her into his arms. 'Come to bed then.'

She hadn't been in his bedroom before. It was the twin of the one she and Lewis were in, with an added balcony on the side of the house corresponding to the window from which they could see the lighthouse. He undressed her and then himself on an enormous sheepskin rug beside the double bed. Diana only had a second to reflect on the times Hilary must have lain in this bed and then she was lying in its embrace with Grant beside her, over her, in her. Everything external dissolved, receded, faded out of existence, as it had once before and they made love and talked and explored each other and made love again on into the night.

Finally she slept and when she woke it was because she was uncomfortably hot. Her body was curled against Grant's and under the sheet he had pulled up to protect them from mosquitoes she could feel the sweat running in rivulets between her breasts and down her thighs. Her hair was wet on the pillow and she eased herself away from him to change her position. He awoke instantly and reached for her as she turned on her side away from him, pulling her in to fit against the front of his body, his left hand coming across to stroke her stomach. She relaxed once more, contentedly acquiescing to these preliminaries to further love-making. She'd burned her boats now and she had no qualms or pangs of conscience. She couldn't let Grant go out of her life a second time. They belonged in a way she had never belonged to Lewis. Grant's hand had ceased its movement and she put her own on his to encourage its further exploration when he removed it altogether and sat up on his elbow, alert and listening.

'What is it?' she murmured drowsily.

'Sh! I don't know. Listen!'

They both waited, he tense and wide awake

now, she not caring and irritated by this interruption.

'I can't hear anything. Come back to me.'

She tried to pull him down but he disengaged himself and slid out of the bed. It was very dark but he didn't put on the light and she could hear him getting into his trousers and pulling up the zip.

'Stay there.' He felt his way across the room, opened the door and disappeared. Diana lay back but the inclination for sleep or anything else had left her. She strained her ears for any sound but, hearing nothing, decided she'd better get up and see what, if anything, was going on. She found her shirt and jeans and slipped them on, then barefoot found her way to the door. The lamp still flickered on the terrace and one of the french windows was open, but there was no sign of Grant. She felt helpless and slightly stupid but not afraid. She didn't know what to do so she sat down and waited. Her eyes became accustomed to the light and everything in the room became clear so that, when Grant stumbled in from the terrace, she could see the expression on his face. It was anxious and he was in a hurry.

'Diana!' he called her urgently and in a whisper, lending a drama to the situation that knotted her stomach muscles.

'I'm here'. He hadn't seen her in the room but now when she rose from her chair he said, 'Thank God. Come quickly.'

She followed him out on to the terrace and round to where the steps led down to the beach. A man in a frogman's suit lay on the top step. He was conscious and all that she could see of him was the oval of his face framed by his helmet, contorted with pain. When he saw the two of them he tried to sit up but a spasm forced him to sink back. His right leg stuck out at an unnatural angle from his body and it was evident that this was where the trouble lay.

'Give me a hand with him.' Grant bent down and said a few words to the man in French and he nodded. 'I'll take his shoulders — get one of those deck chairs. We'll try to get him on it and use it as a stretcher.'

Diana did as she was told and together, with Grant lifting the man's torso, they managed to roll him as gently as possible on to the improvised hurdle and carry him into the house. He fainted once in the process but when Diana suggested getting help Grant said curtly, 'I'm a doctor, remember?' so she shut up. Somehow they got him on the sofa. 'Now,' said Grant, 'let's have a look at him.'

Diana reached out to put on the lamp but he cautioned her with a gesture of his hand

and went first to draw the curtains before he signalled that it was all right to turn the switch. She stood, looking down at the man.

'Who is he?'

Grant ignored her question. 'Get him something to drink — not alcohol,' as she moved towards the drinks. 'He's in shock. Tea, strong and sweet. You'll find it all in there.' He waved vaguely in the direction of the kitchen and she stumbled out and found what was required.

When she returned with the tray Grant was busy with a knife. He had slit the rubber of the man's suit from ankle to thigh on the injured leg and was peeling it back to reveal the damage. Released from its casing, the limb swelled up alarmingly as they watched and Grant felt around carefully until he was satisfied as to the extent of the damage. He straightened up.

'It's a bad break, but I can deal with it. He'll have to rest here.' He thought rapidly. The patient was sipping his tea from a mug held by Diana and her other hand was under his head. Some colour had returned to his sallow cheeks and when he had finished, Grant spoke again to him in French. The man didn't answer but he raised his right hand and tapped the left hand side of his body somewhere in the region of his rib cage.

Diana said again, 'Who is he? Do you know him?'

'Don't ask so many questions. Help me to get him out of his suit. First of all, though, I'll have to put him out.'

She obeyed, waiting while Grant administered an injection and undid the zipper that ran down the front of the man's body. She lifted his head when she was told and Grant peeled back the rubber helmet to show thick, dark, springy curls which fell forwards on to his forehead. Gently they eased the shoulders, first one arm, then the other out of the suit, then Grant took up the knife again, continuing the cut he had made up the leg into the groin to meet the opening of the zip and the rubber fell apart like the casing of a hazel nut revealing the kernel. After that it wasn't difficult to pull his left leg free and remove what was left of the suit.

'Get a blanket.'

She ran into the bedroom, stripped the under blanket off the bed and came back with it over her arm. Naked except for a pair of black swimming trucks, the man lay with his head back, eyes closed with exhaustion and now and again a slight shiver shook his frame. He was of medium height with slim waist and hips, strongly muscled chest, arms and legs and the skin on his body was deeply tanned, contrasting sharply with the pallor of his face. A gold medallion hung from a chain about his neck and nestled in a thick mat of dark hair on his chest. Two wide strips of adhesive plaster held a surgical dressing in place two inches below his left nipple. Diana judged him to be about eighteen or twenty. Grant took the blanket and laid it over the boy.

'I'll have to set his leg,' he said. 'There's nothing more you can do at the moment, my dear. Why not try to get some rest?'

Diana ignored his suggestion. 'Can you do it without an X-ray?' she asked. 'Wouldn't it be better to get him to hospital?'

He was moving about the room purposefully, clearing a space by the couch as he spoke. 'It might be better for him, Diana, but hardly advisable for us.'

He went out of the room and came back, carrying his medical bag, which he put down on the marble-topped table and started taking things out of it and laying them out in neat rows.

'I don't understand what's going on.'

He didn't look at her but went on methodically with his preparations.

'It's better you don't. All you have to do is forget he was ever here.'

She stood her ground. A nameless apprehension stirred in her bowels.

'Grant, who is this man? Grant! Look at me.'

He did so, straightening his back with a sigh.

'I suppose you'll have to know,' he said. 'He's a business associate — you could call him that.'

'What business?'

'Very big business, Goddess. Big enough to make us both rich. You'd like that, wouldn't you?' His eyes shone and she could see how excited he was and she was afraid. 'Come here, I'll show you.'

He beckoned her to come closer and she advanced to the boy, to stand beside Grant. He pulled back the blanket down to his patient's waist and, bending forward, gently got hold of the sticking plaster holding the dressing. With a quick jerk he removed both adhesive and lint. Underneath was an oilskin package the size of a double pack of twenty cigarettes which was strapped to the Frenchman's body with Sellotape. This too Grant stripped off, then, covering the body once more with the blanket, he brought the package over to the table and carefully unwrapped it. Inside was another plastic bag filled with a whitish powder which Grant handled reverently.

* ★ ★ ★

She had to hear him say it although she already knew the answer and to prove to herself that the nightmare was real. 'What is it?'

'Heroin. Worth a small fortune, Goddess, and all for us.'

'How long . . . ?' she stammered.

'Ever since I came out here — and before. That was my reason for coming. They started to get on to me in London. I've had a good run here but somebody betrayed us. He evidently couldn't use his normal delivery route and something must have gone badly wrong for him to have come here. We mustn't be found here with him. I promise you, darling, you're never going to want for anything. I've made my little pile and now it's over. Go and get whatever you need. We'll have to leave almost immediately.'

'What about him?'

'Leave him to me. Do as I say,' as she made no move.

Her brain seemed to be cushioned in cotton wool and she couldn't think straight. Inanely she attempted to reconcile the fact that this man, her lover of an hour ago, was not only a criminal on the run — that in itself blow enough but not sufficient to account for the shuddering recoil she was experiencing — but that he was a peddler of the loathsome corruption that she, as a mother, feared for all the Peters of the world. And now he was offering her a luxurious future on the proceeds.

'Hurry up. We haven't any time to waste.' He was splinting the boy's leg. Still the words wouldn't come but she managed dumbly to shake her head.

He came across to shake her but said more gently, 'Hurry up, Goddess. Don't look like that. You'll get used to the idea. Think of it as any business. We all have to do what we're best suited for. I'm no worse than any other salesman. I'm satisfying a need.'

She found her voice. 'I'm not coming with you. I must have been mad. I thought I knew you.' Her tone was bewildered like a child suddenly puzzled by an unfamiliar mask.

He drew her to him. 'No one better, Goddess. We're two of a kind and you love me, remember?' She felt his body against hers, pressed close from thigh to breast and his mouth came down on hers. She stood with her arms hanging limply at her sides, her own mouth open, and his tongue slid searchingly against her own. After a moment of no response he pressed his knee insistently between her legs, then all of a sudden let her go.

347

'It's no good,' she said dully. She hardly understood herself. It was as if her body, which only an hour ago had throbbed solely for his, were dead and he a stranger. She turned slowly in the direction of her own bedroom.

'Where are you going?' His voice penetrated the numbness in which she was cocooned.

'To pack. I must leave. I can't go with you.'

'And I'm not going without you.' She hardly recognized the menace in his voice. He softened his tone and tried again. 'Be sensible, Diana. Where can you go at this time of night and alone? Darling, it's over. So you don't approve of what I've been doing but it's over. I promise you. If it hadn't been for him arriving out of the blue like that you would never have known and you'd have come away with me happily enough. Damn Victor!'

'Victor? What has Victor got to do with it?'

'He was the one who betrayed us. He was a spy. I discovered today.'

'Don't keep saying 'us'. I want nothing to do with it.'

'Darling, remember how it is with us. We love each other. Don't throw it all away now because you're temporarily upset.'

She looked at him sadly. 'The person I

thought I loved didn't exist. What you do is worse than murder. You degrade and ruin people's lives so that you can live like this. Doesn't it turn your stomach to think those kids you peddle this stuff to might be Peter or your own son, had he lived?'

She'd made him angry and all his efforts at patience evaporated.

'You talk just like Hilary. Women! My God, can one ever expect a practical response from a woman?'

'Hilary? Did she know about this then?' An icy finger traced its way along her spine and she was frightened yet unable to move from the spot where she stood. He was impatient to get away.

'She found out. I couldn't do a thing with her once she knew. She drank, she was hysterical. In the end I was forced to sedate her. That was the only time she was sensible. It was ironical really. In the end she was really hooked herself.'

'Oh God, no!' Diana put her hands over her face. 'Why didn't she leave you?'

'She loved me.'

'God help her.'

'I'm afraid he didn't, Goddess. How unfair life is because the wicked truly flourish like the proverbial green bay tree whereas the worthy, like yourself and Hilary, generally go under for lack of moral fibre.'

'What makes you so sure I'm going under?'

He had moved behind the table and was checking the instruments in his bag. She watched his hands, strong, capable hands that had so recently caressed her, making her want to faint from pleasure. Something gleamed in the right one as he brought it up and it seemed hours before the message connected to her brain that what he was holding was not an instrument but a gun and that it was pointing at her. It could have only been a split second because she heard him answering her in a voice as smooth as silk.

'Because, my dear, you have the choice of coming with me or I'm afraid I shall have to use this for the second time today. I tell you that so that you will know that I mean business. If I am caught, which I don't intend to be, they can already hang a murder rap on me, so I shan't stop at one more.'

Her hand went to her throat and she whispered hoarsely, 'Victor?'

'Yes, Diana. Victor. He deserved it. He was a spy. Now, my dear, you've already said you don't wish to accompany me. Do you now want to change your mind?'

She had to know it all. 'And Hilary? What happened to her? You killed her too when she found out?'

The silence in the room was broken only by the uneven heavy breathing of the man on the sofa between them. She put out her hand to hold on to the drinks trolley as if to steady herself.

'You may not believe me but I didn't kill her. That was an accident. We quarrelled. She was distressed and unsteady. We were on the terrace. She lost balance and went over. That's the truth. I didn't touch her but I could see how it might look and I didn't want a lot of probing into my affairs. Luckily there was no one here, so I made myself scarce and came back later to make it look as if she had been alone. I gave myself an alibi by calling in at Laura's.'

Laura, Diana thought, had tried to warn her. She'd suspected something but couldn't be sure.

The handle of the trolley was smooth under her touch and she ran her fingers back and forth along the beading of the tray in a nervous gesture.

'Who's going to supply your alibi for me?'

'I'm counting on not needing one. You're going to be sensible, aren't you?'

She stood quietly for a moment, her head bent, then with a sigh she raised her eyes to his and shrugged her shoulders in a gesture of resignation.

'I haven't much choice, have I? I'm too young to die. I may as well make the best of you.' She allowed herself a smile. 'Besides — you said it — we belong, whatever you've done. I suppose it's been the ruthless streak in you that I've loved.'

'That's better.' He put the gun down on the table and moved towards her. She held him to her sobbing, and he said, 'There, there,' kissing away her tears. She clung to him more fiercely. His mouth was on her neck and he pushed aside her shirt and nuzzled her shoulder. She pressed his face gently down against her breasts, moaning as if she couldn't bear him to stop. With her right hand she raised the half-full Vodka bottle from the trolley and brought it crashing down with all the strength she could muster against the back of his head. He let go and slid sideways into the trolley, bringing bottles and glasses crashing down around him. His eyes had the dazed look of a K.O.ed boxer trying desperately to beat the bell.

She didn't wait to see if he'd make it. She was through the curtains and out on the terrace and running for the steps before she heard him shouting. The steps were wet and slippery and she forced herself to slow down and concentrate on keeping her feet, expecting any moment to see Grant appear above her. The Vulcan lay in the water below and if she could only get to it before he reached her, she had a chance to escape. She was almost at the bottom when she heard him on the terrace and the next moment she saw him at the top of the steps. He was staggering and had the gun in his hand.

'Diana, stop! You can't get away. If you don't stop I'll shoot.'

She could see him by virtue of the terrace light but she was in the shadow of the wall below and he hadn't seen her yet. He was coming down. She had to break cover. She ran for all she was worth across the shingle that separated her from the stone jetty.

'Diana! Stop, you little fool!' A shot rang out and a bullet ricocheted off the jetty but she was nearly there.

Her heart was pounding and there was a singing in her ears. She leapt on to the stone slab and unhitched the Vulcan in one movement, then she was in the boat. Two more shots missed her and above the roaring blood in her head she heard Grant shouting to her to stop again. Just before she pulled the starter she seemed to hear another voice, strangely like Lewis's. She turned to look back and saw two figures — Grant on the steps, and another person on the beach gesticulating and waving like a madman.

For a split second she hesitated. It was Lewis, and Grant would kill him. She made as if to step out of the boat. She must go to him. At the same moment the bullet hit her. She was still holding the starter cord and the impact swung her round, pulling it sharply. There was a hot wind carrying the smell of burning petrol, a flash and the whole world exploded. She was light and floating in air, then falling, falling as in a dream and she waited in vain for the involuntary jump which would wake her up.

19

It was raining, raining again as it had rained almost unremittingly since her arrival back in England six weeks — two months, she didn't know how long it had been, nor did she care. She didn't mind the rain. It soothed her because it made her feel so far removed from those endless days of sunshine, that summer, another life now remote as a dream recounted by someone else.

The only remaining physical reminder was the operation scar, now neatly healed where they had taken the bullet out of her groin. It had been touch and go, they'd told her, as to whether she would be able to walk again, but now all that was past. She was as good as new. The nurses hadn't been able to understand her lack of reaction. They had clucked and fluttered, uttering consoling reassurances, bracing her with optimism for the future — as if she cared. The numbness was all over her, in her limbs, her spine, her brain.

'It was a miracle she wasn't killed, or at least impossibly burned,' the doctors had told Lewis. 'Had she fallen into the boat instead of out of it when the bullet struck her she would have gone up like the rest.'

Lewis shuddered, remembering the thousand tiny pieces settling on the water that had been all that had remained of the Vulcan. 'The emotional effects of the shock will take time to wear off and are more puzzling. Even allowing for so gruesome an experience, your wife seems to have some deeper psychological blockage, the cause of which we haven't been able to fathom. Be patient with her. You're the one who can do her the most good now.'

'How long will it take?' Lewis had asked.

They had shrugged their shoulders. 'Who knows? It may be weeks — months. There may not be a dramatic change, just a gradual improvement. A lot will depend on you. See if you can get her to talk, take an interest.'

'And if I can't? I've tried, you know, but I don't seem to be able to get through.'

'If the condition continues after reasonable efforts have been made, there are other courses open — electrical treatment, etc., but I feel it won't be necessary. I can only describe it as like flushing a lavatory: we must try to dislodge the blockage then all will flow freely. Don't worry, Mr Holt. She's strong and healthy and from what you tell me, not given to neuroses. She's going to be all right.'

* ★ *

From her chair in the window Diana watched the raindrops falling on the full-blown roses. When she had first come into the nursing home they had been buds. Now most of them were over and the few that remained would be finished after this downpour. The summer was over.

There were footsteps and voices in the corridor, a tap on the door and Lewis came in, armed with a sheaf of chrysanthemums. He had been to see her every day. In the hospital in Spain, where she had been too weak to speak to him, he had sat and held her hand, and when she had been well enough to be flown home he had spent hours with her here in this room, neither of them talking much and both avoiding the subjects uppermost in their minds. Now he came round the end of the bed and kissed her.

'How are we today, old girl?' He didn't wait for an answer. 'Brought these along. Thought your others were about due to be chucked out.'

'They're lovely. Thank you. There's a vase by the basin if you like to put them in water.'

He unwrapped them carefully and jammed them bodily into the container, clearing up paper and a few odd bits of greenery which he put neatly into the wastepaper basket. There was an air of purpose about him today, more of a spring in his step, a feeling of suppressed excitement.

He drew up a chair close to hers and sat down and after a while she said, 'Well, tell me all the news,' because, with some misgivings, she saw he had some.

'I will,' he said. 'In a moment, but first, Di, I've been talking to the medics and they feel that you're ready to come home. They can't do much more for you here. They think the change and being in more normal surroundings will complete the healing process. What do you think?'

She sat looking out of the window while he was speaking and remained in the same position for so long after he had finished that he wondered whether she had taken in anything he had been saying. Finally she spoke with an effort and so quietly that he had to lean forward to hear her.

'I don't know.'

He touched her hand in an effort to bring her back to him.

'What exactly don't you know, Di?'

She shook her head from side to side. 'So many things. How you can want me back. What you were doing on the beach. How you knew about Grant. I don't understand any of it.'

'Perhaps I can give you some answers,' he said gently. 'We've got to talk about it all some day. Do you want to talk about it now? Shall we try to straighten things out a bit?'

She turned to give him her attention. The grey eyes were untouched but they seemed to be searching for something in his. He willed himself not to look away and eventually she sighed deeply and said again, 'I don't know. I don't know anything any more.'

'You should know that I love you and want to take you home with me.'

'Why didn't you want to take me to Barcelona? If only you had.'

It caught him on the wrong foot. He hadn't expected her to go straight in like that but he took the bull by the horns.

'I couldn't. I wasn't going to Barcelona. I want to tell you about it. Do you want to hear?'

'Yes.'

He took her hand in his and, starting at the beginning, gently took her through the whole story. He told her everything. How he had been approached by Andy in the first place, how he had been chosen because of knowing Grant and Bahia Dorada, his discovery of the cave after Victor had told him the lighthouse was being used, the finding of Victor's body and how he had been planted months before at *Encantador* to watch Grant's movements and to tip them the wink in London when they should move in. He described how he had lain in wait for the Frenchman and the plan had gone wrong and he followed him to *Encantador*.

'Grant started to suspect Victor after we found the ring at the lighthouse. His suspicions must have been confirmed conclusively that last day.'

Diana said slowly, 'He had a phone call at Laura's. It was bad news, I could tell. I overheard because I was coming downstairs at the time. He was rattled. He said a patient had had an accident and he had to leave us. In fact what you're telling me is that he went back and killed Victor?'

'He must have done. He couldn't stop the operation and he desperately wanted that final consignment of heroin. It spelt the rest of his insurance for his future and he had already sold it.'

'It's ghastly.' She closed her eyes, remembering how he had returned from murdering Victor to hold her in his arms. 'I still can't believe it, in spite of him telling me so that night. He tried to shoot me.'

'Don't think about it any more. It's over.'

'I must. There's so much I don't understand. It's all too much like a thriller. So much depended on chance. How, for instance, could you be sure he'd take us up — actually asking us to stay in the house? It was beyond the bounds of coincidence.'

Lewis looked down at his hands. 'It wasn't a coincidence. I knew he wanted you.'

Somewhere from the end of a long tunnel came the rushing of a wind getting louder, louder as it came towards her and at the same time snapshots clicked like slides on a projector in her brain. Lewis on his sick bed urging her to go to the bullfight with Grant, encouraging her to be nice to him, sending her out with him to learn to water-ski, accepting with uncharacteristic alacrity the invitation to stay at the villa. All the time she had been fighting to keep their marriage intact, Lewis had been encouraging her to attract Grant, throwing them together for his own ends, using her as bait.

It all unravelled like a piece of knitting until you arrived at the point of casting on. He could have only so confidently anchored the whole plan to her reactions if he had known that she and Grant had already been lovers. He had known about Colombo; he saw comprehension dawning in her face. In her anger and hurt she didn't mince words. She wanted to hurt him.

'You knew he'd had me. Didn't you mind?'

Lewis inclined his head. 'I minded very much. I was aware you had been unfaithful.'

'You were aware I'd been unfaithful!' She mimicked his precise tones. 'Were you also aware by any chance that I regretted it deeply? That I suffered horribly from guilt and that I grew to love and want you? You should have been grateful to Grant because, in encouraging me to be unfaithful, he showed me how I could enrich our marriage. But you didn't even notice.'

'I noticed the difference in you but I didn't want you different. I didn't understand. I thought then, 'No man wants his wife to behave like a whore.' I'd been through that experience before. It wasn't one I intended to repeat.'

She was gazing at him in horror. 'So you stored it up for the future and when Andy called upon your services, you saw how you could make use of it. You didn't give a jot about my feelings, being torn in half between the two of you. You thought precious little about the so-called sanctity of our marriage then.'

He was afraid. It was going wrong. 'Diana, listen. It wasn't that way, or at least, only partly. It's true that I was jealous and hurt and I wanted to pay you back for what you'd done, but above all else, I wanted to prove to you, to myself if you like, that I wasn't a failure. This was a chance to pull off something really big — for both of us. I had to get into Grant's confidence, those were my orders. If you had known you would have wanted me to succeed.'

'Why didn't you tell me then, for Christ's sake? We could have done it together some other way.'

'How?'

'I don't know. You're the Intelligence.'

'There wasn't another way. Diana. He is a killer and, thanks to you and to me, he's now out of the way. Doesn't that mean something?'

'So the end justifies the means? If you knew he was a killer how could you leave me at *Encantador* with him?'

'I didn't know that until I found Victor in the cave. Believe me, darling, I was demented. I knew then you were in danger and I could do nothing. I had to wait then for the Frenchman.'

'It never occurred to you to give the whole thing up and come to help me?'

'I couldn't. I was under orders. If I failed, then everything would be lost. As long as you were ignorant, Grant wouldn't harm you. I wasn't to know the Frenchman would turn up there. As it is, Andrew has made me a wonderful offer on the strength of bringing this job off. I want to tell you about it.'

' 'I could not love thee, dear, so much loved I not honour more!' ' She began to laugh. It was ironic really. Here was Lewis, having such a high regard for his honour and setting so much store on the original loss of hers, and there was Grant, to whom honour had been but another meaningless word, and she had loved them both. One had given her a home, companionship, love of a kind and a son; the other laughter, passion, ecstasy and pain. And both had simply used her. That was the unkindest cut of all. After all, the years she had spent with Lewis, most of them happy and carved out of her endeavour to learn from her experience with Grant, were a sham. All the time she had been trying to build, he had been awaiting his opportunity to revenge her one lapse. She had been a fool — a sheer bloody fool.

He was trying to calm her and she recalled herself with an effort and tried to stop the hysterical laughter. 'Don't, Di. Maybe I was wrong, maybe I should never have taken the job, but I had to have this last chance. All I know is that I've never been so frightened in my life as when I saw you pull that cord and the boat went up, and these past weeks have made me realize how dearly I love you. I can't live without you. I'm not much of a chap for showing my feelings but, if I hadn't loved you, I wouldn't have felt so let down and crazily jealous.'

'And how do you feel now, knowing that until the Frenchman arrived we were making love, that I was going with him, that I had decided to leave you?'

She intended to be cruel in her righteous indignation and yet, as she spoke the words, she wished she could have recalled them. She made a small gesture with her hand as if to soften them, but he wasn't looking at her, but at the pattern on the carpet, his elbows resting on his knees.

Not shrinking an answer he said simply, 'Humble. Sad. Inadequate. He gave you something I never could, never tried. I thought you knew enough about me — ' he spread his hands as if it was useless trying to explain. 'I blame myself. You wouldn't have been in that situation if it hadn't been for me. When I was in that cave I prayed — properly for the first time — I was so afraid for you, everything was a muddle.' He put his head in his hands. 'And then, when I knew that if you pulled that cord you'd be blown to smithereens because I'd booby-trapped the boat to stop him escaping that way, I just saw my world ending.' The words were an obvious effort. 'Isn't it ridiculous? You read that sort of thing in a book and think 'What tripe! How trite!' But the truth is, there aren't any new words. I've never been much of a hand at expressing what I feel anyway. I failed with Klara too. I couldn't provide what she wanted of me, and I hadn't learned to let her give to me. She had so much generosity. Sometimes it's more blessed to receive graciously than to give, you know.'

He raised his head and gave her a long look. There were tears in her eyes.

'Do you still love him?'

'He'll always be a part of me, just as Klara will of you. But love? That's hard to say.'

'You've taught me there's more than one kind, Di. Can we learn from both of them? Are you coming home with me?'

'Can you accept a wife who's behaved like a whore?'

'Must we punish each other or over-indulge in self-flagellation?'

'You haven't asked me the most important question yet.'

The old Lewis would have asked what she meant. 'I'm too afraid to do that,' was what this Lewis said.

She knew there would be many times when

she would be much less sure of her feelings, but sustained by the memory of that moment when she had recognized Lewis on the beach and all that had mattered in the world was that she should go to him, she said, 'Don't be.'

The rain was coming down worse than ever as he stood by the outer door of the nursing home, drawing up his collar before running out to bring the car round. From somewhere came the sound of dishes being clanked around in readiness for supper and down the passage there was a gurgling of water in the heating system and someone flushed a lavatory.

THE END